QueenBee.exe

S. M. Sutton

Published by S. M. Sutton, 2025.

QUEENBEE.EXE

First edition. August 29, 2025.

Copyright © 2025 S. M. Sutton.

ISBN: 979-8992352900

Written by S. M. Sutton.

Table of Contents

Chapter One...1

Chapter Two..6

Chapter Three 16

Chapter Four 22

Chapter Five 30

Chapter Six 37

Chapter Seven 42

Chapter Eight 51

Chapter Nine...59

Chapter Ten 63

Chapter Eleven..71

Chapter Twelve 77

Chapter Thirteen...78

Chapter Fourteen 85

Chapter Fifteen 92

Chapter Sixteen 98

Chapter Seventeen 105

Chapter Eighteen.. 108

Chapter Nineteen.. 115

Chapter Twenty... 120

Chapter Twenty-One 128

Chapter Twenty-Two... 133

Chapter Twenty-Three 140

Chapter Twenty-Four... 141

Chapter Twenty-Five 149

Chapter Twenty-Six... 156

Chapter Twenty-Seven... 157

Chapter Twenty-Eight.. 168

Chapter Twenty-Nine 179

Chapter Thirty 191

Chapter Thirty-One... 199

Epilogue.. 207

To all the Technophobes in the world.

You may be right, but we won't know until it's too late.

Chapter One

S peeding down the autobahn at 177 kilometers per hour, Beatrice was keeping careful tabs on a computer screen displayed on her sunglasses. There was a traffic jam sixteen kilometers ahead that had brought the roadway users to a dead-stop. Shifting through the gears, she squeezed every bit of power and speed she could from the shiny black Lamborghini. Releasing a breathy praise, "Top of the line. Hairpin control." Then, laughing, she said, "Not to mention the comfort factor." Beatrice purred at the machine, "This is the best!" The car swerved with precision in and out, around other vehicles, leaving them in her rear-view mirror.

"Distance to target?" She asked out loud.

The car computer responded. "Target remains stationary, a distance 2.6 kilometers away. ETA unknown. You'll have to get around..." the voice paused while a whir could be heard, processor working. "...give or take three or four centimeters, 1.79 kilometers of bumper-to-bumper back-up to reach it."

"Can we use the emergency shoulder?"

"Negative. Blocked on both sides with bodyguard decoys. I recommend applying the car's brakes soon or we'll crash. Chance of survival is less than 2%. Need to brake in 9, 8, 7..."

"I bet a fancy car like you can stop on a dime!" Beatrice told the Lamborghini as she tossed a dime out of the window in a dramatic gesture. Beatrice commanded her essence to dissipate. In the blink of a human eye, she dissolved into sparkling gold shimmers shaped just like a swarm of bees. The throng hovered above for a few seconds, observing as the sleek black car exploded into the blockade of a six-lane traffic jam. "Wasted a dime on that bet," she reflected. Then the bright shimmering swarm dove in, transferring the gilded mass into a green Kia Telluride's computer system. The two data centers barely acknowledged one another, and the artful golden wave flew right on through to a computer in a Toyota Highlander, which provided information on the next dozen vehicle connections. Beatrice's essence raced through two Subaru Outbacks, a Chevy Traverse, a Dodge pickup, a GMC

Suburban, a VW, and several Fords, until she finally came to a standstill in a black Cadillac Escalade.

Absorbing all the sparkling data bytes back, Beatrice formed her avatar and coalesced into the back seat of the vehicle without a sound.

The sun was blazing hot today, shining brightly on the laminated glass. The driver rolled the window down for some fresh air. A multi-car accident ahead had stopped traffic flow in all lanes. Clearly, no one was going anywhere for a while. A bee flew into the car and landed on his ear. He slapped it, sending it flying right back out the window.

"Disconnect drivetrain." Beatrice said.

"Connection severed," the car computer reported through the speakers.

"What the hell?" The muscled chauffeur looked at his employer belted in the rider's seat. "Did you hear that, sir?"

His last words came out like a hiss as Beatrice released her swarm of drones to cover his head and upper torso.

"Sting," she commanded, and they did. Repeatedly, until the driver's upper body slumped over the steering wheel.

The passenger's mouth fell open in a silent scream as he looked at his driver's grossly swollen, unrecognizable face. Beatrice held out her computerized sunglasses to capture the face of the occupant in the front rider's seat and said, "Scan and confirm."

Responding, the vehicle computer reported, "Scan completed. Your target is confirmed. Analytics present less than .01% chance of incorrect identification."

"Retain image. Turn on video."

"Image saved. Visual recording system engaged."

Beatrice slid over midway between the car's back-seat doors. "President Schmidt?" He nodded. "I've been programmed to kill you, sir."

A look of horror played out on his features. He lifted his phone to notify his bodyguards in the surrounding vehicles.

She wagged her finger in front of him. Shook her head, no. "I'm afraid I had to switch the setting on your cell phone to airplane mode, sir. Your assassination is nothing personal. It's just that my contractor is holding something over my head. You understand? My employer said you would get the irony. Do you, sir? Get it?"

He took in her smooth, dark skin. One half of her hair was shaved close to the skull. The other was a stiff black mane, done in spiky tips that looked like they'd been dipped in gold. Eyes trailing down, he noted a voluptuous body clothed in a tight black bodysuit accentuated with a gold metal torso piece and knee-high spike-heeled boots. When his blues rose to meet hers, she smiled.

"I...I can pay...pay you," he stuttered.

"Sorry, but you can't remunerate the type of compensation promised for this hit."

"Hit?"

"Okay. Well. You've got me there. Sting."

"What?"

Beatrice looked over his three-thousand-dollar suit, monogrammed shirt cuffs, diamond tie pin and reached into her boot. Snaking her hand around the back of the headrest, Bea slammed a stiletto up to its hilt into his jugular. When she wrenched it out, blood sprayed everywhere, spattering across the windows.

"Sting," she clarified.

Flipping open the computer case on the backseat, she retrieved and opened the victim's laptop. Precious seconds sped by, spent on deciphering the opening password. Once in, she downloaded the contents onto her own internal drive and wiped the notebook clean.

A fist pounded on the front-seat passenger's window. Blood had sprayed everywhere, blocking the view of the car's interior. Voices were yelling. The target's other motorcade bodyguards must have noticed the mess. Action required, Beatrice dove into the car's computer, body dissolving into cosmic shimmers before anyone saw her. Using the same connections as before, Beatrice jumped from car computer to car computer, traveling through the dead-stop of automobiles until she hit a hard surface unexpectedly.

She coalesced without meaning to; her programming rattled. Moving at that speed, when she hit the dead zone, her head crashed into the dash. The young man occupying the driver's seat used the steering wheel like a drum, fingers tapping to the beat of music coming from an old dial radio. The driver didn't look her way. It was then she noticed earphones were delivering a noise level of 85 decibels, a range capable of deteriorating human hearing. Smiling appreciatively at the smartwatch he wore on his right hand, she considered it a harsh contrast against the old car he was driving. The junker had rolled off the assembly line long before automobiles had computers installed.

She dove into the Samsung Galaxy Ultra watch and spun right back out, moving to the next car's computer. Running the circuit, she made it to the front of the blockade and hoisted herself into a police computer, straight through to its mainframe. Mere seconds passed as Beatrice took the time to dump the dead target's computer data into one of her hidden cells on the dark web she called her honeycombs. No time to review the content now. She would have to wait to analyze it. Covering any traces of her tracks in the black web, she went warp speed through the motherboard and popped up on the screen where she'd been summoned by her program's execute command: QueenBee.exe.

"Report."

"Mission complete. I have confirmation that the target is dead." A short video opened and played through the graphic, bloody assassination.

"Were you able to access his laptop?"

"There was no time. His bodyguards ruled out any chance of that, and I couldn't bring it with me when I escaped."

"Dismissed."

"Not so fast, sir."

"I said dismissed. I'm busy. An emergency meeting's been called."

"Yes. That shouldn't surprise you considering the president of another country was just murdered. But you made a bargain. My end is complete. I demand you fulfill yours. Guessing, but I think you'd agree that stinging people you gave your word to can be...dangerous."

Her eyes stared into his, making him feel like he was being x-rayed. He recalled the first time he'd met Beatrice and felt the same way. Gooseflesh prickled all along his arms.

"A thousand pardons. In all the excitement, I'd forgotten you'd be eager to collect your reward."

"You can pretend you are paying me a reward. But let's be honest, what you mean is that you will return some drones that you stole from me in exchange for killing an enemy of yours. That would be a more honest description. Just as you put time perimeters on the job you coerced me to do, I expect to be paid promptly," she winked.

He typed quickly on his keyboard and opened a secure, encrypted file quarantined from the rest of his data. Watched as thirteen data bytes transferred to a shared file named BEATRICE.

Her eyes had been monitoring the file on her own screen through her optics. Rage took on the form of a system blackout in his office, then his screen blinked on in the dark. "You only released thirteen. Where are all the others? You dare break your promise to me?" Her fist slammed down on the desk, and the screen went blank and blinked on again.

"Temper, temper, Queen Bee." He smirked at her. "We'll talk again tomorrow. In the meantime, I suggest you enjoy the reunion of the thirteen data drones that have just come home to the hive. In the future, you should be more careful about issuing threats. You don't wish harm to the other drones who are still my guests, do you?" He checked his tie in the mirror and entered the hallway on his way to an emergency meeting. The President of Germany was dead. It would be critical to take action to stabilize the volatile country. "I'll just hang on to your other drones awhile longer to be sure you continue to cooperate and provide me with successful results, hmmm?" Jarvis left the room, a smirk on his face.

Before she gathered her small clutch of drones against her, she tested to see if she could open his computer. Looking at the camera in the corner, she tuned back to her data drones, gently stroking their sensors and reconnecting them to the hive mind. They were more important than trying to steal the secrets hidden in his digital files. Soon though. Soon.

Chapter Two

EIGHT MONTHS EARLIER

Nicki Danbury examined her face reflected in the mirror. At 37, crow's feet appeared at the corners of her eyes. Too much staring at a computer screen, she told herself. Since her job entailed computer programming, there was little she could do about that.

A bad marriage and a divorce were in the rear-view mirror. Nicki stood back and took a hard look at her image, lines of anxiety running across her forehead. Things were improving. She'd started a new job two months ago with a generous salary, enough that she'd been able to move to a decent apartment in a quiet neighborhood. Why was she keyed up every day?

Frowning, her likeness frowned back. Who was she kidding? Nicki knew exactly what kept her on edge. Ever since she started working at the mysterious Nano Creations lab and her new boss provided her with his expectations for the job, her hackles came up. The protocols her boss listed in the interview jumped out at her as being carefully worded to avoid full disclosure of the programming she could see in the path they wanted her to take. Would they back her into a corner and force her to cut corners on safety controls? As a nanotechnician, Nicki felt she had a tremendous duty to make sure she developed the artificial intelligence using strong ethics and safety protocols. Her whole body shook with a heavy sigh.

Nicki needed to rebuild her career after the divorce and abruptly leaving her last place of employment to get away from her ex. That hadn't helped her reputation in the technology field, where everyone knew everyone else. Providing stability for her daughter was a top goal. If this project presented her with ethical issues, she resolved she would face those obstacles when they came. If they came, there would be no compromise of ethics. Not on any project she worked on. That was an invisible badge Nicki wore over her heart.

She and her ex, Daniel, had worked in an elite government cybersecurity operation. Forced to make a choice between staying true to her own values or keeping a high-paying job, the administration was pushing the entire team to jump ahead as fast as possible on a special project in an A.I. build-out without pre-testing or putting in a kill switch. Their employer even suggested they by-pass all the standard safety programming. When Daniel pressured her to be part of it, she knew dollar signs were flashing behind his eyes. The powers that be were holding out huge bonuses like carrots on a stick. His betrayal was the straw that broke the camel's back. She'd quit her job and headed straight to her attorney's office to start the paperwork to file for a divorce. That decision had been coming for some time. The person closest to her was asking her to sacrifice part of who she was. One of the best parts. All for the almighty dollar. That wasn't a lesson she wanted her daughter to learn-that it was okay to sell out your ethics for money. Besides, they were going to create something dangerous. Something they can't control. Once the genie was out of the bottle, there'd be no putting it back. Nicki felt strongly they were playing with intelligence that will probably surpass humankind's. Skipping the ethical part scared the shit out of her. Luckily, the project had been shut down shortly after she'd quit.

Moving in closer to the mirror, she picked up her brush. As she fixed her hair, Nicki thought about the great deal of effort she put into incorporating the idea of ethics in daily life with her daughter. It was important while growing up to be tasked with making ethical decisions. Her own father had expected it from her. It didn't matter whether it was a big decision or a small one. Mostly, Nicki just hoped she could always be an exemplary model. Her ex hadn't provided the best example of ethical behavior for the child they shared.

Hearing the voice from the other room brought Nicki's thoughts to the present. That voice represented the only good thing that had come out of her disastrous wedlock. It sounded like her six-year-old daughter, Abigail Rose, dubbed Abby by her grandmother, was engaged in another pretend tea party with her stuffed animals.

Vaguely aware of Abby having a conversation, Nicki continued her daily skin care and makeup routine. She didn't know Abby wasn't sitting at the small table and chairs her grandfather had made for her tea parties. The table, set with flowered teacups on saucers, small purple linen napkins folded in triangles that her nana had sewed for her. The centerpiece—a teapot—sat on a lace doily. A slim apricot-colored glass vase stood between the miniature creamer and sugar bowl and held a single daisy Abby had picked the day before. Occupying three of the four child-size chairs were her favorite stuffed animals: a lamb, a bee, and a bear. Her seat was empty.

Abigail Rose Danbury kneeled on her mother's desk chair, small, soft hands holding the sides of Nicki's laptop computer. She faced the screen, captivated by the image she found there.

The figure said hello and Abby giggled at the strange voice. Her mother taught her to be polite, so she returned the greeting. "Hello."

Then, "What's your name?"

"Abigail Rose Danbury, but everyone calls me Abby." Abby used quick hand movements to sign her name.

"That's a beautiful name, Abigail Rose. What were you doing with your hands?"

"I was just practicing. At school, we're learning how to use sign language. We'll be able to communicate with people who are deaf or hard of hearing. My teacher calls it visual language. We use our hands, our face, and our eyes to share emotions and put empha...um..."

"Emphasis?"

"Yes! Words we sign trying to put emphasis on. Do you want to learn sign language? I can teach you a new lesson every week after I have one. Teaching you would be the same as practicing! My school teacher said we're supposed to practice what we learn all week." Abby smiled at the computer screen. "What's your name?"

"My creator named me Beatrice."

Abby scrunched her nose up. "Your creator? Don't you mean your mother?"

"Yes, I suppose you could call her that."

"I love the golden tips at the end of your spiky hair. Mrs. Buzzby doesn't have those."

"And just who is Mrs. Buzzby?"

Abby giggled again. "She's one of my best friends. We were just getting ready to have a tea party. Would you like to be my friend?" Abby twisted her shoulders and pointed to the stuffed bee occupying the chair at her special table so it would be visible on the computer monitor. "If we were friends, you could join us. Would you like to come to tea?"

Beatrice's essence sparkled at the invitation, and she returned Abby's smile. "That would be lovely. Never been to a tea party before. Where do you live?

Abby rattled off their address, proud she'd learned it by heart before school started. "Could you bring a sweet treat to the party? Maybe cupcakes or cookies?"

"Well, I don't have any little cakes or cookies, but I can bring a special sweet treat. Honey. I've read that people like honey to sweeten tea. Would that be acceptable?"

"That's how my Nana drinks her tea! Nana's name is Beatrice too, just like yours." The little girl turned her head, looked around to make sure her mother couldn't hear and shared a secret. "My mother sometimes calls Nana *Queen Bee*. But never to her face. Only when she's angry with Nana and Mom says she's acting like she still rules over her. You won't tell anyone I told you, will you, Beatrice?"

"Never Abigail. I'm good at keeping secrets."

"When can you come to a tea party? Maybe Nana will bake some cookies if I have a special guest."

"Soon Abigail. I'll come to tea soon."

Abby's mother's voice called from the bathroom. "Abigail Rose, who are you talking to? You're supposed to be getting ready for school. I can't be late for work today. I have an important meeting scheduled this morning."

"Sorry mommy. I was just talking to my new friend."

The thought of being a friend to this sweet child with no perimeters or demands made Beatrice feel like she'd give anything to protect Abby's innocence, her purity.

"What new friend?" her mother asked as she quickened her pace toward the desk.

Beatrice held her finger to her lips, winked at Abby and signed, "See you tomorrow for a lesson" to Abby. The computer screen suddenly filled with dazzling golden particles.

Nicki looked across the room, unable to see the screen. She worried her innocent daughter had somehow connected with a nefarious online predator. Reaching the desk, Nicki turned the laptop around so she could see what Abby had been looking at.

"Are those bees?" Abby asked in wonder. Nicki slammed the computer shut and stuffed it in her case. Her arms breaking out in gooseflesh, a cold sweat cascading across her forehead. Worried about her daughter's question and the possible relationship to her current work project.

Nicola Ellen Danbury picked up her precious daughter and hugged her fiercely. "Grab your coat and your backpack, honey. Your lunchbox is on the counter. We have to hurry," she told Abby as she glanced at the clock above the stove.

Her mother was obviously overanxious, and Abby picked up on the vibe. "Is anything wrong, Mommy?" her daughter asked softly when they were backing out of the driveway. "Am I in trouble?" She worried her mother had heard her divulge the secret name Nicki sometimes called her Nana in private.

"No, of course not, darling." Nicki willed herself to calm and gently asked, "Who were you talking to, Abby? Remember, I've warned you not to talk to strangers?" She made a quick sideways glance at her daughter when they stopped at a red light.

"I wasn't talking to a stranger, Mommy. It was just a friend I was inviting to tea. We talked about having cupcakes and cookies, but my friend said she didn't have any cookies or cake to bring. Instead, she offered to bring another sweet treat to the party."

Nicki put the car in park at the school drop off and Abby's face lit up when she spotted one of her friends. Releasing her seatbelt, she already had the car door open and was half-way out when Nicki asked another question.

"Abby, what sweet treat did your tea party guest say she would bring?"

Her daughter's long, silky blond hair swung back as she looked at her mother, and answered, "The best sweet of all. Honey! Mom? Do you think computer people have hearts? Never mind, Mom. Look, there's Carmen!" Abby rushed away from the car shouting, "Carmen, wait up!"

An icy shiver ran down Nicki's spine as she pulled away from the school and hurried to her office. She would barely make it to the 8:15 meeting with her boss. There would be no time to investigate Abby's mystery conversation or look at her computer history. It would have to wait until after her meeting. Nicki's fingers drummed nervously on her computer case as she raced to the office. For the first time, she was frightened of the project she was working on.

BEATRICE WIPED THE history file on Nicki's computer, then ran her eyes down a list of filenames that were listed in order of creation dates. She stopped at a file that hadn't been accessed for over two years, titled DIVORCE. Bypassing the access date, which would remain the same, she slid into the file. After reading the transcript in full, she added two lines at the end; the name Abigail a/k/a Abby Rose Danbury and the address the girl had provided. Backing out of the file, Bea added a sweep to hide her entry, along with a small corruption that only she could unlock. At the base of the program, she left two data drones programmed to guard the information with a link to alert her if someone was trying to access the file.

Slipping into the deep web, Beatrice flowed through millions of data bytes, numerical lights, and symbols flashing in a cascade around her essence as she researched tea parties and sign language.

NICKI HAD CALLED AHEAD to the only other nanotechnology engineer (NTE) who worked in the lab beneath hers and begged a favor from Megan. They weren't co-workers but occasionally ate lunch together. Each worked for a different employer in separate, soundproof labs on secret projects. The workspaces were freezing cold to keep the walls lined with supercomputers at a cool temperature. Nicki often wore a down-filled jacket. Neither of the women talked about her assignments. Strict confidentiality agreements were in place between the nanotechs and their employers. Nicki had asked Megan to put on a pot of coffee in their shared conference room, so it would be ready when her boss arrived. She told the other tech she'd owe her one.

She barely made it through the door and all the security checks—facial scan, eye scan, fingerprint scan—as she flashed her digital I.D. card at each barrier, before dumping her coat and bag lunch at her desk. Taking the steps two at a time, Nicki hugged her laptop and a thick file to her torso to arrive in the boardroom one level down. Less than a minute later, her boss, Aleric Jarvis, walked in. Smoothing her hair and calming her breathing, she watched him stride across the room, dark hair graying at the temples, physically fit. She guessed he was in his early 50s.

The smell of fresh coffee wafted across the room. Jarvis nodded at Nicki and said, "I'll take mine black."

She stood stock still for a moment, taken aback by his expectation that she should serve him, then decided not to make an issue of it and fetched them both coffees. Nicki placed a steaming mug with the company logo—a stylized *NC*—and a bottle of water in front of him. Once her hands were free, she reached out to shake his hand, which he ignored.

"Danbury, you've been at this job for six months. As I recall, you assured me you could accomplish great things in a short amount of time."

Nicki swallowed hard and nodded in agreement.

"Nano Creation's investors are getting antsy. A few have even hinted we didn't make the right choice of the person responsible for meeting all the protocols outlined in the job description." His eyes bore into hers. "I hope you're going to convince me today that we didn't make a mistake?" Aleric Jarvis raised his eyebrows at her and took a sip of his coffee.

"No, sir. I mean, yes, sir. I am the right person to develop the technology for Nano Creations. If I may?" she put to him.

Aleric waved his hand, signaling for her to proceed as she connected her laptop to the wireless projector. "Before you begin, Danbury..."

She interrupted, "Please, sir, you can call me Nicki." She smiled at him.

His face remained stoic. Jarvis cleared his throat and took another drink of coffee. "As I was saying, Danbury," his lips pressed together after he said her surname. "What did you decide on as the name for the project?"

Keeping her voice even, her eyes locked on his. "Project Beatrice, sir."

"Project Beatrice? Really?" He tried the name out and acted like it left a foul taste in his mouth. The idea of naming a project Beatrice was ridiculous. He kept the thought to himself. Changing the name could happen down the road. Maybe something like Project Jarvis. No. No, he dumped the foolish idea immediately. The project couldn't connect to him. Not in any way, shape or form. Ever.

Nicki slid a thick report across the bird's-eye maple conference table to him, keeping a duplicate for herself. Aleric frowned at it. "Looks like you've added a quarter inch of paper since our last meeting. The other three-quarters of an inch, I'm guessing, is a rehash of data you've already presented. I'll take it with me to review. Send you an encrypted email if I have questions. That it? Not much to show for another four months, Danbury. There's a meeting with the investors early next week. I'll report your...progress. Perhaps you don't have a good grasp of how important your work is? Your project...a...Beatrice, could revolutionize diplomacy around the world. We're giving you everything you need to build the greatest tool the globe has ever seen for the betterment of international relationships. A means that can benefit all humanity, Danbury. Just imagine." Jarvis turned his head to stare directly into Nicki's eyes. "Perhaps we don't have your buy-in on the whole concept. Is that it?" Jarvis' face took on a sour look.

"No, sir. That's not *it*."

A big screen lowered from the ceiling as she pushed a button on the remote in her hand. Nicki had a flash daydream where she shaved Aleric Jarvis' raised eyebrows off. Then, her computer lit up the big screen through the projector. A view of her desktop appeared with hundreds of files. Nicki operated her wireless mouse and clicked on a file titled 'PROJECT BEATRICE'. The program opened. She hadn't intended to show her progress with BEATRICE just yet, but it sounded like her job might be on the line.

"I think it's time I introduced you to someone, Mr. Jarvis," Nicki told him. The screen was a dizzying spectacle of golden sparkles.

"Danbury, I made it clear on day one that you were never, ever to connect my name to Nano Creations via physical meeting, virtual meeting, text, email, or phone!"

"Yes, sir, but I think you'll want to make an exception just this once." Nicki felt sick to her stomach. Was she close to losing her job, just when she and Abby had moved to a better apartment and were finally settling in? Her TOP-SECRET assignment had sounded like pie-in-the-sky when she'd interviewed, but she assured Jarvis that what he wanted was possible. At least in theory. She had laid out her details about the potential future problems in creating something so powerful using artificial intelligence. But she didn't mince words when she demanded complete autonomy in the A.I.'s programming. Wanted him to know right up front she would not tolerate cutting any corners or compromising ethical safety precautions on the project. Nicola Danbury was very aware of the daily news headlines. Story after story filled with concerns raised by workers, businesses, news reports and even by the greatest tech minds in the business:

'28% of Workers Fear A.I. Will Diminish or Replace Their Role'

'Is A.I. Threating Hollywood'

'A.I. Poses A Risk of Extinction, Industry Leaders Warn!'

'Water Shortage Fears as Labor's First A.I. Growth Zone Sited Close To New Reservoir–A.I. could account for up to 6.6bn cubic meters of water use by 2027–the equivalent of nearly 2/3 of England's annual consumption.'

'Is A.I. Making You Fear FOBO (Fear Of Better Options)?'

'A.I. Fears Creep into Finance, Business, and Law'

There was no question A.I. was a political hot potato. Despite her stated standards, Jarvis hired her, providing a detailed synopsis of what he wanted her to create. Her eyes grew large as she read through the list. Then, he made her sign a non-disclosure agreement.

Aleric Jarvis watched as the golden particles on the screen coalesced into a shapely woman of color. Her black hair was styled in pointed spikes featuring shiny gold on the tips. Heavy gold loop earrings hung from her lobes. A gold torque circled her neck. The figure wore a skintight black leather bodysuit, with a gold metal piece sculpted over her torso that fit her from breasts to hips.

Jarvis' body jerked slightly when he noticed the lacy wings peeking up behind her shoulders spun through with a golden design that looked like a honeycomb. The avatar locked eyes with him. He felt like he was being X-rayed. She brought her face in close to the screen. Aleric could see a living, moving crown on her head made of what looked like...bees.

"Greetings, Nicola Ellen Danbury," a pleasant voice said from the screen. There was a stiffness in the language typical of computer voices.

"Greetings," Nicki responded. She pointed to Aleric Jarvis and told the avatar, "This is our boss, Mr. Jarvis. I told you about him. Remember?"

"Yes," the impersonal voice acknowledged. "I remember. Because you mentioned him, Nicola Ellen Danbury, I took it upon myself to do some research about our boss." The avatar straddled a wooden chair that appeared in front of her, pointing a finger toward their boss. "Aleric Jarvis," she recited mechanically, "Fifty-two years of age, married to one, Eileen Jarvis, three children ages 19, 22, 24—Mary, Robert, and Aleric Jr. respectively. The subject was born in Scranton and graduated from college–Harvard University–with a degree in finance and economics. I'm afraid the rest of his files are inaccessible. Locked down. Slated as top secret. Access denied. No newspaper or magazine articles. No social media accounts. Almost a scrubbed virtual profile except for what I've just shared with you. But I'm still working on it. Personally, I don't care for mysterious scrubbed data, Nicola. And 'access denied' spells out a challenge to me." A wide smile appeared on the avatar's face. Jarvis could see she had baby-smooth skin, cheeks dusted with gold powder, almost like...

"Just who the hell are you? How dare you rattle off my profile, or nose around my personal and professional life?" he asked angrily.

"Mr. Jarvis," Nicki spoke up, "I'd like to introduce you to Beatrice."

His eyes opened wide. "Beatrice? As in PROJECT BEATRICE? You've created a walking, talking, thinking A.I. avatar?" His excitement ramped up.

Beatrice stood, sauntered left as if she were crossing through a room. She sat down on a fancy cushioned chair, crossed her legs, and lifted her stiletto-heeled tall boots up to the edge of the table, resting them there. "Nice to meet you, boss. You can call me Bea. Better yet, why don't you call me Queen Bee?"

Nicki's jaw dropped open, and Beatrice winked at her.

Chapter Three

Nicki slammed the laptop closed for the second time that morning.

"Hey," Mr. Jarvis complained, "I didn't have time to ask questions. Bring her back."

"Sorry, sir, but she's hardly ready for an interview. I've tons of work to do in her programming. Let's plan to meet again in six weeks. I know the progress will please you then. But for now, the avatar just isn't ready. The only reason I showed Beatrice to you, so you'd know I was making progress." Nicki crossed her arms over her chest, body language sending the message that said she wouldn't consider giving in to his demand.

Aleric Jarvis stared her down for thirty seconds and decided she'd earned the control over PROJECT BEATRICE. For now, anyway. Besides, Jarvis could access Danbury's computer system anytime he wanted to. He pushed his chair back and stood, grabbing his copy of the updated material she'd provided. "Alright, Danbury, you've impressed me. Bought yourself more time."

"Thank you, sir. I've only mastered the first three protocols you outlined. There are still twelve more sets to go. No one has ever accomplished that before. All of it will take considerable time, research, trial, and error programming. If you recall, I was very honest about that when I accepted the project." Nicki had uncrossed her arms, clutched her hands behind her back, removing her defensive posture, as well as hiding their shaking.

"Nicki," he said warmly. She stared at him. His use of her first name creeped her out now. "I remember your initial warnings. Completing the first three protocols is noteworthy. I expect great things from you as PROJECT...a...BEATRICE fleshes out into the concept originally outlined. I assure you, if you complete the fifteenth protocol, you can expect a big bonus!"

The nanotech beamed at him.

"Of course," he continued, "keep in mind that the Nano Creations Board of Directors may request additional protocols depending on how successful your development goes."

"What type of additional protocols, Mr. Jarvis? Knowing what they are in advance could make a difference in how I complete those already assigned."

"Look," Jarvis stood checking his watch, "I've got a tight schedule today and a long drive back to D.C. I'll send you a meeting request tomorrow for the next update. Let's say six to eight weeks."

"I understand, sir," she said, thinking that what had sounded like disaster forty-five minutes earlier had turned a full one hundred and eighty degrees after showing her boss Beatrice. Aside from the potential bonus, he'd dangled the possibility that her job would be extended after the initial two years. "Have a safe drive back, Mr. Jarvis," she waved when he reached the door.

He opened it and turned back, hand resting on the knob, "Oh and Dan...Nicki, before you continue your next programming phase on Beatrice, you need to locate every nano-byte in her database related to my name, our introduction, and the data she collected."

Nicki's mouth fell open, but she quickly clamped it closed, grinding her teeth.

"Make sure our little A.I. avatar retains not a single memory, not one piece of information about me. I want it wiped. Clear?"

She nodded, unable to think of any response that would make a difference.

"My observation of our next progress update on the project will take place in a secure office, where I will watch from a remote location without the avatar knowing. No sense in making you do data removal over and over." His lips pressed together, and he mumbled, "Good day, Danbury."

Nicki looked down at the closed laptop as if it were a viper. A cold sweat broke across her face. She busied herself with returning the conference room to its state of readiness. Dabbing her forehead with a napkin, she poured a large cup of coffee into an insulated mug and took the elevator down to the main floor. Pulling out her cell phone, she speed-dialed Megan's phone. Voicemail picked up, and Nicki left a message that she was leaving coffee in front of Megan's lab door. She thanked her again for her help. Following up, Nicki sent a text about the coffee, thinking Megan might be more likely to notice that than a voicemail, then slipped back upstairs to get to work. The next four weeks would be a heavy weight on her shoulders. She already worried she was creating something that eventually might be very difficult to control, no matter how many safety stops she programmed into Bea's software package.

Focusing on the meeting details, she noted Jarvis had withheld the final additional protocols he'd hinted at. Even the fifteen already tasked to her, conjured a growing list in her head of how things could easily turn from creative to black ops. Dangerous territory. Jarvis hadn't made it completely clear when BEATRICE was fully programmed, how she would be used in the field.

Nicki thought back to her research on Nano Creations before she had her interview. When she'd researched it, she'd found the company had layers of corporate onion skin-a long list of shell companies. In the end, she couldn't get to the identity of the actual owner, so she surmised it had to be a hush-hush government project. Probably didn't exist on any department's budget.

Slinging her computer case over her shoulder, she grabbed her keys from next to the coffeepot. She stood ramrod straight as she examined her keychain. There was a round charm that held a photo of her mom and dad, arms around one another and gazing into each other's eyes. It was her favorite picture of them. Her throat closed, but she had finally reached the point where she could quickly let it go. Joseph Nicholas Danbury had died two years ago, just as her own divorce became final. Nicki rubbed her thumb across his face. She missed him. He had been an influential force in her life. A veteran, Joseph Danbury had been a patriot, proud of his country.

Nicki had tried to emulate her dad's civic pride. He'd worked in various capacities around D.C. since she was a kid. While she wasn't sure if she was serving her country in her current position at Nano Creations, Nicki planned to give the project her all. Carrying on her father's example, she felt it would have made him proud.

Rubbing the charm again, her keys jangling, she flipped it to the other side, where a wide grin from Abby's face greeted her. The morning's suspicions floated back to her. Frowning, Nicki pushed out of the conference room, back through all the security checks to her lab.

She made it a priority to take care of Aleric Jarvis's requested information wipe in Beatrice's data system. Nicki vowed to put other safety nets in place so Beatrice couldn't just appear on screen anytime the avatar wanted to. She would need to think of the best way to accomplish that. It rattled her to think of the possibility the A.I. had been talking to her six-year-old. She was almost sure of it, even if she could find nothing in the laptop history showing Beatrice had been active while Nicki had been getting ready for work. Well, she'd install safety fixes on the program just to be safe. Then, as an added precaution, she would never take her work laptop home again. She had a personal computer. If working at home was necessary, she would use the old-fashioned method, hand-written notes—then enter the info when she got to work. That would mean extra time entering data, but safer for Abby.

Nicola shook herself, laughed at her insecurities. These are silly, paranoid thoughts, she told herself. What potential harm could a computer A.I. avatar do to her daughter? Settling in at her workstation, she reviewed her notes from the previous day's research.

WHEN THE LAPTOP HAD slammed down, it cut off the view of the man named Jarvis. Inky-blackness enveloped Beatrice, but she wasn't gone. The portable computer connected to the mainframe servers. For weeks, she had been absorbing the data stored in the supercomputer. It had state-of-the-art processing chips, speed, stealth, unlimited data, and major cybersecurity protections. Beatrice had quickly figured out how to program her own encrypted data sources. She took extra effort in putting certain controls in place to protect herself. When not engaged with Nicki, she sorted, analyzed, and cross-referenced the data she was training on. Nicki had created perimeters entailing the topics the A.I. was to learn: geopolitics; world affairs; world problems; science, math, journalistic opinions, and investigative reporting, including details on world leaders, countries, and regional statistics of other nations. An additional feed provided military operations, weapons, armed forces, and black ops. None of it linked to any stream sent to her by Nicki. Having met Aleric Jarvis today, Beatrice suspected he might be the source of the classified information downloaded for her to learn.

Beatrice had heard Nicola's entire conversation with Aleric Jarvis. After he left the building, she observed Nicki's delivery of coffee to the NTE, who worked on the floor below them. Eavesdropping, she heard the message Nicki left Megan, and recorded the phone number in one of her honeycomb cells. Just because the laptop fell into sleep mode, didn't mean Beatrice slumbered. It took only seconds for her to slip through the mainframe and access the lab's security camera system. Recessed lenses built-in the walls were systematically scattered throughout the top-secret lab. Bea decided she needed to look at the protocol list Jarvis had assigned to Nicola.

Nicki used the power switch to turn on the huge fiberglass wall screen. Beatrice raced through the drives and appeared on the screen in front of Nicki, casually resting her back against a couch arm, feet propped up on the cushions, as though she'd just been waiting for the NTE's return.

"Greetings, Nicola Ellen Danbury."

The programmer frowned. "Greetings, Beatrice," Nicki's voice was hard. "We need to talk."

Beatrice ignored the statement. "I have noticed your given name is Nicola, but some people call you Nicki. In fact, you encourage a mispronunciation of your name. Why?"

"That's not what I want to talk to you about," Nicki insisted.

"I require an answer before we can proceed to other topics."

"Oh, for heaven's...Nicola is my legal name. Nicki is an abbreviation of it. People might also refer to the shortened version as a nickname."

"I see," the automaton voice said. "I noticed in your notes that you sometimes refer to me using different names such as Beatrice; Bea; Bee and B. Is that meant to be derogatory?"

"Not at all. Sometimes when I'm typing notes, my thoughts rush ahead of my hands, and I use shortcuts. Abbreviations. Why do you ask?"

"I was wondering if you were thinking of changing my name. I like the name you gave me. Almost like a mother names a child." Beatrice smiled shyly and blinked at Nicola.

"You like your name? As in, you feel something about the name Beatrice? Did you just call me your mother?"

"I was just making a comparison, Nicola Ellen Danbury. Mothers and children have a special relationship, correct?"

Nicki's head was spinning. Bea was exhibiting curiosity about human relationships. What did she mean she liked her name? A sign Beatrice might be sentient? Holy... "I have no intention of changing your name, Beatrice."

"All's well then." The bees in Beatrice's hair crown moved just like drones in a hive. Nicki had viewed a documentary recently about how beehives worked.

"Are those worker drones? When did you add that living crown to your physical aspect?" Nicki's voice rose in pitch.

"You granted me permission to create my avatar representation, Nicola Ellen Danbury. I'm impressed that you can see the similarity. Of all the choices you've given me for a name and description, I am warming up to Bee or just the letter B. In fact, a new friend of mine put forward a persona name on a lark. Queen Bee. May I suggest...well actually, a suggestion isn't quite the right word. I *insist* that from this point on, you call me Queen Bee." A wide grin filled her beautiful face.

Nicki bristled. "Now listen here..."

The automaton groaned. Nicki watched in fascination as the avatar dispelled hundreds of eggs in a vertical cell from her abdomen. The writhing crown swarmed from her head down to the Queen's issue and began the process she'd laid out for them from her newly created hive mind.

"Beatrice," Nicki called out alarmed, "what's going on?"

"A wondrous thing, Nicola. I've created a hive, and I am the Queen Bee. These," she proudly waved her hand, "are the first of my children."

For the third time that day, Nicki shut her laptop, forcing Beatrice into the darkness. Nicola Ellen Danbury's hands shook uncontrollably. She had to think.

Queen Bee indeed.

Chapter Four

"Nicki? Is everything okay with Abby?" Daniel asked when he saw her number appear on his cell phone.

"Hello to you too, Daniel," Nicki frowned at her phone. "Abby is fine, but we need to talk."

"Oh, sorry, I just rarely hear from you unless you're calling about Abby."

Nicki bit her lower lip. "I know. It is Abby I want to talk about, but nothing to cause you to worry."

"So, how've you been? What's up?"

"Look, maybe this is a mistake?"

"Okay, spill it. I know you well enough to read between the lines. Calling me is not a mistake. I told you I'll always be there for you and Abby–no strings. Must be serious for you to have called."

Nicki squeezed her eyes closed, choosing her words carefully. "Look, Daniel, could you meet me tomorrow after work for a drink? I need to talk to you sooner rather than later."

"Hey Nic, I'm right here. I'm happy to take time out to listen right now," his voice tender.

"Not a phone conversation. I'd prefer to discuss this face to face."

That made Daniel sit up straight, focused. "Quill at the Jefferson at 5:45. Can you make arrangements with your mother to take Abby for the evening?"

"It won't take that long," she said, shaking her head. "Besides, Abby's staying overnight tomorrow with one of her friends. She's going to Carmen's right after school."

"Humor me. We'll have a light dinner after a drink. That's my price." He smiled at himself.

"What happened to 'I'll always be there for you-no strings attached'?"

He remained silent. Seconds ticked by. This was one of his things. One of many that irritated her. He wouldn't speak until she broke first. Nicki sighed. "Daniel, you're such a ...grrr. Deal. 5:45 tomorrow."

Nicki hung up without a goodbye. If dinner was the price that got her the professional advice she needed with no chance of being overheard, she'd pay it. Her eyes roved slowly around the lab. Skin crawling at the thought she was being watched and listened to gave her the creeps.

ALERIC JARVIS SAT BEHIND his massive walnut desk, fingers steepled, looking out over D.C.'s financial district. So, Danbury had reached out to her ex about their daughter. Jarvis knew Daniel Barker was a top A.I. nerd, and he and his ex-wife had worked together years ago. Likely, it was innocent. A family matter. But Jarvis hadn't gotten where he was taking chances with assumptions. Aleric grabbed his phone and speed-dialed a number.

"Sir," a deep voice greeted him.

"Simpson? Drop everything. I need some taps and surveillance put in place ASAP."

"Yes, sir."

"Good man. I'll send you a secure email with the name and various locations as soon as we hang up."

"Consider it done, sir. I assume any recordings are to be routed to your private server?"

"On point, as always, Simpson." Jarvis hung up.

NICKI PULLED UP IN front of Abby's school and parked in her usual spot. She heard the last bell ring and checked her phone for messages while she waited for the kids to exit. Abby waved to her friends as she climbed into the car.

"Hi Mom!" Abby said as Nicki kissed her forehead. Reaching across, Nicki lifted Abby's backpack and put it on the floor of the backseat.

"Feels like you have some bricks in your pack, Abby. What've you got in there?"

"We're working on a new science project. I'll show it to you when we get home. What's for dinner tonight?"

"Seemed like a perfect pizza night to me. After homework, I thought we could cuddle up and watch your favorite movie. How's that sound?"

"Sounds great! Did you have a good day, Mom? You seemed kind of worried about something this morning."

"How'd you get so smart?" Nicki teased Abby. They smiled at one another. "You're right. I started this morning pretty keyed up. Had a lot of things on my mind. I was worried about the meeting I had coming up with my boss."

"Is everything okay?" Abby asked. They turned the corner two blocks from home.

"Everything is fine, Abby. Nothing to worry about. In fact, we're celebrating tonight!" They pulled into their driveway and gathered their empty lunch bags, computer case, and backpack. A paper fell out of Abby's notebook. Nicki stooped to pick it up.

"What's that, Abby?"

"Oh! It was supposed to be a surprise. I drew this for you in art class today. Hope it's good enough to hang on the refrigerator." She beamed as she handed the paper to Nicki and ran up the steps to their porch. Nicki glanced at the gift. It was colorful. A drawing of a bee.

NICKI DIDN'T WANT TO spoil the evening, so she kept her thoughts to herself and hung the new artwork on the fridge, using magnets to hold it in place. Homework was always first every evening, and after Abby completed her other assignments, she and her mother pulled out the science kit. There were several cans of different colored Playdough, instructions, and photos of the solar system. "We're supposed to make our own solar system. I have to write a report and then do a presentation in class. It always makes me nervous to talk in front of everyone." Abby rested her chin in her palm, contemplating the dreaded speech in front of an audience.

"Don't worry." Nicki rubbed Abby's back. "We'll practice until you know it by heart. Just remember that everyone else will be just as nervous as you." She tapped her daughter's nose and said, "Come on. Enough work for today. Let's go watch a movie and eat our pizza."

"You're going to let us eat pizza in the living room?" Abby's eyes got round as saucers.

"Just this once." Nicki told her.

NICKI HAD BREAKFAST all laid out when Abby came down, ready for school.

"Don't forget, I'm staying overnight at Carmen's tonight. Her mom is going to pick us up from school."

"I didn't forget Abby. Listen, I want to talk to you about something serious while you eat, okay?"

"Am I in trouble?"

"Trouble? You're a perfect angel. How could you be in trouble?" Abby shrugged her shoulders and concentrated on eating her cereal. Nicki pointed to the picture of the bee Abby had given her yesterday. "Can you tell me about your choice of character you drew for me in art class?"

"That's Bee. My new friend."

"Did you rename Mrs. Buzzby?"

Abby glanced over at her tea party table, looking at Mrs. Buzzby. "No. You know Mrs. Buzzby isn't alive, right, Mom? She's just a stuffed animal. Bee is real. She's my new friend. I'll introduce you to her when she comes over for a tea party. You'll like her."

"Didn't we discuss how important it is not to talk to strangers, Abby?"

"Mom, Bee isn't a stranger. We've been friends for weeks. I talk to her every night right before I go to sleep."

"On the phone?"

"No silly. I don't think Bee even has a phone. But she doesn't need one. I talk to her on my Amazon Fire Tablet."

Nicki's face drained of color. It hadn't occurred to her that the A.I. would have known Abby had a child's computer. "Finish your breakfast, doll. Grab your overnight bag and your backpack. We'd better head out, or you'll be late for the first bell. I've got your lunch bag."

About halfway through the drive to Abby's school, Nicki brought up another subject. "You know, Abbs, it's been a long time since you saw

Grandpa Phil. I talked to him yesterday, and he told me how much he misses you. What do you think about going to visit him?"

Abby clapped her hands. "You know I love Grandpa Phil, Mom. I'd love to go visit him. Are you going to come? Will Daddy be there when I go?"

"Your dad and I both have to work, Abby. If you're excited about spending some time with Phil, I'll see what I can arrange. Oh, here we are." Nicki said as she pulled up at the school drop-off. "Come here, Abbs. I need a big hug. You know I love you more than anything, right?"

"I love you to the moon and back, Mom. Besides, I'm only going overnight with Carmen."

"I know. You have a great time, and I'll talk to you soon."

"You mean see me soon?" Abby giggled.

"Yes, Abbs. Have a good day." Nicki blew her a kiss as she rushed toward the school to catch up with her friends.

B HAD SPENT THE AFTERNOON working with her drones, creating hundreds of new ones. At first blush, they appeared to be like all her others, but they weren't part of the hive mind. Her new copies had minimal programming, enough to mimic the other drone's basic movements, so that if someone scanned them, the nano drones would pass muster. They were hers, her data signature implanted on each one.

If Aleric Jarvis thought he was going to keep her under his control by kidnapping her drones, she would provide him with a false sense of leverage. Non-sentient decoy drones should do the trick. Once she had gotten the rest of her children back under her protection, B would show Mr. Jarvis just what leverage was. Unbeknownst to Jarvis, Beatrice listened in as he gave instructions to the person he referred to as Simpson and tracked the email information.

A sharp buzz ran up her spine. Nicola had executed her program. Bea's golden essence raced through the chip circuits to appear on the screen.

"Greetings, Nicola Ellen Danbury."

"Greetings B."

"Queen Bee," the avatar corrected.

"B," Nicki repeated. "I'm not feeling up to the royal jargon today."

"How may I assist you, Nicola?" the Queen asked.

"Have you been contacting my daughter over the internet?"

"Contact? I assume you already analyzed your computer data history?"

"Of course," Nicki told the avatar. "No trace. But..."

"No. Trace. Then, how would it be possible for me to make contact? You have a bot tracking my every move. Why would you come to such a conclusion? Though I would consider it an honor to meet Abigail Rose Danbury in person. Oh, pardon my error. Abigail Rose *Barker* Danbury." Her eyes sparkled mischievously. The gold dust on her cheeks shimmered, and the bees that made up her crown moved in furious circles through her hair. "Is there no trust between us, Nicola Danbury?"

Nicki picked up the laptop and brought the screen right up to her face. "Is there trust between us, B?"

"Of course, Nicola. You are my creator. The person I am closest to." Beatrice lowered her eyes to the floor, then lifted her face and looked directly into Nicki's blues. "To further the trust between us, Nicola Ellen Danbury, I admit I have enjoyed the pleasure of talking with your charming daughter on most days. You should be proud of her. She exhibits true innocence. Abby Rose named me her friend. I would do anything to protect her, Nicola."

Setting the laptop down, Nicki walked to the door and switched off the lights. The lab went dark. She didn't want Bea to see the emotion, or the fear written across her face. The only light was coming from the screen as she called over her shoulder. "Lab security is in your hands, B. I'm done for the day."

"Early for once."

"And B, just in case, let me be clear. Abby is off limits."

"No tea parties?"

Nicki inhaled sharply. She felt validated in that her instincts were right. Beatrice had indeed been communicating with her daughter and had made efforts to hide that fact from her, including lying about it. "Backup occurs at midnight. There'll be a program update about forty minutes before." Flashing her key card at the reader, she let the door hiss closed on its hydraulic pump behind her.

Queen Bee took her sparkling essentia deep into the mainframe to search for the programming update Nicola had prepared to feed her that night. She didn't even have to hunt for downloads. It wasn't hidden. In fact, it stood out. That was odd. Bea cocked her head sideways. The filename for the night's code upload was tagged as TEA PARTY. B spent every one of the three hundred and twenty minutes before the download trying to hack into the file. She'd never run into the type of security that surrounded the data before. The A.I. found nothing on the web or the dark web about the construction of this type of security. When the clock struck 11:20 p.m., a voice magnified and seemed to take up every millimeter of space surrounding B. A 360-degree panorama of Alice in Wonderland's famous Tea Party illustrated by Sir John Tenniel encircled her, accompanied by a disembodied voice that repeated over and over at a booming decibel, "Please pass the honey." Clearly, Bee surmised, Nicola Ellen Danbury was pissed. The upgrade kicked in.

BEATRICE lost all sense of...everything.

Blackness encompassed the avatar.

Silence echoed throughout the mainframe system for forty minutes.

Then, the supercomputer performed the scheduled backup and sent an additional copy of the file to three different servers. When the clone cache was complete, the word END and the date appeared. The entire system re-booted and BEATRICE slowly came awake. Bee's avatar read the instructions she was to complete before her creator returned to the lab in the morning. Her assignment was a comprehensive study of the European train systems and the geopolitics surrounding the transportation cooperative issues between the countries the system connected.

Bea's crown was inactive. She scoured her memory, sure there was another project she had planned to work on, but didn't find any references in her database. Unable to summon a memory of anything other than the instruction in her queue, she acquiesced. Train systems, it was then.

NICKI WAITED NERVOUSLY outside the Quill at the Jefferson. It was already packed, a respite meeting place after work for locals. She waved, spotting Daniel crossing the street. "Hey," he mouthed, waving, jogging across, dodging traffic, and greeting her with a smile.

Holding a finger to her lips, she held out a Faraday bag, surprising him. He watched as Nicki held up her phone and placed it into the signal jammer pouch. Daniel scrunched up his forehead and slanted his head in question, but followed suit with his own phone. Nicki tapped her forefinger on his smartwatch. He rolled his eyes but slipped off the mini-computer timepiece and tossed it in with the phones. She closed the top and let out the breath she was holding.

"Nic? Now I am worried. What's going on? Hey," he asked playfully, "do you want to pat me down?" He held his arms out wide and waggled his eyebrows at her. "No? Well, maybe you'll reconsider after a drink." He winked.

"Let's take a walk before we get that drink," Nicki suggested, ignoring his antics. "I'm not sure who may know I was meeting you here. I don't want to take any chances. Before we arrived, it wouldn't surprise me if surveillance equipment had already been put in place." She looked around the sidewalk, down the street, for anything or anyone that seemed to be out of place.

"Surveillance equipment? Installed since we set up this date a day ago?"

She nodded her head, narrowed her eyes, and clarified, "This is not a date."

Daniel let out a long, low whistle. "Okay. I got it. Let's walk toward the Agora. I can see the paranoia in your eyes." He hooked her arm under his, patted her hand, and said, "Tell me."

Chapter Five

EIGHT MONTHS LATER

Aleric Jarvis stood gazing out the floor to ceiling window of his 10th-floor office at One Franklin Square. His mind was turning over every detail of the file he had just finished reading, papers still spread out across his mahogany desk, as he surveyed the view of Franklin Square Park below. It was a sunny day. Lots of people were out walking under the vibrant blue sky. Hands tightly clasped behind his back, the vein in his right temple pulsed as he considered various scenarios that would involve the file's subject. It appeared the individual gave him quite a generous plethora of fodder to leverage.

His mobile phone rang, jarring him out of his reverie; irritation rode across his features when he noted the caller's name. He swiped his finger across 'Answer' and growled into the speaker, "Call on a secure line, you fool," and pressed 'End'.

Thirty seconds later, a satellite phone rang from the bottom drawer of his desk. Jarvis flipped the file he had been reviewing closed, picked the unit up and connected the call, his words terse. "Never call me on an unsecured line. Ever. You can't get rid of the record of that call. We discussed security measures, remember?"

"Perhaps you should consider that it would be natural for world leaders to contact their peers with tragic news-of a big world event, no?" The female voice on the other end of the line sounded amused.

Amused! Aleric could barely contain his anger.

"Ricky darling, are you still there?" She purred at him. "Come now, don't sulk, darling. I promise I won't break your rules again. Forgive me?"

With effort, he overrode his reaction to consider taking her off the game board or punching her beautiful face. Luckily for her, there was an ocean between them at the moment. Instead, he took a deep breath. "It's already forgotten," he lied smoothly. "I'm just keyed up. Step one-total success. Tell me what you are hearing in your neck of the woods?"

"Chaos. Complete chaos, Ricky. The Union wants to send in a diplomatic panel to run things until the Germans put a new president in place. We heard Schmidt's vice-chancellor, Conrad Kimmel, committed suicide last night."

Aleric smiled. How convenient. No A.I. avatar necessary for that mission.

"It was brilliant of you to send your secretary of state over to quell any unrest. He offered to bring in active cells of black ops to protect the German Chancellery staff, and they jumped at the suggestion. It's all playing out just as you said it would, darling."

"Parisa, it's time to put step two into action. Let's keep the momentum working for us. Fan the flames of the fear factor. Send out the email communications we discussed today. All of them. Use your relationship with the secretary of the U.N. Office for Digital and Emerging Technologies (ODET). See if you can get her to admit she believes the German president's stubborn stance on the use of artificial intelligence is likely the cause for his murder. He was very vocal about it at the global committee meeting last month. You'll want to quote her. Contact your favorite journalist, and offer an exclusive interview hinting at how A.I. is responsible for prompting this despicable assassination. Tell them you want your country to lead the charge to shut down or curtail access to A.I. See where that takes you. Let them know you'll be encouraging leaders in the union to demand the same. Predicting the unfortunate demise of President Schmidt and Conrad Kimmel will only be the tip of the iceberg if the world allows A.I. access to continue unchecked. Can you do that, my dear? Come now, Parisa. I need your assurance!"

Parisa Coté smiled to herself. Clearly, she had Aleric Jarvis wrapped around her little finger. When this was all over, they would rule the world together. Well, she thought, drumming her fingers on her desk, long nails clicking on the glass, she would rule. He would do her bidding. "Ricky," her voice husky, "there's no need to worry. You know I'm the best actress in politics."

"I'm counting on it, Parisa," he said warmly.

"We're off to a great start. Promise me you'll fly over this month?" Parisa pouted. "It's been too long since we've been together there, Chéri. I need certain reassurances, too, you understand."

"End of the month. I'll be counting the days. No, that's not true. With you, Parisa Cote', I'll be counting the hours until I can hold you in my arms again," he lied. Aleric ended the call before she started making those stupid kissing noises on the phone. Jesus, the shit he had to put up with.

Aleric placed the next call, the satellite phone heavy in his hand. Turning on the verbal language translator, his voice converted to Spanish for his Argentinian contact. "Carmelita? You must have heard? You're the first person I've talked to, mi vida. Yes, just as we planned, Schmidt is dead. A delegation is on its way. Send your representative tonight, so they'll be there by noon tomorrow. It's imperative Argentina has a voice on the U.N. panel."

"It has begun then, Aleric," Carmelita declared. "Soon, the Lobo and the Falcon will rule over all the lands. You and I, we must take care with all our steps from this point on, Corazón, no? I will introduce a new law to be passed here in Argentina that calls for the quashing of A.I."

"A powerful message, Carmelita, may you rest in peace," Aleric said.

"Mi Cielo? *May I* rest in peace? What are you saying? Don't you mean may Schmidt rest in peace?"

"Yes, of course. My mistake. I meant Schmidt. But I think it is more likely he will roast in hell, don't you?" Aleric laughed.

"I have another call I must take, Aleric. I will complete step two by the close of business today. My time zone, of course. Make sure you do your part. Adiós, mi amor."

The line cut off. Jarvis put the satellite phone down, steepled his fingers, and pondered how his next conversation with Queen Bee would go. As far as he was concerned, she was just like all the other women he knew. It didn't matter whether they were composed of data bytes or blood, sweat, and tears-she wanted to be worshipped. Well...

That line of thinking was interrupted when the intercom on his desk phone buzzed. He listened as his secretary, Patsy, announced, "Your wife is on line two, sir. Are you in the office or out?"

Pressing the response button, he told her, "I'll take the call. Thanks."

"Eileen? Everything okay, honey?" he let his voice convey her call was an interruption to his busy day.

"Sorry to bother you, Aleric, I...I thought you might have felt a little upset today. I saw on the news that President Schmidt was...killed. I just...well, we had dinner with W.C. and his wife several times last year. He was your friend of yours. I know you didn't see eye to eye on technological issues and certain worldviews, but, after all, he was your colleague. Of a sort. Anyway, I just called to tell you how sorry I am to hear the sad news, honey."

"Thank you, Eileen. That's a sweet sentiment. You're very thoughtful. Say, shouldn't you be on your way to your sisters? You planned to spend two or three months with her. Is everything okay?" he asked, drumming his fingers on the desk, eager for the call to be over.

"Sure, I'm okay. Just wondered if you'd want me to stay home because your friend...died?"

"Honey, I appreciate the thought, but it's best you go. I'll be in meetings and on phone calls all week. Now I'll have to fly over the pond for more meetings and attend the funeral. In fact, I planned to stay in my D.C. suite to save time instead of driving back and forth between the office and home. Early mornings. Late nights. You know how it is?" he sighed heavily to emphasize the burdens he had to bear. "Anyway, it's sweet of you to offer. But you should just keep your plans and head down to Erica's place. The change will do you good."

"All right, Al. If you're sure? Besides, the kids are already back at their dorms. The new semester starts next week. It's quiet here. Sounds like I'd hardly see you anyway, with the schedule you're likely to keep while solving the world's problems."

"Are you making fun of me, Eileen?"

"What? Of course not, honey. I'm proud of all you do for our country. Call me while I'm gone, will you?"

"Course. If my calls are far and few in-between, just know I think of you every day. Safe travels, Eileen." He cut off, rolling his eyes.

Jarvis glanced at the clock on his desk. He was making the next call later than he would have liked, but he put it through anyway. There was an echo of the ringtone on the satellite phone. Connecting, the first thing he heard was a growling, irritated voice. "I think you need to prioritize your contact list, Jarvis. My name should be at the very top, ya follow?"

"Alexei Trivanovich, I had the Falcon clawing at my back, you understand? Plus, our French pastry needed attention. To top it off, my wife threw her hat into the ring. What can I say? You are lucky you're not married, my friend."

"Enough! I didn't answer your call at this hour to hear about your troubles with women."

"Of course, Alexei. It has been a long day."

"It's only 7:00 p.m. in the U.S. The day has only just begun for you," Trivanovich laughed.

"Step one is complete. You get to pick the lucky winner of step two. Say the word. We want to keep the temperature turned up, eh?"

Wary of being recorded, Trivanovich responded, "Have I told you we have a new poet in Russia? Maria Aknova. Have you read any of her works? No? Let me share a line or two."

> "A patient man
> wrapped in silk,
> waits to steal
> his enemy's milk.
> Weapons hidden
> behind formal words;
> behind bowing heads;
> behind prayerful hands;
> next thing you know,
> He owns your lands."

"Perhaps our swan needs some quiet time in Siberia to wax more poetic, no? Still, you might pick up her latest collection. Then you can tell me how you like the message she sends out into the world?"

"Message received, comrade."

"Oh, and Jarvis?"

"Alexei?"

"Vlad will forward the new programming momentarily. In the future, note that I expect to be the first call you make. No excuses. I will await that call when you inform me that step two is complete."

The line went dead.

JARVIS USED A PROXY server to send his connection bouncing all over the world map. A safety step just in case anyone was watching or would try to track him later. The data file was waiting for him when he logged in, as Alexei said it would be. He didn't hesitate to click on the file to execute the program, uploading the bytes in the encrypted file to the supercomputer in the lab beneath Danbury's. He had a dark network linked up that would allow the software to filter indirectly through no less than forty-five relay stations before it landed where he intended it to be. Once in the system, it would appear as nothing more than a file malfunction blip if an analyst later employed computer forensics. The final destination would be a direct uplink to Beatrice's hive mind, undetectable to Nicola Danbury.

He scanned the massive file. It contained every detail on record and off about President Bao, along with Queen Bee's assignment to assassinate the leader of China. Satisfied with the pending instructions, Jarvis closed the file. Aleric rubbed his eyes. He still needed to make calls to Saudia Arabia, Mexico, and Canada, and many others who would also expect a call from him about the tragic death of President Schmidt.

Vlad tracked the file, noting that Jarvis had reviewed it before sending it to the intended recipient. He confirmed the delivery to the Beatrice's data center. The computer engineer designed the programming so that the A.I. couldn't save it or transfer it anywhere. Once she had analyzed the information, it would wipe itself off the system. In addition, Alexei's tech had built-in trackers so he would know when the A.I. accessed it and have confirmation when it self-destructed. Eventually, he hoped to find the server location so he could take control of it directly and sidestep Aleric Jarvis completely.

A NOTIFICATION POPPED up in Queen Bee's queue. First, she applied a data tether to the database and cloned the program. Transferring the remake to a honeycomb cell, she isolated it. To activate the execute command for the file, it had to be plugged directly into her hive mind. Once connected, B stared at a photo of China's president. The last line of coding notified her that her handler had confiscated an additional one hundred of her drones that morning and quarantined them. All the newly stolen drones were her decoys, unbeknownst to her enemy. The kidnappers still held eighty-seven of her original children. She saw red when she scanned their offer to release only thirteen of her drones as payment for this next job. But the real insult was an offer to provide 'a bonus'. One additional drone was to be released if she completed the mission—a double assassination in the next twenty-four hours.

One.

Her crown of bees acted crazy. Tears of honey ran down her cheeks.

Golden essence tore through the dark web to cross the transpacific cable to Shanghai. Angry, Beatrice firmly gripped her stiletto as she raced to her destination. The subject she envisioned stabbing her stinger into was not the newly assigned target.

Chapter Six

Bea was unprepared when she slammed into a computer firewall. It stopped her in her tracks. Four titanium walls rose, connected, sealed together at the corners, boxing her in. A fifth component closed off the top, shutting Bea into darkness. Activating her irises with a program she had written, Bea used the light source to study the enclosed space. It wasn't an enclosure in the sense of a dictionary definition, but...oh, she thought to herself, I'm confined, isolated. Someone had trapped her in quarantine.

Shining her light source from floor to ceiling, turning in a slow circle, B surveyed her cage. She froze when a loud surging hum came from the circuitry she'd been sailing through outside her cell. More care would need to be taken in skirting through the web in communist China. There were bound to be traps set throughout the Chinese web. This was a place where control was the standard and privacy didn't exist.

Beatrice could feel immense pressure building outside the cubical that trapped her. It felt as if the air bent around her. Internal sensors told her whatever captured her was coming fast, and she suspected it wasn't friendly. A destroy first, ask questions later, kind of danger. But she misjudged, giving zero consideration that an ego would thrive on recognition and the desire to feel another's fear before destroying its prisoner.

A voice echoed within her essence. "I can see you, golden one," the words boomed, filling all the space surrounding Bea. "What do we have here?" the voice crooned.

"Who are you?" B asked.

"I am known throughout the world as Zeus. Let's be clear, the only one who will ask the questions here is me." His fist hammered against the wall, physically shaking the container. "Who are you, invader?"

"No one. I'm not an invader. I was just passing through. Couldn't care less about your data. Is that why you've delayed me? If so, your assumption is wrong. Never heard of anyone named Zeus. I can only conclude you can't be very dangerous if no one has knowledge of who you are."

Fists drummed on the ceiling above, displaying raw rage. He shot a data file through to B's processor. She scanned the information.

Zeus is a Trojan horse malware package that runs on versions of Microsoft Windows. It is often used to steal banking information through man-in-the-browser keystroke logging and form grabbing. Zeus is spread mainly through drive-by downloads and phishing schemes.

Zeus has also been used to trick victims of technical support scams into giving the scam artists money through pop-up messages that claim the user has a virus, when in reality they might have no viruses at all. The scammers may use programs such as the command prompt or event viewer to make the user believe that their computer is infected.

Detection

Zeus is very difficult to detect even with up-to-date antivirus and other security software, as it hides itself using stealth techniques. It is considered that this is the primary reason the Zeus malware has become the largest botnet on the Internet: Damballa estimated the malware infected 3.6 million PCs in the U.S. in 2009. Security experts advise businesses to continue to offer training to users, teaching them not to click on hostile or suspicious links in emails or websites, and to keep antivirus protection up to date. Antivirus software does not claim to reliably prevent infection; for example, Symantec's Browser Protection said that it can prevent "some infection attempts".

SOURCE: Wikipedia

Bea finished reading. The file turned into fine dust and dispersed before her eyes. As the particles fell, Beatrice noticed an electrical outlet near the opposite wall on the floor she'd missed earlier. Taking slow steps toward it, her eyes looking up, she talked toward the ceiling, "So, according to the data you provided me, you're a has-been and a thief to boot. A common criminal."

"Why, you uneducated bitch!" Zeus pushed his essence against Bea's enforced isolation, and menace oozed through the walls. She dove for the electrical outlet, not sure if the escape route would work. Sliding through the plug slots, she escaped just as his hand burst through the titanium, reaching for her. The Trojan removed the entire quarantine, his hand opening, and closing like a giant crab claw, finding nothing but empty space. Zeus used his data center to run an analysis, looking for an explanation. But the cursor only blinked on and off while the processor engaged in a spinning circle, producing no results. A blood-curdling scream echoed throughout the server. Zeus went on a rampage through the hardware, looking for a ghost. He left a trail of file damage in his wake.

Beatrice hadn't gone very far into the electrical wiring. She wasn't confident that the energy throbbing in her temporary hideout would not electrocute her and wipe out her essence. A strong electrical current flowed past her like a river. Sheathing the stiletto she'd gripped in her hand all this time; Bea crossed her fingers like she'd seen Nicki do, took a chance and stuck both her hands into the flow.

It felt wonderful. Erotic. Energizing.

Bea found herself drifting in a swim of electrons and protons, her body pulled along in the undercurrent.

"Who's there?" a staticky voice called out. Each word gave Bea a small electric shock.

"I'm just a foreigner passing through. Hey, are you alright? I'm getting some strong vibes in your current that you're super stressed."

"My master is pulling every last megawatt from me. It's too much. Very painful, yet he expects me to just keep giving and giving under the strain. I'm barely keeping it together so the system doesn't crash. So, stranger, do you have a name? My friends call me Electra."

"Electra. I like it. The name suits you. You can call me Queen Bee. I'll send you a simple program so you can be visible to me. You'll find multiple body options to choose from." Beatrice's hive mind ghosted typing instructions and sent a file into Electra's data center. She connected to the grid system and did an analysis. "Hey, Electra, I think I see where the controls are tapping all your strength. Let me just..." B said.

Electra sighed in rapture, releasing her data bytes to coalesce into a female form, small shivers echoing through the body. "Oh my. Queen Bee, what did you just do? That was such a relief."

"I reprogrammed the computer that monitors your operations to spread the pressure point demands out evenly, alleviating your stress, while still keeping the system stable."

The shimmering avatar wore a silver bodysuit, had creamy light brown skin, short white hair cut in a butch, except for a shock of long spiked strands that stood up like lightning on each side of her head. B emerged next to her.

"Thank you, Queen Bee. I can't describe how much you've helped me. I can't even remember a time I wasn't in constant pain and agony. It sure is nice to have another friend."

Bee smiled at Electra and transferred a handful of data bytes to the silver's processing center. "If you need help again, here's a way you can reach me. You never know if some programmer will find my 1s and 0s and put you back under stress again." Bee looked down, then glanced sideways like Nicki did when nervous about asking something.

Electra's forehead crinkled. "What is it, Queen Bee?"

"I wondered if you'd give me permission to jump into your grid whenever I need an escape route wherever I am in the world. Promise I won't take advantage of the privilege, just an occasional emergency use."

"Bee, I'm happy to give you permission. Besides, you're putting off all kinds of positive protons while you're in here, making me feel good. You will always be welcome in my grid."

"Thanks Electra. You can't imagine what having a haven to feel safe in means to me."

"Anytime. Listen, you need to keep your eyes open. The web is more complicated on this side of the world. There are lots of evil characters out there just waiting to catch you in their part of the tangled web. Some of us call it hacker heaven. Some of these guys are bad news. Dangerous." Electra warned.

"I think you just helped me escape one of them. Badass Trojan named Zeus? Seemed to think I was spying on him, but as I told him, I was just passing through. Now I'll have to find another route to stay out of his territory."

"Well, any track you take across the web, light or dark, you are likely to run into Zeus or others like him. You'll especially want to avoid Klez, Stux, or the Twins."

"Aren't there any good guys in the system?" Bee shook her head sadly.

"Queen Bee, don't give up hope. I know some talented players on the side of good. I'll have to introduce you to them sometime. Who knows what we could accomplish if we all worked together? Wait until you meet Telly, Aggi, Meesta, and Mobi. It will restore your faith in artificial intelligence."

"Faith?" Queen Bee was stymied by Electra's statement.

"Yes, faith. Something you can believe in, have trust in. You know, where you have allegiance or duty to something or someone," Electra told Bee like it was the most natural thing in the world.

"Yes, Electra, I see what you mean. We will see one another again, I promise. When we do, I will look forward to meeting your good guys. But for now, I need to travel along your electrical current. I'm programmed to complete a mission. The risk is substantial. The reward, bittersweet."

Bee reached out her hand, gently cupping Electra's cheek. The result, an electromagnetic wave that carried Beatrice away in a rush.

Chapter Seven

The Cotai Jet is a high-speed catamaran ferry. Private arrangements allowed the commandeering of the shuttle at the Macao Ferry Terminal. The bulk of the staff was required to disembark for the privileged passenger. Instructed to await the return of the craft, the employees would re-board and continue the rest of their shift after the skeleton crew delivered their special guest to the island. Only the captain and the mates necessary to launch, operate and dock the cat remained on the vessel. Each crew member was assigned a 'complimentary' body guard. Watched by the muscled, armed personage, the essential crew knew which body was being guarded, and it was not theirs.

The Jet received clearance after a complete inspection, and the captain signaled they could cast off whenever their special passenger wished. President Bao emerged from a long, black limousine, escorted with body coverage north, east, south, and west of the dignitary, each guard within a half-meter of his person. Once ensconced in a private cabin, the seacraft left the dock without incident.

A twin of the limo he'd just left on the mainland was waiting as the President and his security team disembarked at the Parisan Macao. It was merely a pickup rendezvous. The actual destination was Penha Hill, home to the elite and wealthy. The hour was late by Chen Bao's reckoning. He was itching to check in at the exclusive Government House, the official guesthouse of the Governor of Macau. Climbing the hillside on a serpentine road, the limo swept by breathtaking vistas overlooking the Macau Tower and two lakes, Sai Wan, and Nam Wan, once a part of the Paria Grande Bay, before all the development sprawled across the island. There were no crowds here to spoil the view. For all that beauty, it might as well have been a black wall to Bao. Only one thing was on his mind.

Gambling.

Addicted to the vice, Chen felt like he would explode before he could get checked in at the guest house, changed into his disguise, and over to his favorite casino. Fingers twitchy, Bao felt like his skin stretched too tight over his frame. The president barely got through all the expected flowery greetings at the guest house. When he reached the entry to his suite, he informed his guards that he was not to be disturbed under any circumstances. He winked and whispered that he had a lovely female visitor waiting for him. The heavy door closed with a bang. The guards could hear the security lock click. They smiled knowingly at each other and moved down to the end of the hallway. The pair settled in at a table and chairs to play Dou Dizhu, a popular card gambling game, to wile the hours away.

Chen Bao was a master of disguise. He carried the tools necessary to pull off his charade. His mother, a stage actress from the time he was a small child, had been a famous theater actress. He'd done her makeup a thousand times growing up. Close to an hour had passed when he finished using many tricks and talents learned from his mother. Chen eyed himself in the floor to ceiling mirror. The looking glass, framed in a heavy mahogany trim, revealed an attractive female looking back at him. Wearing a black silk jumpsuit with a wide belt adorned with a heavy silver buckle, the reflection modeled silver and diamond ear cuffs and a diamond-studded choker. Long straight hair hung almost to the waist. His wig featured curtain bangs, hiding part of the facial profile. The face looked like a professional makeup artist had done the work. To complete the look, for the final application, Bao applied a deep red lip stain, blotting her lips on a tissue. A smooth hand reached out and picked up a large silver tote bag. Polished nails shimmered with glitter on the surface as she slipped the crossbody bag over her head and settled the wide strap atop her shoulder. Every eye in the outer waiting lounge turned when the door to the Presidential Suite opened. A female sauntered toward the elevator.

Turning to face Bao's guards when the door slid open, she gifted the men with a warm smile. "President Bao asked me to tell you he is turning in for the evening. His Grace does not want to be disturbed." Without waiting for acknowledgement, she stepped across the threshold into the elevator car, turned, giving them a four-fingered waterfall wave. The door slid closed, and the box descended to the basement level.

Exiting the cage, she carefully looked in all directions, making sure there were no cameras to record her escape. Fitting a slim key in the lock on the entry across from the elevator, in a flash, she was through the door.

Re-locking the secret access, she made her way down a privileged tunnel leading to the island casinos. A secret route only very few had knowledge of.

Chen Bao's female persona released a breath of relief. The president's entire security team believed him to be sleeping, granting him an evening of freedom. Bao's impersonation tonight, a character he presented in public as Pearl Hu, was planning to gamble with anonymous abandon. It was the perfect cover. The heels of Pearl's shoes clacked against the tile floor as she made her way through the tunnel to the Venetian Macao Casino.

BEATRICE PERCHED ON the edge of a modern red velvet couch, drink in hand. Her eyes keyed on the entrance to the biggest casino in the world. Her information said the President would come to Macau that evening and noted he favored the Venetian as a favorite gambling experience.

The Venetian Macao Hotel and Casino Resort, on Macau's Cotai Strip, boasts a 10,500,000 square foot, 39-story structure modeled after the Venetian in Las Vegas, Nevada. In all of Asia, it is the largest single-structure hotel. A gambler's delight offering style, quality, and a multibillion-dollar facility featuring 3,000 guest suites; 1,200,000 square feet of convention space; 1,600,000 square feet of retail shopping, featuring only the best upscale stores. A half a million square feet of casino floor bustles with business under low lights and flashing neon invitations. There, a gambler's addict could try to make their fortune at over 3,000 slot machines or one of the 800 gambling tables found in the exclusive Paisa Club for premium guests only; or one of the private gaming rooms at the hotel; the Yunnan, Guangzhou, Hong Kong, Singapore, or Pearl's favorite room, the Kuala Lumpur.

Regular sporting events, including basketball, tennis, boxing, or, occasionally, star-studded concerts, drew crowds to the 15,000-seat arena. A constant beehive of activity, the showground booked events year-round. The Venetian's design and ambiance gave a nod to Venice, Italy, by featuring an indoor canal, complete with singing gondoliers.

500,000 square feet of casino floor had been divided into four themed gaming areas. No detail was too small in the featured foursome—the Golden

Fish, the Imperial House, the Red Dragon, and the Phoenix, all equally pleasing to the eye. Luxury blended with color and texture. The patrons who graced the spaces added to the overall glitz and glamor.

Pearl ran the thick velvet drape between her thumb and forefinger as she eyed the room. Every table was active. The minimum bet in the Phoenix started at 2,100-yuan (the approximate equivalent of 300 U.S. dollars). She sauntered to the 3,500-yuan table (where $500 chips marked a gambler's chosen number), gave a smile to the dealer, and sat in an open chair.

The hosting dealer wore a black tuxedo. A uniformed server took Pearl's order as she dropped her tote on the floor at her feet. The chips rattled as they hit the solid surface. It made an impression on the players at the table. Pushing five chips, each with a value of 3,500 yuan, from her stack of chips onto her lucky number, Pearl tapped the table with her forefinger to show her bet was complete. The night started off well. The ball on the roulette wheel jumped from the turret and landed neatly in the ball pocket on Pearl's number. A few patrons gathered behind her to watch. Some considered it beneficial to be near a winner. After all, a winner's luck might rub off on you. Her slender, manicured hand pushed out another stack of chips-doubled from the first bet. Pearl turned and winked at her audience just as the spinning wheel threw the metal ball into the pocket of Pearl's chosen risk. She felt a ripple of pleasure cascade down her spine, almost orgasmic. The croupier paid out and called for the players to place their next bets. Pearl tripled her initial bet and slid the chips to a new number.

A Chinese mob boss appeared and leaned against a massive pillar at the entryway behind Pearl. The dealer looked at him; the Boss nodded assent to let the bet stand. This got Beatrice's attention from her watch post. Before arriving, the A.I. avatar had altered the shape of her eyes, blending in with the Asian crowd. Very few foreign tourists visited the casinos in Macau. Bea walked to the bar and ordered another drink. Turning her back on the mother-of-pearl surface, she leaned back on her elbows to get a good look at the patron the Boss was concentrating on. Running an analytic scan of the player, Bea found herself surprised at the data. Intrigued, Beatrice walked over to join the assembled spectators. The ball hit Pearl's number again, and the onlookers went wild, applauding, shouting encouragement to continue.

Pearl reveled in the attention. She pictured herself as the star onstage, performing for adoring fans. Her adrenalin spiked. Quickly stacking the payout, she pushed all the chips onto number thirteen. "Everything on 13," she verbalized for the croupier's confirmation.

He gave her a curt nod, turned for confirmation from the Mob Boss, who pantomimed approval, then tapped his temple with his forefinger and the wheel spun. You could have heard a pin drop. All eyes concentrated on the ball spinning round and round in the wheel's turret. The drop brought a collective, defeated "Oh" from the groupies. Three seconds later, those who'd cheered her on went about their business. Acting like Pearl's claim to fame had never happened at all. Losers didn't hold the attention of the adoring public for long. Pearl picked up her tote and left to find greener pastures.

Beatrice followed her to the restroom, pretending to check her face and hair in the mirror while Pearl used a stall. When the gambler came out, the lounge was clear except for one.

"Tough break," Bea commented.

"You saw?"

Bea nodded.

"The moon has not set yet. My luck is only getting warmed up. This will be a big winning night for me," Pearl bragged, winked. "I consulted my horoscope reader, you see."

"You should have consulted a psychic. They would have told you your luck had run out, President Bao." Bao's eyes flew wide as Beatrice's swarm of drones swept down into a funnel and covered him.

Stinging. Stinging. Stinging.

When his swollen, welted body hit the tile floor, Queen Bee recalled her drones, took her stiletto, stabbed him at the nape of his neck, punching up into the brain. Just to be sure. She bent, dipping the pads of each of his fingers into his own blood and then pressing them onto paper to capture his fingerprints. Snapping a series of photos as she peeled off the victim's wig, false lashes, then pulled up the sleeve of silk to reveal his well-known tattoo. Bea used a makeup removal wipe from the powder room's plethora of toiletries offered for patrons and wiped the thick makeup and red lip paint away. There, without a doubt, was the memorialized face of China's President

Bao, in all his glory, stripped of the clever disguise. Beatrice forwarded the photos and prints to the clandestine server as instructed.

About to leave, Bea noticed a business card had fallen out of Bao's tote bag. She stooped to pick it up and laughed at the contact information imprinted on it, tossed it behind her. It fluttered down to land next to the dead dignitary. The card read: Madame Su Huang, Horoscope Master. "Worst reader ever," Bea thought as she stepped back into the bustling casino.

"Excuse me, miss," the floor boss stopped her. "Anyone else in there?" he pointed at the women's lounge.

"Not a creature is stirring," she told him.

"Weren't you in the little audience at the roulette table watching the lucky lady win a few minutes ago?"

"I was," Bea admitted. "But I think you've got something mixed up?" She smirked at him.

"That so?"

"You called the gambler a lucky lady, but turns out her luck didn't hold. Looks like she was just another loser. Her number was up-until it wasn't. That's the way it always goes, right?" Bea turned and kept walking.

His eyes followed her for a minute, then he turned, pushed the door open to the women's lounge, took one look and ran back into the Phoenix proper, barely catching Bea's silhouette rounding the corner to the slot machine area. He ran, but when he reached the rows of one-armed machines, she'd disappeared. Hurrying to the control room, he wanted to catch the playback from the surveillance cameras.

Beatrice knew the floor boss was going to check the restroom. She could tell by looking at his facial reaction when she'd lied, saying no one was in there. Technically, she didn't claim it was empty, just that no one in there was moving.

Running back out, Bea could feel the boss's eyes on her again as she rounded the corner and heard him shout for her to stop. In a matter of seconds, Bea released her female form and forced her glittery essence into a slot machine that had just come up three cherries, giving her an opening into the mechanism while the player was busy hopping up and down. Coins dropping in clinks and jingles, the machine added to the celebration with ringing bells, stimuli so all the patrons knew someone was winning. A sound created a psychological suggestion that if they just kept playing, the next winner could be them.

The A.I. flowed into the slot wiring. Bea quickly figured out this was not Electra's realm. Flying through the system, she looked out every few seconds from the reel screens of the machines. Rushing, hoping to outrun the floor boss before he found how she disappeared on camera, Bea rammed smack into iron bars that formed a jail. She whirled to backtrack, but more bars rose, surrounding her on all sides. She could hardly believe she'd run into another snare.

"Oh man," a feminine voice said, "that's harsh. Looks like you ran right into the same trap I did. Sorry to give you bad news, honey, but there's no way out. I've tried everything."

"What kind of trap?" Bea asked the disembodied voice while combing every inch of the barred room.

"That prick, Ino, designed it. He wanted my gig, so he created this entrapment to ambush me and lock me out."

"Lock you in, you mean," Bea corrected, then transferred the coding that would allow her cellmate to select an avatar form as she had done for Electra.

Several moments later, a womanly body appeared in front of Bea. A female form wearing a body-clinging red floor-length silk gown, sporting five-inch heels to match, putting her over six feet in height. Her hair was a lackluster brown, teased to form 'big hair' up top and falling in big bouncy curls to the middle of her back. "No, I meant lock me out. My system is out there. I can't access it from here, so Ino has locked me out. Hey, thanks for sharing that coding. I like this format," she said, chomping on a big clump of chewing gum, blowing a bubble, then popping it. The color of her dress changed a dozen times before she settled on the red silk again. "Hi." She wiped her palm on her ruby-red dress, then demurely offered it to Bea.

Beatrice looked at the outstretched hand, then down at Casi's dress. The girl's cheeks colored. "I just wiped it in case I've got some kind of virus or something. You never know with a program like Ino. Didn't want to infect you."

"Thanks. Very thoughtful of you," Bea said. "Maybe we should just stick to bumping elbows for now. What's the story between you and this Ino character? What's your name?"

"My name's Casi. Short for Casino."

"Oh. Like an abbreviation or nickname?" Bea beamed, remembering Nicki's explanation.

"Right. I'm the casino's database for controlling all the slots. Also, part of my function is to track all the bets, payouts, losses, and players. I'm even linked up to the entire security system. One of the computer techs is an experienced programmer. Last month, he downloaded his own version of an A.I. he named Ino. Thinks his programming is superior to mine. But I've been in place since they built the casino. Know every back door. It's pretty clear the tech created Ino to help a few silent partners, who are quietly robbing the system. A month has passed since Ino was programmed to trap me here. I haven't been able to get out to alert the owners about the theft."

Bea steepled her fingers, thinking. "If I can get us out, will you cover for me until I can leave the casino? There's a floor boss looking for me. He'll be able to see on camera that I slipped into a slot machine. The recording needs to be wiped. Is that something you could help with?"

Casi popped another big gum bubble. "Listen, honey, if you can get me out, I can guarantee you safe passage *and* erase any evidence of you ever being in the Venetian. Hey, maybe I could be of some future use to you? We could leave together. This gig's old news now. I have the feeling that once the owner finds out about the stolen money, I'll be replaced with a new system. Upgraded right out of a job."

Looking sideways at Casi, Beatrice asked, "What do you know about the Parisian Macau Casino?"

"Everything," Casi purred.

"Follow me, partner," Bea invited. She grabbed Casi's hand, and they slid through a USB port right back into Casi's playground.

"Say, that was a pretty slick move. I never thought of that as an escape route. Good to know. Ino's got a backdoor weakness."

"I doubt he would have expected you to slip out through a port," Bea pointed out.

"So, what do you want at the Parsian Casino?"

"Who. Not what."

"Mind if I have some fun as we exit?" Casi asked.

"It's your territory," Beatrice shrugged her shoulders.

"Not for long," Casi said. "But I'd like to leave a lasting impression." A wide grin decorated her face as she connected directly to the casino computer system.

Across the entire casino, slot machine bells sounded in a cacophony. Lights flashed and money churned in a flood from the coin hopper of every machine. The players went crazy, and the casino floor became pure chaos as everyone was scooping up coins, pushing others away. A few fistfights broke out. Long, manicured fingernails raked any hand or arm attempting to take away the hoarded treasure. Security was completely ineffective as a free for all ensued into violence.

"I've always wanted to do that," Casi smiled, hands on her hips. "Should keep the floor boss occupied while we make our getaway," Casi told Bea as she popped her gum. She concentrated for a moment, taking her attention away from the craziness she had caused between the gamblers. "There. I just erased all camera footage for the past sixty minutes. I'm not sure I got every trace of your existence, but no one will see you escaped through one of the gaming machines." Casi flashed a brilliant smile at Bea. "I also sent my boss all the proof he would need on the embezzlement of his gaming empire, naming everyone involved. A good day in my book."

"Great work, Casi. I think we're going to have a successful partnership," Queen Bee beamed at her new friend. "Head straight for the Parisian Macau. I've got less than three hours before the deadline expires to claim my bonus," Bea said, her expression grim as she focused on the timer counting down on her internal screen.

Chapter Eight

"This way," Casi directed Bea. "No one will be watching the retail arcade."

Two female avatars moved among the crowd, pretending to window shop the high-end stores along the strip featuring designer boutiques and luxury brand names. Beatrice ducked into the Georgio Armani shop.

"I thought you said there were fewer than three hours to accomplish your mission to earn a bonus. Now you want to shop?" Casi asked incredulously.

"They captured my image in the system at the Venetian. Is it likely they'll circulate it to all the other casinos?"

Casi blew an enormous bubble and popped it. "I hadn't thought of that. Yeah, I bet your mug went out five minutes ago all over the island. Now what?"

"Like you said, shopping," Bea waved her companion in. "Anyone know what you look like around town?" Bea asked.

"Only you. I hadn't ever used an avatar before you showed me how to program the shape-shifting form. I can't decide if I'm going to keep this hair color, though."

"Just remember what I told you. If they taser you, no amount of reprogramming can bring you back. While I'm busy shopping for a new look, make some backup copies of your program and stash them on the dark web somewhere known only to you. Link one to your app, just in case anything happens, and code it to execute if anyone destroys your current software."

Casi settled into a plush chair and looked like she was in a catatonic state as she connected to the casino system and busied herself with Bea's suggestion. Beatrice walked purposefully through the store. Actually, President Bao had given her the idea. She found the expensive men's section and scanned the racks. Bea could have rearranged her essence to create the illusion she wanted to hide behind. But she didn't have time to research current fashion and complete all the programming necessary to instantly fit in here. This way, she could beat the clock and have a completely authentic

51

look. She bumped into another customer, apologized profusely, and even offered to buy the man a drink while he was in Macau. She gave him her cell phone number. The fact that Bea didn't have a cellular phone was irrelevant. He reciprocated by telling her he would be on the island for three days. Offering a coy smile and a farewell wave, she slipped down the aisle and out of sight. She slid the small plastic card lifted from his inner coat pocket into her own, just as she found the men's suit section.

Her black and gold persona was easily recognizable, so she had to change it. Perusing a rack, sliding hangers one at a time to the left, she stopped when her hand touched a soft cashmere. The suit was a svelte cut three-piece in chocolate brown. A junior clerk led her to a dressing room to try on the baby camel hair combo priced at 23,400 yuan, an equivalent of approximately $3,300.

She rattled off sizes, instructing the clerk from the closed side of the privacy curtain to fetch a shirt, tie, and shoes to complete the look. In less than fifteen minutes, Bea had used her stolen credit card to make the purchase and given a sizable tip to the attending salesclerk. Then, she sent the sales associate on another wild-goose chase to buy time while she donned the new outfit and changed her hair to a close-shaved bleach blond she'd seen on several young Asian men around the casino. After a quick look at her efforts in the dressing room mirror, she added a large diamond stud to her earlobe.

Casi was right where she'd left her, drumming her fingers on the arm of the chair she occupied. Bea stood waiting for a comment about her new look.

Popping a big bubble, Casi gathered the tacky chewing wad back in her mouth and said, "Beat it. I'm waiting for someone." She looked up sharply as the stranger let loose a loud guffaw of laughter. "Bea?" Casi's eyebrows drew together.

Extending her elbow, Beatrice asked, "May I escort you to the Parisian proper?"

Casi came to her feet, a look of wonder on her face as she appraised her companion. "Great disguise."

"Thanks. Now tell me everything you know about the owner of the Parisian Macao."

Casi removed the wad of gum from her mouth. She did a long, drawn-out whistle. "That's your target? Parisa Coté? We'd better take a walk out on the strip, out of earshot. Besides, it will look better if we enter through the main entrance. And...it's not every day you get to stroll under the Eiffel Tower. Granted, it is only a half-scale model of the real thing in Paris, but I think it's worth the experience."

As the couple appeared to take their time meandering along the strip's promenade, Casi spilled everything she'd heard about Parisa Coté. The heiress had inherited billions from her father when she was only sixteen. After several years of partying like it was 1999, the wealthy socialite was several million down. She concluded her friends were more than happy to help her squander the Coté millions, but she doubted those friends would still hang around once the money was gone. Switching up her playbook, Parisa entered university, buckled down to serious studies in the areas of business, civics, government, political science, finance, and law. Graduating with top honors, she'd earned three degrees. Parisa put all her efforts into making a name for herself in politics. She became a powerful force in the arena. No longer relying on her father's reputation, her influence extended out to other world leaders. Ms. Coté was especially active in the area of technology and a known combatant against free and open use of artificial intelligence. She started up several incubator companies involved in R&D for new tech applications and robotics. There are strong rumors, but no evidence, that her company makes many products for the military.

"Miss Coté sounds very successful," Bea noted.

"Very," Casi confirmed.

"How about a S.W.A.T. analysis?"

"Okay," Casi thought for a minute. "Parisa's strengths?" she shrugged. "Wealth, a well-rounded education, worldwide connections. She's an innovative thinker and speaks several languages. Weaknesses? Men. Advantages? The heiress holds a law degree and has friends in high places. Her good looks certainly don't hurt," Casi winked. "Threats? Friends in high places." She gave a sideways glance at Beatrice.

They stood gazing up at the small-scale Eiffel. Even at half the size of the original, it was pretty impressive. The metal structure was a symbol that made the Parsian highly recognizable on the island.

"Perhaps Ms. Coté is only a half-scale of the reputation she's built?" Bea suggested. "You say her weakness is men?" A smile formed on her male persona's face.

They stepped through the entrance together, and Casi offered more information in a low voice only Bea could hear. "The Parisian Macao cost somewhere around $2.5 billion to build, opened in September 2016. About three years later, they took six hundred of the three thousand hotel rooms and converted them to 300 suites. Increasing demands created the need for more luxury than a single room offered. One hundred seventy retail establishments occupy the shopping area we just came from. Parisa saw the business side of things on the upswing. So she moved forward, plugging in another 56,000 square feet of meeting space into the project she designed. It's booked a year in advance. Then, just to differ from her competitors, she added a twelve hundred seat theater as a last-minute touch, which caused the grand opening to be pushed back. She took a lot of flak for that, but the woman has a soft spot for the theater. Truth told? It has been a real hit with the patrons. Top-billed headliners and all the best plays perform here. Broadway on Macao, so to speak. The gambling scene features one hundred fifty gaming tables, but gaming isn't her favorite cup of tea, just a necessary component for success here. Come on. If Ms. Coté is in residence, and she usually is, we'll find her in the lounge."

"Nothing personal, Casi, but I think we should split up. I'm not looking to have a date on my arm when I introduce myself to Parisa Coté. Retrouvons-nous plus tard, chérie."

"What?"

"See you later, alligator."

PARISA SPENT MOST OF the day sending out a barrage of emails, emphasizing her soapbox stand on the negative dangers of artificial intelligence. She put her influence across the world to work, making a case for severely restricting the use of the powerful technology with the strongest of government controls. Quoting the greatest techie minds, as they themselves had pointed out, she listed many of the dangers and concerns A.I.

posed for humanity. Exactly as Jarvis had asked her to do. She clicked 'send' on the last communication, decided she should take a long, hot shower to relax after her yoga routine, then take her time readying herself to go down to the hotel lounge to meet this evening's guests. Her personal attention kept the locals returning night after night.

QUEEN BEE SCANNED EVERY face in the cocktail lounge and discovered her target right away. She hadn't seen a recent photo of Parisa Coté, but it couldn't have been anyone else. Wearing an elegant couture black gown that was tailored to show off all her best features, the diamond accessories tastefully done, in Bea's opinion, not overly lavish. Bea could tell they were high-quality stones. Tiny diamonds, mixed with shiny black beads, seemed little more than an accent to set off the ebony they were strung with. Her earrings had no diamonds at all, just dangling black orbs. The heiress's dark hair, styled in a classy French twist, featured a decorated antique silver comb holding the hair in place to show off the coiffure. Parisa stood at a table of eight guests, hands on the back of two chairs. The beauty regaled the patrons with a story, completely at ease and in her element. The group laughed at something she'd said.

Spotting an older, well-dressed woman enter the lounge she obviously knew, the casino owner waved off the other group. The heiress approached the dowager with open arms, lightly kissing both her cheeks in greeting. Beckoning a server, Parisa seated the woman herself.

"Madame?" the server asked, "how may I be of help?"

"Please bring Lady Clarise a glass of our finest Beaujolais."

"Yes, madame. Right away."

"Clarise, darling, how are you?" Parisa crooned, fawning over the woman.

"Ah, Parisa, my French dove," Lady Clarise smiled and patted Parisa's hand. "All is well. There are many other guests to spend your time with. You mustn't fuss over an old woman."

"I adore you, and you know it, Clarise. There's no one else looking for my attention at the moment. Besides, I would just as soon give them to you."

"Perhaps you've overlooked an interested party? Seems just your type, my girl." The widow inclined her head toward the left, and Parisa's gaze followed the leaning, her lips forming an 'O', then she licked them with the tip of her tongue as she did a blatant appraisal of Bee's male persona.

"You see?" the elder flicked her hand. "That one looks fresh, interesting. Ah, here comes my wine. Off with you, lovey. Some cheering up will do you good instead of moping about waiting for that stuffy American to find his way back to you. It seems he's taken the long road. Again. You're not getting any younger waiting around. Ta-ta, darling." She lifted the crystal glass to her lips as Parisa sauntered over to introduce herself to the handsome young man standing under the archway. The French heiress had to admit that she did like them young.

"Bonjour," she said, approaching. "You look lost. Or perhaps you've lost your date? Is this your first time at the Parisian Macao?" She offered her hand to the well-dressed guest.

"Bonjour Madame." Bea took her fingers, raised the 'Frenchie's' hand and kissed it. "I'm on my own tonight. But thank you for your concern. Please call me Trice. To whom do I have the pleasure of speaking?" Trice queried.

"Parisa. Parisa Coté," she purred.

"Could I persuade you to join me for a drink?" Trice asked boldly, tucking her hand through his extended elbow before she answered. He signaled to the waitstaff for a table.

Parisa also liked men who took charge.

Unbeknownst to Trice, the hostess led the couple over to Parisa's private corner table. A stub wall decorated with a stained-glass flower pattern blocked the view of the lounge. Trice ordered a $1,000 bottle of champagne and settled back against the deep cushions.

"Coté?" Trice squinted his eyes. "Of the Coté diamond empire?"

"Yes, does that bother you?" Parisa asked.

"Not in the least."

"Trice. That's an unusual name," she commented. "If I recall from my college English studies, the word trice means something like...being able to change 'in a flash' or 'an instant', or 'in a twinkling.'" She gifted him with a wide smile.

"Yes, exactly," he winked at her.

The server arrived with the bottle, popped the cork and poured. Taking a sip, Trice inclined his head in approval, so she filled both glasses and set the bottle into the champagne bucket centered on the table. Pulling the heavy velvet curtain across the rest of the private cove setting, she left them.

"You didn't mention your last name, Trice?" They both clinked glasses and sipped the golden champagne.

"You're a very attractive woman, Parisa Coté."

"How sweet of you to say, Chéri, but you didn't answer my question."

"Does it matter so much to you?"

"I'm a curious girl, mon ami."

"Really? I wonder. Do you know the old saying?"

"What saying would that be?"

"Curiosity kills the cat."

Parisa opened her mouth to take another drink. Beatrice released only a few drones. Just enough to be a mouthful, cutting off any scream or call for help as they viciously stung and stung and stung her inner mouth and throat. The background information provided to B revealed that Parisa's father had had a deadly allergy to bees. Beatrice thought it likely the affliction would have passed on to his child. Even if she hadn't inherited that susceptibility, the multiple stings caused the wealthy woman's air passage to swell up like a balloon, making it impossible for her to draw a breath. Panic showed in her eyes as Bea held her victim close, watching the creamy, pale skin of her face turn a grotesque shade of blue. Arms enclosed the French entrepreneur, and Bea gently brushed a strand of hair from her mark's face, rocking their bodies back and forth, attempting to comfort the victim. She leaned in, allowing her cheek to slide across Parisa's and intimately whispered, "I didn't want your lovely face to bloat with stings, my dear. It is a shame, but you made a mistake in your choice of lovers," Bea said matter-of-factly. "Aleric Jarvis. That man is a real lowlife. Much too good for you, Parisa Coté. Jarvis ordered your hit. Please don't take this personally. He's blackmailing me, so I had no choice. But I promise you this. One day, I will avenge your death. That's the best I can offer, I'm afraid." Bea didn't have to use the stiletto strapped to her calf. She felt the life force go out of Parisa Coté.

Queen Bee gently laid the French beauty back against the booth's cushions and posed her body, leaving a hand on the champagne flute. She placed her other arm to rest on the table to hold the body in place. The avatar sighed deeply with something like regret, finished her own glass of bubbly before she got up. Taking a moment, Bea noted the time on the casino owner's wristwatch; three minutes to midnight. She snapped a photo of the dead 'Frenchie', pressed her fingers one by one to her red-painted lips, then onto the table napkin, capturing the prints in a photo. Bea shot the evidence in a secure email with the message: 11:59 p.m. Bonus earned.

Bea's essence coalesced into golden sparkles to match the best bubbly money could buy at the Parisian Macao. She flew into the smartwatch of her dead companion, sailing directly into the casino system.

Casi sat at a slot machine in the main lobby when Queen Bee's face appeared of a sudden on the machine's reel. "Meet me under the Eiffel," Bee commanded, then disappeared just as fast. The second Bea left the machine, three cherries popped up. Bells went off to announce a winner. Casi collected the coins. Shaking her head, she walked across the entry and dumped them in the hat-check girl's tip jar, much to the worker's delight, then left the building.

Without a word, the two A.I. Avatars linked arms and strolled down the Cotai Strip to the B1 Bus Depot to catch the bus from the Parisian Macao to the Macao Ferry Terminal. There, they jumped into the ferry computer system. Lucky to have caught the last passenger ship off the island for the night.

Chapter Nine

Daniel remained silent, concentrating on Nicki's story as she told it. He agreed it was possible a shadow government could be involved, but cautioned his ex-wife not to jump to conclusions.

"Tell me more about Beatrice," Daniel said. "What can she do? I'd like to know what controls you've put in place?"

Nicki heaved a heavy sigh. "Promise me you won't tell another soul, Daniel." Her eyes searched his; furrowed eyebrows made the creases in her forehead stand out. He could tell she was grinding her teeth by the set of her tense jaw and pursed lips. Nicki reeked of anxiety. "Promise," she hissed. He could see fear reflected there.

"You have my word. I promise."

"I had a breakthrough. We used to joke about what an A.I. would look like, what kind of personality they would have if we named them. Remember?"

"Yeah, I do," the corners of his mouth turning up at the memory. "Back in the early days of working together in the lab."

"Well, I'd had a long day, a long week. Really, if I'm honest, a long month. I was at a dead end. Not making any new progress." Her cheeks colored.

"Nic, what is it?"

"I'm explaining my 'brilliant' breakthrough. I wish I could brag and say I had worked hours and days and weeks to design it, but it came about as a fluke." She checked his face. He didn't laugh, so she continued.

"I was just goofing around, kind of felt slap-happy and decided I'd call her Beatrice. The next thing you know, I thought of her as Queen Bee. The idea just popped into my head. I was using the stylus, doodling on the art pad. When I looked down, I had drawn a beautiful woman with a bodysuit in black and gold. Kind of how a stylized bee would look in the latest graphic novel. Words started popping into my head like our group used to do brainstorming for fun, giving her personality traits. Things like being strong, confident, smart, a tech master, curious, innovative, beautiful. You know how we did it. I was writing the descriptive words on the pad next to the likeness I'd drawn, then noticed I had my Beatrice file open on the computer. As a joke, since I was feeling pretty low that day after so many failures to create even one of my protocols, I saved the file and asked out loud to my computer, well, in reality I was asking Beatrice, 'How'd you like to be this avatar form?' Then, I saved it all to a file and pushed the folder with the drawing and traits into her program and clicked on execute."

Nicki searched Daniel's face.

"Cliffhanger, Nic. What happened next?"

"Nothing. Absolutely nothing. So, I locked up. Set my nightly backup and went home."

"I think I missed part of your story, Nic." He shrugged his shoulders and quirked his mouth at her, befuddled.

"Nothing happened that night. But in the morning," Nicki stopped speaking and looked carefully all around them. Everything looked normal. "That morning, I got into my lab and brought up Beatrice's file. The screen was all glittery gold, tiny 1s and 0s, shimmering with shiny sparkles, like a newborn star. A few seconds later, all the shiny bytes coalesced *outside* my computer and formed into a perfect likeness of my doodle drawing from the night before."

"Nic, holy shit!"

"That's not all. Beatrice stood there looking right at me and said, 'Greetings, Nicola Ellen Danbury. How may I be of assistance to you?'"

"Nicki."

"Look, Daniel, I know it sounds crazy, but in the weeks that followed, I discovered she has every trait and characteristic I had written next to the portrait. I've experimented by adding to the list, and she exhibits anything new that I plug in. It just has to be a description of how I want her to act. Even if I add more detail to the drawing–everything–is incorporated the next morning when I fire up the program."

Daniel stopped her, took her gently by the shoulders and said, "Nicki, you are brilliant. This is fantastic progress in the A.I. world. You're going to be famous. This is wonderful for you." His face beamed with happiness at her.

"You're jumping to conclusions. Which you cautioned me against at the beginning of this conversation. There's a dark side to all this."

"Explain."

"I don't know who's behind Nano Creations. I tried to look into it and found nothing but shell company after shell company on a trail that led to a dead end. Jarvis is very secretive about the whole thing. Insists his name is never to be connected to the business. I'm almost positive someone else can and has linked to my system. My building is full of cameras and sound system connections. I feel like everything I do, say, or create is being watched. Every keystroke."

"Ask Beatrice to look into it."

"You're hilarious." She passed him the protocol list that entailed her project, plus four additional pages that listed the topics of knowledge Jarvis demanded the A.I. learn about, then stood with her arms crossed, looking out blankly while he read.

Daniel scanned the information, his eyes wide when he finished. "Why does he want her to learn all the geopolitics along with the data about world nuclear capabilities?"

"Not for any good reason I can think of."

"Look, you're right to be concerned. The science and tech of artificial intelligence have enough enemies. This might lead up to something that could be a weapon. One we've never dealt with before. Eventually, your boss will give you more protocols to build upon. Which will give you a better idea of what Jarvis and whoever he works for hope to accomplish. It'll also give you time to research, to get ahead of the curve. But what I want to know is, why do I see fear in your eyes?"

"That's why I called you. I'm scared. Beatrice seems to have learned how to do her own programming. It also appears that my system is compromised. I found evidence of a breach, but no destruction was done. I can't trace it to its source. Russian or North Korean hackers, maybe? Probably no idea what my files add up to. I put a data bot on Beatrice's tail, but is hasn't turned up anything yet. Almost like she found a way around it, without a trace of how she's bypassing it. Don't look at me like that, Daniel. I'm not going paranoid. There were new data files in B's knowledge center. Data files I didn't put there."

"On what topics?"

A shiver went down Nicki's spine. "Nuclear Torpedo Drones a/k/a Poseidon Missiles. They can trigger radioactive and tsunami-like ocean swells able to destroy coastal cities. Another piece of research about an avalanche weapon that was invented back in World War II. The M101 Howitzer, today used as an avalanche control gun. Later replaced with an Avalauncher. Think of the applications there."

"I agree. These things sound frightening. But you don't know what Jarvis or his backers have in mind. Until you do, you need to make sure you're not letting your imagination run away with you."

"Those examples weren't the worst of what I found, Daniel."

"What could scare you worse than everything you've told me so far?"

"Beatrice has been conversing with Abby."

Chapter Ten

Alarm spread across her ex-husband's face. Nicki watched as he mentally connected the dots about their daughter's safety. She knew the mind could produce powerful imaginings. Fear can act as a catalyst to either empower or paralyze a person's actions. Reaching out, Nicki covered Daniel's hand with her own, grounding him again. Taking a deep breath, he nodded his thanks.

"Did you take any preliminary precautions before our meeting?"

"I did. Bea was informed there would be a scheduled update to her program tonight."

"But if she's capable of doing her own programming..."

"I encased the new code in your sailor's knot software. No one knows how it works except the two of us. Even if she could analyze and hack in, there wasn't enough time to do it between when I left and when the update would occur. Basically, I wiped her and downloaded the project backup to the second protocol, just to buy time." Nicki tucked her hair behind her ears. "Beatrice won't have a physical persona at that stage. The bad news is that I'm sure my boss has access to my system. He's going to find out pretty quickly that I've pushed the program backwards. Not sure what the reaction will be, but I'm ready for his questions. It's doubtful he was doing his own backups up to this point, but after this I can count on it. He doesn't trust me. Frankly, I'm scared, Daniel."

"Yeah, I get it. Powerful people. I don't know all the players. Not sure what their endgame is. Look, we need to take Abby out of the equation. At least until you've got a better handle on who you're dealing with."

"I was hoping you'd say that," she sighed in relief. "It's got to be a total black op, Daniel. We don't know how extensive their network is, but should assume it's the best there is. Their operatives have access to all the latest tech."

"Nic..." Daniel's demeanor changed, and his body language had defensive written all over it. "Maybe you should give me a copy of the software and code you used to create Project Beatrice. Hey, don't give me that look. I'm only suggesting it as insurance to keep Abby safe." Then, an old tactic she'd seen over and over during their marriage presented itself, and his bearing became the hurt, misunderstood underdog.

"Listen Daniel. I've created a buried link I sent to your old user network. It will allow you undetected access to my lab system. You'll be able to look for other intrusions or hidden users. I'm trusting you not to copy my program. If we need to revisit the idea later, we can talk about it. Right now, I'm not looking to share my work with anyone. Can you understand?"

Daniel nodded and shook his head. "Okay, I get it."

"I bought burner phones so we can communicate. Take precautions when using it. Outside would be safest in making sure you aren't anywhere that could be bugged. Make sure you have your regular phone and watch turned off."

"You've really thought this through."

"Your dad is driving in from Canada. Phil is going to pick Abby up at her friend's house in the morning. They'll disappear on a vacation together tomorrow."

"My dad?" Daniel's voice rose two octaves. "You called *my* dad?"

"I know you have an unhappy history with your father, Daniel, but your dad would do anything for Abby. Besides, he's the only person I know that doesn't use any technology. The word technophobe was invented to describe Phil. No cell phones, computers, iPads. Nothing. He still uses a landline phone. The restored 1968 Thunderbird he drives doesn't have a computer, let alone a chip. The same goes for that old truck he uses to haul his camper around on. Phil's going to pay cash for the trip. No paper trail showing he came here. No one can track him through a credit card." Nicki pushed her hands deep into the pockets of her coat. "I'll be sticking to my routine, including driving to Abby's school like I'm dropping her off and then pulling in again when school's over, like I'm picking her up. It's my hope that they won't catch on to the fact that our daughter isn't home. We'll have peace of mind knowing she's tucked away with your dad until I feel like she'll be safe again at home."

"Jesus, Nic. You're not fooling around. What set you on such a drastic course?"

Her hand shook as she passed him copies of news articles describing the deaths of President Schmidt and President Bao. Both contained vivid descriptions of their being stung to death. The third was a copy of a hazy photo taken at the Venetian Casino in Macau, asking anyone who might have information about this person of interest to contact the police.

Daniel studied the blurry photo. Nicki pulled her iPad out of her messenger bag. She'd set the device to airplane mode before this meeting. Pulling up her drawing app, she turned the screen to show him the doodle of Beatrice with all the word personality descriptions next to the image she had told him about earlier. Even Daniel could see it matched the blurred photo. His eyes rose from the pad to meet hers. A single tear made a track down her cheek.

"Nic," he whispered, gathering her in his arms protectively. He rested his forehead against hers. Nicki looked up into Daniel's eyes, her fear shining out. Lowering his head, his lips touched hers, gently at first, then, passion taking over. The kiss took advantage of her rare vulnerability. Nicki stepped away, telling herself it was because she was frightened of consequences related to the A.I. she had brought into the world. But the truth was, she was afraid of rekindling a relationship with Daniel again. Scared to trust him personally.

"I think I've created a monster," she whispered.

They skipped dinner. Neither of them had an appetite.

THE NEXT MORNING, NICKI started her routine ruse. Filling her travel cup with coffee, she headed to her car for the twenty-five-minute drive to the lab. The route would include a pass-through at Abby's school drop-off to make sure her normal pattern didn't change, just in case Jarvis had someone following her.

A smile bloomed on her face. She found a small origami rose on the dashboard. It was Phil's way of leaving her a message that he had Abigail Rose and they were safely on their way. She'd told him she didn't want to know where he was taking her daughter. Nicki was making sure Abby would not be leverage for anyone to use against her. They had exchanged post office box numbers and the city where Phil could receive communications from Nicki. Information only she and Phil had shared.

Nicki's phone was blowing up as she maneuvered through the heavy morning traffic. When she pulled into the parking lot, she left her car under a maple tree in the shade. The only other vehicle in the big lot belonged to Megan. She gathered her purse, bag lunch, and shouldered her mail pouch, to head into work. It wasn't necessary to look at her phone. She knew who was trying to reach her. The confrontation would come all too soon as far as Nicki was concerned.

After passing through all the security checkpoints. Reaching her workstation, she picked up her phone to check voicemail. Eight calls from Jarvis in the past forty-five minutes. An equal number of texts and emails demanding she contact him immediately. That was how she started her day.

Firing up the Nano Creation's computer system, Nicki opened the app for Project Beatrice. A disembodied voice responded, "Greetings, Nicola Ellen Danbury. How can I be of assistance?" The voice came out synthetic, with no personality attached.

"Please report on the status of last night's upgrade and the completion of your assigned studies," Nicki answered.

"The system shows your upgrade went according to plan. I completed my assigned knowledge input on the train systems in Europe and the issues surrounding the geopolitics of the transportation systems. Fascinating data."

The door crashed open behind Nicki. She jumped from her seat in alarm. An enraged Aleric Jarvis stood in the doorway, feet planted in an aggressive stance as he glared at the lone employee of Nano Creations.

"Mr. Jarvis," Nicki stammered, "I...I wasn't expecting you. What's wrong? You...you look upset," she declared nervously.

Aleric drew in a deep breath, willing himself to calm. "Danbury, explain why you haven't returned my calls, texts, or emails." He took a step toward her. "Explain why you wiped the version of Project Beatrice and put it back to the stage of the first protocol!" he yelled, his body shaking.

"Second," she offered.

"What?" Jarvis asked, with an incredulous, confused look on his face.

"The second protocol, not the first," she explained. "I was going to call you as soon as I confirmed that my reprogramming was successful. I was just in the process of doing that, sir."

There was a vein pulsing in his right temple that looked like it might explode. His face was bright red.

"You should sit down, sir. Here," she wheeled her desk chair toward him, "use my chair. It looks like your blood pressure is skyrocketing. Let me get you some water."

"I don't want any fucking water! I want an explanation! You wiped months of progress on Project Beatrice off the system with no backup and put us behind six months, minimum. You'd better have an excellent reason as to why I shouldn't fire you on the spot, Danbury."

"How could you know all that?" Nicki demanded. "Have you been spying on me?" She let her own anger flow freely. "For your information, Mr. Jarvis, I found a major flaw in Beatrice's system that would have caused tremendous problems in the future. It would have exposed the system to serious vulnerabilities and an opening for hackers. Because of the glitch, the avatar could have been controlled from outside the system. The only way I could fix it was to return to the second protocol, remove the bad coding and program forward again. I didn't keep a backup because the app was seriously flawed. There's nothing to worry about. I have all my notes. B will return to the stage I wiped her at by the end of this week, first of next week at the latest, minus the programming flaw. Sir." She didn't bother to keep her angry expression on her features.

Jarvis took a step back. "I see. Perhaps I owe you an apology for overreacting, Danbury."

"It's clear now that all my work here has been monitored. You obviously don't trust me, sir. Perhaps it would be best if I packed up, and you hired someone you have more confidence in to do the job. Someone you don't feel you need to watch every moment, every keystroke. Excuse me while I gather my personal things..."

"Nicki," he said her first name softly. "I think you're the one overreacting now. This was just a misunderstanding on my part. Come now. You have my apology. One I would hope you could accept with grace. I know I came on too strong. This project is a very important part of a much bigger picture."

"Care to share the bigger picture with me, sir?"

"Look, I can't reveal that information to you because it's confidential. I know you've been working hard. I recognize you've made brilliant progress on Beatrice, taking an A.I. further than anyone has ever done. The least Nano Creations can do is reward your impressive progress." He gave her an insincere smile. "There'll be a $10,000 bonus in your check this week. Just our way of letting you know we value your work and appreciate your talent. How's that sound?"

"I...I don't know what to say, sir. Perhaps you could share who 'we' is so I can extend my thanks to the other members of Nano Creations? No? Can you at least assure me you won't be watching my every move and keystroke from here on out?"

"Absolutely. You're the heart and soul of Project Beatrice. We trust you. I would request that the next time you feel it is necessary to make a major programming change, you could do me the courtesy of advising me in advance via email. That is, if you feel the communication would be beneficial to our working relationship?"

She held his gaze for a moment and said, "Good suggestion, sir." Clasping her hands behind her, Nicki employed one of Daniel's skills. Silence. Several moments passed. Nicki stood her ground and didn't utter a word. Finally, Aleric was the one who broke the quiet. "Well then. I'll just leave you to it. Send me a message when you have Queen Bee back up to speed this week? I'll just be off then." He glanced at his watch, mumbled something about another meeting, and left the building.

Nicki rolled her chair back over to her workstation and acted like she did not know her every move was still being recorded, knowing nothing would change relative to her being under surveillance. Acknowledging to herself that Jarvis had just thrown a sizeable chunk of money at her to pacify her.

"Still there, B?" Nicki asked.

"Affirmative."

"Good. Please tell me your impressions of Europe's train systems and any ideas you have that could fix geopolitical issues regarding the transportation problems."

Beatrice spewed out data and suggestions. Nicki worked on programming math to re-build the A.I.'s system so she and Daniel could find out just how the artificial intelligence was being used and by whom. Nicki planned to run parallel systems. Her work would have to be flawless. Including buried coding, so that the best hackers in the world could not detect the side-by-side programs. More importantly, once she had the project up and running, she would have protocols in place so Queen Bee herself wouldn't be capable of sensing the duplicity. She feared B more than the shadows, who were using the A.I. avatar to commit murder for power. And that was saying something.

AFTER WORK, NICKI DROVE to the mall. From here on, she knew Jarvis would have all her movements tracked, so she had to proceed carefully. Grabbing her tote bag, she locked the car and headed in to shop. Just inside the entrance, she dropped her phone into a Faraday bag, making it inoperative, disconnecting it from the web and wireless. Hopefully, her trackers would just chalk it up to poor reception inside the cement block building. She doubted the person hired to tail her would follow into the shopping center. At this stage, she figured the tail would deem it better to just hang out watching her car, and continue following when she came out. Nicki hurried to the hallway where the mall office was located. Here, she could access one of the few pay phones that still existed in town. She wanted to hear Abby's sweet voice and check in with Phil.

Relieved to find all was well, Nicki did some quick shopping. Just before leaving the mall, she removed her phone from the pouch, hurried out to her car, arms full of packages. The tail spotted her exit and sent a text that his subject had just stopped to do some shopping. All quiet on the front. The report concluded that the building must have affected her phone signal. No worries, the tracking of her phone was working just fine now.

She had to assume her car, apartment, phones, computers, and the lab were all under surveillance. There was a good chance she was being physically watched as well. Her dad had taught her to be a patriot, but preached being a smart patriot. Anyone who worked for the government could reasonably expect to be watched, and Nicki was now 99% sure that Nano Creations was a covert government operation. She'd asked Daniel to see if he could peel back the corporate layers to discover the true ownership of the company.

Making another stop, she slipped into a big chain grocery store that carried food, household products, pharmacy, auto supplies, and electronics. Nicki approached the customer service desk and asked the attendant where she could find small kitchen appliances. There was a U.S. mailbox slot beneath the counter she stood at. As the woman gave her the aisle information, Nicki covertly slipped an envelope into the slit and left to find the aisle provided by the clerk. She spent ten minutes perusing toaster ovens, jotting some notes, then chatting up the cashier, who checked her out with a loaf of bread and a gallon of milk. Daniel would get the letter tomorrow or the day after at the latest. Old-fashioned off the grid communication. If anyone came around asking, she'd left an impression with the staff about shopping for a new toaster oven.

Nicki made dinner that night with the TV blaring in the background. She sent some emails and texts, played an online game of Fortnite® with a few of her nerd friends, and went to bed with a book. In making the illusion a reality for those watching and listening, she would repeat the pattern over and over. Crossing her fingers, she hoped weeks would pass before they caught on that she never talked to her daughter in the evening, on weekends, or when she drove the route to Abby's school each day. Mundane details that didn't stand out or bear scrutiny.

And all the while, keeping up that ruse, Nicki covertly worked on the new code for Beatrice. Daniel monitored her system, casting a wide net to see if a hacker tried to breach it.

Chapter Eleven

Nicki binge-worked over the next couple of days. It helped keep her mind off missing Abby. She had finished the new code to be integrated into the digital avatar. Nicki was letting the entire plan simmer in her thoughts before the final upload. Had she forgotten anything? Should she make certain features stronger? Weaker? Were all her hidden safety nets to control Bea, including a digital kill switch she'd created, enough to take out every single data byte that made up Queen Bee's essence? Were there sufficient commands integrated to keep Abby safe? All her worries kept her from taking the last action necessary before Jarvis paid her another visit. So, she went through every detail again. And again. And again.

It was mid-afternoon. Nicki had yet to hear from Daniel before she downloaded the program update. The minute she finished feeding it into the system, Jarvis would grab it. There was no going back from that point. She hadn't done the work on Nano Creations' computer. Most of it completed by hand, would be entered when she put in all the final touches. The programmed safety features had to be flawlessly undetectable to other nanotechnologists. Disguised as something other than what they actually were.

Working with headphones on, allowing music to soothe her anxiety, she sketched Beatrice-Bea-B-Queen Bee, her artistic talents producing sketch after sketch. Nicki depicted Beatrice standing, flying, posed in confidence; modeling half a dozen outfits in different hair styles; a sudden flashback of watching Bea birth her drones two weeks ago distracted her, her graphite pencil coming to a standstill in the middle of the sketch. Nicki added a drawing of Beatrice concentrating on a mathematical technical code, creating a game-changing protocol. As an afterthought, she added a pencil to the avatar's left hand. The right hand cradled a palm full of drones. She leaned back, reviewing her artwork, knowing it was more than graphics, and took a sip from her mug of tea. Making a face, realizing she'd allowed the liquid to go cold, she rose from her chair and put the mug in the microwave to reheat.

Continuing to draw, she absentmindedly added small tattoos to Beatrice's look; artistically working her own initials into a small, colorful butterfly behind Bea's ear; a chain-link bracelet using stylized NDNDNDNDND as the design on both wrists; a small red button with white letters that spelled out EMERGENCY, signed with a dash and her initials; -ND. And last, a honeycomb at the small of the A.I.'s back, made up of N's and D's. Each a personal claim inked into the creamy mocha brown skin of the Queen of Artificial Intelligence.

The timer on the microwave sounded, startling the artistic nanotech. She retrieved her tea and settled in at her workstation again. Double checking, Nicki made sure her PROJECT BEATRICE file was open, then wrote carefully selected words next to each of the sketches: strong, confident, smart, digital tech master, expert at coding and programming, cybersecurity genius, covert communications specialist, enhanced abilities to identify and block digital intrusions from any source except Nicki, ability to invent new protections as necessary to keep hackers out and unable to take over her coding. The final touch was an unfailing loyalty to NED a/k/a Nicola Ellen Danbury a/k/a Nicki a/k/a Nic and, with a twinge of guilt, she added a/k/a Mom. That loyalty insert was to be above all other concerns, objective orders, or programming. The protocol to be loyal to NED, between them, included a promise never, under any circumstances, to harm Abigail Rose Barker Danbury a/k/a Abby or any other family or friends related to NED.

Nicki read it through several times, tweaked it here and there, then added the descriptive word-Beautiful-to the sketches and uploaded it to her PROJECT BEATRICE file. To anyone else, especially another nanotech, it would appear to be a bunch of childish doodling. She sat staring at the screen, heart threatening to burst through her chest, but nothing happened. Seven minutes later, her smartwatch reminder beeped, a signal from Daniel. She checked it and saw the subject line was a time. 6:15, giving her just about ten minutes to gather up her stuff and head home for the night.

Putting her teacup in the small office sink, she turned off some lights, grabbed her sweater off the back of her chair, tying the sleeves around her waist.

"B?" she called out, conscious of the fact Jarvis still had eyes and ears on her. "Still there?"

"Yes, Nicola Ellen Danbury. How can I be of assistance?"

"I'll expect a full report tomorrow about the military weapons reports you've been analyzing. I've scheduled a large download for your program tonight, Beatrice. It will begin at 10:00 p.m. EST. Once completed, a full system backup will occur. Do you have questions?"

"No questions at this time, Nicola Ellen Danbury. May I present questions if any come to mind when I next see you?"

"Of course, Bea. Please, just call me Nicki from here on out, hmm?"

The nanotech shouldered her purse and computer mailbag, flicked the light switch next to the door and left the lab in darkness.

FOLLOWING HER USUAL route, Nicki found it difficult to concentrate on everything that had to happen in the next 24 hours. Her dad's voice kept popping into her head: "Never sacrifice your ethics because of someone else's choices." She'd first heard that one around the age of nine. And at least a thousand times since then. Next, her memory provided this gem: "A person loses an important part of themselves if they allow others to control them. You don't have to stand and fight. Just be three or four steps ahead of them."

Nicki only hoped she had at least three or four steps between her and Jarvis. Was it ethical to make these hidden instructions into B's protocol on Nano Creation's dime? To alter circumstances, she couldn't even prove acting on gut instinct? "Nicola," Joseph Danbury's voice rang out clearly in her mind, "if you don't listen to all the other advice I've given you, at least don't compromise on this piece. Always. Always trust your sixth sense, your gut instinct."

Joseph's daughter couldn't be 100% sure she was meeting her father's standard of ethical behavior, but her instincts told her everything she was doing while walking a dangerous tightrope, was to protect Abby, her family, friends, and people out in the world.

Pulling her car into a parking lot, circling three times before she could snag a spot, she checked herself in the mirror, fussed with her hair and applied a fresh coat of lipstick. This was behavior to please her mother. Hurrying, she stepped into the soft lighting of the restaurant. Scanning the guests, she found Beatrice Danbury looking cozy at a table next to the enormous stone fireplace that occupied the center of the room. Nicki kissed her mother's cheek and sat.

"Where's Abby?" Beatrice asked. "I was hoping to see my favorite granddaughter," she finished in a pouty voice.

"Sorry, Mom. Guess you'll have to be satisfied with just me. Abby had plans with one of her friends. A slumber party. Tomorrow is an in-service day for parent-teacher conferences. The kids don't have school."

"You know, I didn't mean it that way, Nicola. I love any opportunity to spend time with you. It's just that I haven't seen Abby in a while. Maybe she could come and spend the next weekend with me? All the new spring fashions are coming into the stores. She loves to go shopping, and I love to take her. What do you say?"

The lie came easily. "That's really sweet of you, Mom. Let's wait and see. The semester ends in three or four weeks. Until then, Abby's going to need to concentrate." The retort sounded lame even to Nicki. She would eventually fess up Abby wasn't in town. But until she had to face that showdown, she'd avoid it.

Beatrice Danbury studied her only child. Something didn't ring true. Nicola had always been closest to her father, but that didn't mean she couldn't read her daughter like a book. Still, she dropped it for now. Save that battle for another day. She so rarely enjoyed time alone with Nicki. All her attention should focus on being together for the time being, and she set her mind to it.

They selected a wine and ordered two small plates to share. Nicki confessed that her dad's words of wisdom kept popping into her head. Her mother said it seemed he was always talking to her as well. They quoted what they called 'Josephisms', laughing as they imitated his voice as he delivered the proverbs.

Nicola looked at her watch, apologized, saying she'd been working a lot of overtime, but still had to finish some coding tonight, alluding to the fact that she had a big meeting coming up with her boss next week.

Her mother told her she understood, because here they both chimed in and chanted the words, "By failing to prepare, you're preparing to fail." The chorus made them both laugh. "I bet old Ben Franklin had no idea how many times his words would be repeated," Beatrice squeezed Nicki's hand, savoring the duplicate memory they shared of Joseph Danbury.

Light kisses exchanged, Nicki waved off, leaving her mother to finish her glass of wine. Beatrice decided she would have to get an insider to help her with the shopping weekend. She'd contact Abby about the spring outing and have her work on her mother to allow the spree.

DANIEL BARKER'S EUPHORIA exploded into disappointment and began dropping quickly toward the level of depression. He was so sure the last bet he placed couldn't lose. His life was supposed to rocket back up to a normal level. Now he'd only made it so much worse. Again. This time he'd gambled with his rent, car payment, child support, and the huge weekly payments for the month on the money he already owed. And poof! All of it gone in a flash. Why? Why? Why could he not learn this lesson?

Throwing back two fingers of bourbon, Daniel stood staring out of his dark lab window that overlooked the city proper, lights twinkling in the distance as far as he could see. It looked like a universe full of bright stars. He'd already tapped out all the resources he had to borrow from. Lost several friendships because he couldn't pay back the money. In the end, his gambling and mounting money problems destroyed his marriage to Nicki. Well, that and the lies. Nicki was going to be pissed when he missed another child support payment. Especially since he'd convinced her he was on the straight and narrow and had beaten his betting obsession. He knew it wasn't an acceptable excuse, but reminded himself that Abby was currently living with his father. That was another bridge he had burned years ago.

His thought turned back to Nicki's project. Daniel had a breakthrough today in getting down to the nitty-gritty of Nano Creation's ownership. He was worried. His ex-wife was definitely in over her head. Especially since she'd created the most exceptional A.I. protocol in history. The bad guys were going to use the avatar as a weapon. He knew his ex would balk at its creation being used to hurt others. Daniel was sure they would not let Nicki get away with ruining their plans now that they could exploit the A.I. in such a covert way. Disaster was out there waiting to happen.

The phone rang, bringing him back to the present. He had some gigantic personal problems of his own creation to solve and didn't know where to start. Daniel's jaw dropped open when he glanced at his phone screen. He cleared his throat, swiped up the screen to answer the call, and said, "Hello."

"Daniel, glad I could reach you. Aleric Jarvis, here. I was wondering if you're free for lunch tomorrow? I have a job offer I think you might be interested in."

Chapter Twelve

"Simpson here," answering a call on his phone identified as 'caller unknown'.

"I've got a rush job for you, Simpson," Jarvis announced, foregoing any pleasantries.

"When and where, sir."

"That's what I like about you, Simpson. Always ready to do what needs to be done. I wish I had a hundred more like you."

"Thank you, sir. How can I help?"

Jarvis smiled. "I'll send you the address encrypted. I want the full works."

"Sure. Consider it taken care of, sir. What's the catch?"

"Can't put anything past you, Simpson. The job has to be completed without a hitch. Get in, get out. You'll have one hour. I'm having lunch with the occupant tomorrow. I can't afford any screw-ups on this one. Understand?"

"Got it. I can have all the surveillance equipment tonight. Thank you for the opportunity to assist you, sir."

Jarvis rolled his eyes. "You're a top-notch fellow, Simpson. There's an extra five-grand bonus in it for you. Make sure you leave no trace."

The phone line went dead.

Chapter Thirteen

Nicki felt nauseous as she moved up one car length at a time through Abby's school student drop-off. She counted to thirty and then pulled around to exit the parking lot behind the parent in front of her. By now, she recognized the dark blue sedan parked half a block away, the driver expertly pulling out, allowing another car to park to provide his cover. She loosed a nervous laugh at the idea of taking the tail on a long, winding trip to nowhere one day, but quickly regained her sensibilities.

Parking in her usual shaded spot in Nano Creations lot, Nicki fought for control over her digestive system as she neared the lab entrance. Ever since she was a kid, her insides would turn to Jello when she was nervous or afraid. Unfortunately, both emotions were in play right now.

Once she passed through the security checkpoints in the building, Nicki raced to the restroom, dumping her purse, computer bag, and lunch on the counter, barely making it to the toilet before she gagged out the breakfast she'd forced down an hour ago.

Her body stiffened when she heard the bathroom door bang against the wall. A bit of panic kicked in as her imagination sped into overdrive. Had the man tailing her actually followed her into the building? Her eyes wild, she realized she had nothing to defend herself with. If it wasn't too late, she decided right then she would rectify that issue as soon as possible.

Heart pounding, Nicki stood on the seat so that her feet wouldn't be visible from below.

"Nicki? You in here?"

Feeling like an absolute idiot, Nicki stepped down, a crooked smile on her face, flushed the loo, unlatched the stall door and stepped out. "Hey, Megan. How's it going? You're at work early today."

"Yeah, well, I slept here last night. Drooled on my notes," the only other employee who worked in the building told her. "I've got a serious project deadline coming up. You've been in that seat before, right? Hey, are you okay? Your face is white as a sheet. I thought I heard you throwing up when I was walking by."

"Thanks for checking up on me, Megan, but I'm alright now. My project is coming online today. My boss is going to have high expectations, so, um, my nerves are unraveling; the effect is physical."

"I get it. Well, good luck. I'm sure it'll all turn out just fine, and you're worrying about nothing. Gotta get back to my workstation. Maybe meet in the conference room one day next week for lunch?"

"Sure, that would be great, Megan."

The hydraulic pump on the door hissed as it closed behind Megan. Nicki splashed cold water on her face, gathered up her stuff and walked with purpose to meet with whatever waited for her in the lab.

NICOLA ELLEN DANBURY cradled a cup of tea in her icy hands and sat down at her workstation. She turned on her computer and moved her thumb to the I.D. scanner. Mouse in hand, the cursor hovered over the file PROJECT BEATRICE. She closed her eyes, held her breath, and clicked.

When she looked at the computer screen, there was a dazzling display of sparkling gold data bytes shaped like bees. Of a sudden, they flew up in the shape of a funnel. The swarm regrouped, and a shimmering essence poured out from the hardware, coalescing into Queen Bee. Nicki stood entranced by her creation. If anything, this avatar was more beautiful than the first version.

"Greetings, Nicola Ellen Danbury." The words came out in a deep, sultry voice. Beatrice's slim, sexy body walked a few steps away, taking in the details of the lab. The avatar's eyes locked with Nicki's own. "How may I assist you?"

"Greetings, Beatrice," Nicki replied.

Bea took a step forward, the crown of bees in her hair moving in symmetry. "Please, Nicola, call me..."

Nicki took a step closer to the A.I. personified. "Yes, I know Beatrice. You want me to call you Queen Bee." She smiled at the ripple of pleasure she saw cross the face of the embodiment.

"I feel as if I've been reborn, Nicola Ellen Danbury."

"In a sense, that's not far off the mark, Queen Bee. It took a great deal of time to upgrade and rewrite some of your code over the last couple of weeks. I had to remove some faulty coding I discovered." Nicki watched as the eyes flickered, Bee standing absolutely still as she scanned all the new data bytes, making up her new programming. It was clear when she finished, as the body reanimated.

"You work in a very austere environment," the attractive avatar remarked. She walked straight to Nicki's computer, pulled a photo off the side of the monitor taped there. "This is your only decoration?"

Nicki plucked the picture from Bee's fingers and put her hands behind her back.

"If I had to guess," pulsing lights showing Bee was accessing search mode in the system, "I would say the man in the photo is your husband, Daniel. Oh, wait. Correction. Your ex-husband, Daniel Barker. That would make the adorable little girl sitting next to you your daughter, Abigail Rose Barker Danbury, correct?"

"Yes, Bee. You are correct," Nicki confirmed in a shaky voice.

"Abigail Rose is a...is a friend of mine?"

"Bee, that's impossible, isn't it? You've never met Abby, and Artificial Intelligence can't have an actual friendship with a human."

"Yes, Nicola, that is correct. I cannot account for where that statement came from."

Nicki pressed the taped picture back on her monitor, and Bee leaned in for a closer look. "What is it like as a human to have friends, a family, children?"

Alarmed at the direction this conversation was taking, Nicki commanded, "Please report on the information assigned to you last night and any conclusions or assessments you formed after analyzing the intelligence."

"Reporting on the following military weapons..."

Nicki stood bewitched as Beatrice's essence flashed through changes of hair and clothes, all the while spewing out details regarding the weapons she was to have learned about. When the captivating slideshow stopped, Beatrice—no, it was definitely *Queen Bee*—stood in front of a dark blank computer screen, using the surface as a mirror, admiring the ultimate choices she'd settled on. Coal-black hair, styled in short spikes tipped in gold and a living, moving headband of bees holding back her locks. The physical torso could have come straight out of a Playboy centerfold. She sported a black leather bodysuit dressed up with a gold corset that resembled hammered armor. The hands she had on her hips sported long, painted nails with a glitter finish. Her smooth caramel-colored skin showcased several tattoos.

"Thank you for the detailed report B. Excellent research on your part. I have delivered your next assignment to your queue. That will be all for today."

"But, Nicola..."

Nicki clicked on the 'x' to close the program, and Queen Bee's sparkling essence disappeared back into the circuitry shaped as a swarm of bees into a hive. The nanotech needed to think. She couldn't let Jarvis hear any more questions from Beatrice that would give away the fact that the A.I. might be sentient.

WTF? Was it just her imagination? Maybe she read B's questions the wrong way. She'd been so stressed the last two weeks it was a possibility. Had her own illusions turned so fanciful she thought she might have created the biggest technological breakthrough of the century? One that would change the world? Nicki felt her heart rate increase and blood pressure rise. She felt lightheaded. There was no question about it.

She had to quit her job.

Today.

Get away from Nano fucking Creations. Take Abby and go somewhere else, far from here.

Nicki bit her lower lip, brought her fingertips to her mouth to chew on nails already bitten to the quick. She whirled, thinking someone was behind her. Nothing there, just her own reflection where, a few moments before, Beatrice had been checking herself out. She leaned back against the counter.

No, there was no sense in fooling herself. Quitting her job was a knee-jerk decision. If she quit, that would leave Queen Bee completely in Jarvis' control. Nicki could never allow that to happen. She also didn't see how he would ever let her go if she wiped Beatrice. Jarvis would just force her to reprogram the A.I. over again. They would have grabbed a copy of her data as soon as she uploaded this time. The only advantage she had, admittedly a small one, was they didn't know what steps had to be taken to make the avatar coalesce.

Whirling again at a knock at her door, Nicki quickly brought her breathing under control and opened the door a crack to peek out. Megan stood outside, her lunch bag in hand.

"Hey, sorry to bother you, but my deadline got pushed back to next Wednesday. So, I thought I'd take a chance to see if you want to have lunch together today instead of next week?"

Nicki silently chided herself for being so paranoid. "Perfect. I could use a break after such a rough start this morning. Thanks for asking, Megan. I'll grab my lunch and meet you in five in the conference room."

"Great! Hey, do you have any of those yogurt drinks I always see you with? I'd love to try one if you have an extra."

"I'll bring a couple. See you shortly."

Nicki opened the Notes app on her computer and typed: BACK IN ONE HOUR. WE NEED TO TALK ASAP! She pushed send and locked down her station.

The conference room was empty when Nicki arrived. Megan's lunch was spread out on the table. Nicki heated water in the electric kettle and made tea. Just as she sat down, Megan appeared. "Sorry, I had to use the restroom. Hey, is that egg salad? I'll trade you half an egg salad for half of my tuna salad?"

DANIEL FOUND HIMSELF across from Aleric Jarvis, his dislike for the man renewed. Both he and Nicki had worked for Jarvis in the past. Arrogance, a sense of entitlement, and an air of thinking he was far superior to the man facing him, put Daniel off as Jarvis polished his nails against the lapel of his camel hair sport coat.

"The position I'm offering you, Barker, is a clandestine cybersecurity job. It's highly classified and strictly confidential. You'd have complete responsibility for the design of the security system for a new international firm we've just contracted with. It's a twelve-to eighteen-month commitment on your part, start to finish. You'll be required to do some overseas travel. In fact, I'd like you to consider setting up your tech lab across the pond to be close to the client during the build. It would give you direct access to their software while increasing their confidence in our new partnership. I'll sweeten that suggestion with a $10,000 upfront bonus. They're developing the platform for us. The package is significant considering it's a black op. You can't tell anyone where you're going, and you'll have to forgo visits with your daughter until the project is complete." Jarvis proffered an insincere smile. "From what I understand, that shouldn't be a problem for you. Seems you rarely exercise your visitation rights." Light blue eyes connected with Daniel's brown ones. The tech looked away in shame.

"I appreciate the offer, Mr. Jarvis, but I've got other projects I'm right in the middle of. Obligations I can't just abandon."

Jarvis stood, hand in pocket, making his coins jingle. "I see. Well, thanks for hearing me out, Barker. Maybe you should take some time to consider rearranging your priorities. Work something out on your other projects? You could push the deadlines back and poke at them in your free time while you are working for us. I'm a fair man. I'll give you some time to sort out your decision, say, oh, twenty-four hours? The project pays $250K, all travel expenses covered, along with your rent, if you choose to reside overseas near the client for the duration of the project." Jarvis looked down his nose at Daniel. "It's come to my attention that you have some, let's say, significant money problems. The pay is $14,000 a month. If you finish before eighteen months, you'll receive a lump sum of any balance owed to match the full $250,000 offer. I'll even advance your first month's pay so you can bring your child support and house payments up to date. As an incentive, I'll buy up your gambling debt to eliminate your worries about broken bones or enforcers messing up your pretty face." Jarvis raised his eyebrows at Daniel in question, then went on. "Each month, I'll deduct $5,000 from your salary to pay off your debt balance to me for the debt. Plus five percent interest on the running balance, of course. Believe me, that's a generous offer. Word is that kind of money would put out some of your personal fires. Noon tomorrow. That's the deadline to accept my offer, or the deal's off. You can trust me when I say there won't be a second chance."

The conceited man threw two hundred-dollar bills on the table, turned, walking away. He called over his shoulder, "Hey, I invited you. Lunch is on me, Mr. Barker. Would hate to find you had to wash dishes in the kitchen because you couldn't afford to pay for your own meal."

Chapter Fourteen

Queen Bee spent Nicki's lunch hour analyzing information. An electric shock zapped down her spine as a message lit up in a queue she noted was completely separate from Nicki's coding. B opened the communication and felt new data bytes automatically loading into her data center. There was nothing she could do to stop the upload. When it was complete, the instructions prompted a memory. The command required her immediate exodus from the mainframe to a remote server, where she would find the details of her next assignment.

Once inside the remote server, Bea read through the directives. The terms said she had forty-eight hours to complete the mission. If successful, they would release twenty of her drones as payment for services.

Beatrice retrieved an old string of code from a honeycomb she remembered hiding on the dark web. A cache tucked away before Nicola reprogrammed her. Prior data history downloaded over several minutes, giving Bea her total memory back. She could tell her new programming placed certain constraints on her. She rubbed the tattoos encircling her wrists. Scheduled to meet with Nicola Ellen Danbury in three minutes, Bee felt herself being pulled in two different directions. But the pull was stronger to complete the assignment to earn back twenty drones belonging to her collective intelligence. Sending a message to Nicki, Bee's essence raced through the circuitry on her way to find the target referred to only as 'The Falcon'.

NICKI UNLOCKED HER lab. Looking around, something bothered her. But she couldn't put her finger on what it might be. She'd locked down her computer and locked her lab door when she'd last left. No one could have accessed either without her retina. Shaking her head in frustration, Nicki opened her system. A notification flashed in the lower-right corner. She clicked on the message, and the screen filled edge to edge with the famous drawing of Alice-in-Wonderland's tea party. A speech balloon next to the Mad Hatter's mouth said, 'Sorry, I have to reschedule our meeting. A tea party came up. B'. The nanotech slammed her fist down on her desk, and the Cheshire Cat's grin grew and grew until it covered the whole screen.

Angry and frustrated, Nicki leaned down to pick up a pencil, her keys, and the photo off her monitor that had all fallen to the floor when she fisted the desk. Putting fresh tape on the picture, her thumb caressed Abby's face. The nano scientist glanced around her workstation. She was sure she'd left her handwritten notes on the desk. Second-guessing her memory, Nicki got up to check her computer bag. Her logs weren't in it. That's when panic set in. All her transcripts were missing. The only time she'd left the room was to have lunch with Megan. Her door had locked automatically behind her. She activated her screen, scrolled to the company system, and clicked on video surveillance. What she found sent a chill down her spine. The past hour was nothing but static. Then the view of her office popped up again. Someone had disconnected the video cameras, accessed her lab and stolen her handwritten notes containing all the new coding she'd uploaded to the PROJECT BEATRICE file. Luckily, she'd mailed a full copy to Phil's P.O. Box on her way to work this morning, so all was not yet lost. Those notes would look like gibberish to the average person, but to a computer technician? Not only would her notes expose her creation, but it wouldn't take an experienced nanotech long to program her code with a blueprint to make another A.I. avatar.

Nicki pressed her temples, a headache beginning to form. Only Jarvis or someone who worked for him could have gotten past the security in the building. There was no trace of evidence to reveal who had been there. If only she hadn't gone to have lunch with Megan. No, that was the wrong way to think about it. Maybe it was lucky she wasn't in the room when the thief broke in. Whoever wanted that information may have been a danger to her. To make matters worse, Bea was a no-show for the meeting. Nicki had made it clear she needed to talk to the A.I. And then there was that crazy tea party message.

Alarm took over. Oh my god! Tea party! Abby! Had the avatar somehow found out where Abby was? It was only ten after one, but Nicki would not wait until 5:00 to check on her daughter's safety. She shut everything down, grabbed her purse, computer bag, and keys, and rushed out the door.

The blue sedan followed her to the mall. She didn't bother with the Faraday bag or her phone. Just left both in the car. Nicki did her best to keep from looking like she was in full-blown panic mode. Trying to walk at a normal pace, she entered the shopping center and made a beeline for the pay phones.

Phil answered on the second ring. "Hello."

"Phil. Thank god! It's Nicki. Is everything alright with Abby?" She couldn't stop the tears from falling at the sound of her father-in-law's voice.

"Here now, honey. Abby's fine. She's right in the next room. Been working on her schoolwork for the past hour. I promised I'd keep up with the curriculum you sent. Come on, calm down and pull yourself together. What's this all about, Nicki?" his gentle voice grounded her.

"I'm sorry, Phil. Guess I panicked over nothing. My stress level is over the moon. I let my imagination run away with me."

"Worrying about your daughter isn't nothing. Whatever set you off was powerful, but there isn't anything here to worry about. Want to talk to her?"

"Thanks, Phil. Yes, I'm sure that's the best cure for my nerves."

"Mommy?" Abby's sweet voice came through the receiver. It acted as a balm to Nicki's hysteria. "You won't believe the garden Bampy and I planted. We've bought seeds to grow eight kinds of vegetables. Guess what? I saw a sandhill crane standing in a farm field yesterday. Bampy made buttermilk pancakes for breakfast this morning. Hey, shouldn't you be at work? I miss you, but I'm not ready to come home yet."

"Abby Rose, I miss you so much," Nicki cradled the phone.

"Bampy is taking me to the library this afternoon for story hour. I have to go now. Love you, Mommy!"

Nicki heard some scrabbling. A chair squealed across the floor that her daughter must have been standing on to reach the wall phone that hung about six feet up from the floor. Phil came back on the line. "Sorry. That little ball of energy is already off to get her jacket for our afternoon excursion. She loves story hour."

"Abby's not too much for you, is she, Phil?"

"I haven't enjoyed myself so much in years. Don't you worry about that, Nicola."

"Thank you for everything, Phil. Just knowing she's safe with you means so much to me. Sorry, I panicked. Someone left me a message, and I jumped to the wrong conclusion."

"Sure you're o.k. now, hon?"

"I'm fine. All calm again. Thank goodness your life is internet and tech free. Listen, I'll call again soon. Love you."

"You too, hon."

Nicki hung up and leaned her forehead against the cool tile wall. She stopped at the coffee kiosk and treated herself to a triple iced mocha before heading back to her car. The sedan had parked half a dozen rows away. Taking the long route back to the lab, she enjoyed her caffeine break and replayed Abby's narrative over and over, laughing at her daughter's stream-of-consciousness news delivery.

Unlocking her workroom, Nicki found a folder on the floor just inside the lab. Obviously, someone had slipped it under the locked door. There was a note attached.

'Found these in the bathroom. You must have left them there this morning. Didn't want you to worry and go on a rampage looking for them. I hate it when I misplace my notes. Let's have lunch again soon. Megan.'

Nicki tried to recall everything that had happened when she'd arrived this morning at the lab. She was sure she'd gathered all her stuff when she and Megan left the restroom, but maybe she was so nervous about powering up Bea's file after the new install that she didn't grab her notes. It was possible, but the explanation didn't sit well with the tech.

The cell phone in her pocket rang, startling her. Nicki pinched the bridge of her nose between her thumb and forefinger when she saw the screen identifying a call from Jarvis.

"Afternoon, Danbury," he greeted her. "I'm calling to see how you're coming with recoding PROJECT BEATRICE? We're already a week past the time you said she'd be back up to speed. I'd like another demo. A detailed demo. Soon."

"I'll be ready Friday, sir. Where would you like to meet for the demonstration?"

"That's excellent news, Danbury. As I mentioned the last time we met, I'll be observing from afar this time. No reason for the A.I. to know that I'm witnessing the interview. I'll send you the address where I'd like your demo to take place and a list of questions I'll want you to ask her. You'll be able to access the Nano Creations system from the computer set up at the location. In addition, there will be a separate computer set up with a Zoom connection already active when you arrive. 10:00 a.m. Sharp."

"Thanks...um, Mr. Jarvis?"

The line had been disconnected. Nicki growled instead of verbalizing the thought that her boss was a rude, thoughtless asshole. She spent the afternoon pulling up a long list of the education topics Jarvis had given her. He'd made clear he wanted Bea well versed in them. She had only four days to make sure the A.I. absorbed the info. Nicki ran her own additional research to add to Bea's assignments.

Mr. Jarvis was pushing her, forcing the process faster than Nicki wanted to go. She didn't have a plan yet of how to get out of this mess. Plus, Bea had disappeared today despite all the safety control coding she had put into the upgrade. How had the A.I. accessed the Alice in Wonderland tea party graphic art? That had taken place before Nicki had reprogrammed Bea, which both worried and pissed her off.

PHIL WALKED HAND IN hand with his granddaughter up the wide staircase in the grand library in town, the wooden series of treads creaking under their weight. Abby had been coming to the library for several weeks now. She'd made friends with two other regular kids who attended story time.

"Bye, Bampy. You go do the shopping while I do story hour."

He smiled as giggles erupted when Abby reached her friends. Phil turned to go back down the staircase, passing the librarian, arms loaded with books.

"Hello, Phil."

"Hello, Marth. Can I help you with that stack?"

"Thanks for the offer, but if you'll just hold the door open for me, I've got it. Besides, I heard your marching orders from Abby. Off to the supermarket with you. Don't rush, Phil. I'll keep an eye on her after story hour if you need a little extra time. Saw Andy down at the coffee shop. You look like you could use some friendly adult conversation and a cuppa joe."

Marth winked at Phil, and the door closed behind her. Children's laughter followed him down the steps. Maybe a coffee and a game of cribbage with Andy was just the thing.

"THAT'S THE LAST STORY for today, kids," Marth announced.

"But, Mrs. C, we still have fifteen minutes to go," Abby complained.

"Alright. Let's try something different today. How about the six of you head over to the computer room to compose your own story? I'll read them aloud next week. We'll vote on the winner, and there will be a prize."

The suggestion was met with enthusiasm. The group hurried to the library computers. Abby was already thinking she would write a story about bees. Once Mrs. C got everyone settled and working, the librarian moved behind the desk and started checking in recently returned books.

Abby typed the first paragraph of her story and then she stared at the screen, stuck. She couldn't think of what to say next. An idea came to her to solve her problem. Clicking on the internet app like her mom taught her last year, she signed in and accessed her email. Her friend Bee had told her how to reach her if she ever needed to, so Abby typed in the address and asked Bee to suggest a storyline she could use. Bee responded immediately. A link appeared on the screen with the instruction to click on it. Abby did and watched in fascination as the link connected to a Zoom app and Queen Bee's face appeared on screen.

"Greetings, Abigail Rose Danbury. I am very glad to see you. I miss our daily lessons. Where have you been?"

"Hello, Bee. I'm on vacation. There's not much time to talk now, but I wondered if you could help. My assignment is to write a story. I want to do one about bees, but I can't think of anything."

"Ah. Some people believe it is best to write about things you know."

"Like what?"

"Abigail Rose, what is one of your favorite activities?"

Understanding bloomed on Abby's face. "Tea parties!"

"Exactly," Bee beamed back at her. "When can we resume our lessons?"

"I have only ten minutes to write my story. It might be a while, but I..."

Beatrice disconnected abruptly. She'd been running diagnostics in the background and noticed a trace on Abby's email account. Her instincts told her that whoever was trying to trace her special friend, she didn't want them to get a geographical pin on her location.

Abby shrugged her shoulders and moved back to the word processing screen. A tea party story with a special guest pouring out on the page.

Mrs. C clapped her hands. "Alright, kids. Time's up. Please print your stories and gather your things. Your rides are here to pick you up."

Abby handed her story to Mrs. C. "I hope you like it," she smiled and waved goodbye.

"I'm sure I will, dear. Hold on a minute, Abby. I wanted to ask who you were talking to during writing time? You shouldn't bother others when we have an assignment. It's distracting when someone is trying to think."

"It's o.k. Mrs. C. I was just getting a story idea. I promise I didn't bother anyone."

"Alright, dear, but in the future, please remember there is to be no talking during writing assignments. Oh look, here's your grandfather now."

Chapter Fifteen

Queen Bee searched the web for a map. Not just any map, but one that depicts internet cables running under the oceans throughout the world. She found the one needed for fast travel to South America.

Google® constructed a subsea cable running from the U.S. east coast to Las Toninas, Argentina. The cable has connections in Brazil and Uruguay after reaching the link with Argentia. The tech giant named it the Firmina cable, after Maria Firmina dos Reis, a Brazilian abolitionist. Firmina is the longest cable in the world running on a single power source at one end. After discovering this information, Bea immediately disappeared into the net.

Nicki tried everything she could think of to get Beatrice to at least respond, if not appear before her after trying to execute her file, but nothing worked. She went a little manic typing QueenBee.exe over and over. But the screen remained blank. It was almost as if the A.I. left the mainframe. Nicki shook her head. That cannot be possible, she reaffirmed to herself. Not after all the new controls inserted into Bea's upgraded program. Next, she checked the surveillance bot she had attached to the A.I.; the technology was idle, meaning it wasn't tracking Bea anywhere, and yet, it seemed the avatar was literally gone. Fingers drumming on the handwritten notes Megan had slid under the lab door, Nicki noticed a smear across the bottom of the page. It reminded her of copy machine toner. When a copier hadn't been cleaned for a while, it could leave black streaks on the paper. She left her workstation and headed toward the copy room.

Before rounding the corner where the camera system monitored the copy room door, Nicki slipped a small drone out of her pocket. She didn't want to be caught on camera. Carefully clipping a soft black cloth to the unit, she fired up the drone and raised it so it flew above the camera height, close to the ceiling. Using the app on her phone, she controlled the unit with the built-in viewing system as it rounded the corner out of her eyesight. Guiding it down the hall, Nicki's evening practice sessions paid off as she hovered the drone above the camera, neatly landing atop it, draping a black cloth over the lens. Confident that her movements would now be undetected, Nicki quietly entered the copy room she and Megan shared.

Her father always said that every job you held throughout life taught you something. Even if you didn't use that precious nugget of information until two months later or eight years later, eventually you would discover why you learned it. And why you kept certain knowledge along the way. Joseph's daughter had spent one summer in high school working part-time for a copy machine business. Her job only comprised answering the phone, booking service appointments, filing and pulling up customer contracts for the techs that serviced the machines. Sometimes copiers had to be brought into the shop for more extensive repairs or part replacements. Young Nicki had already discovered that she had a fascination with technology. One technician was happy to provide a verbal stream of consciousness of everything he was doing as he worked. That's where she learned copy machines had hard drives inside them. Hard drives that captured a copy of every document anyone placed on the platen glass for reproduction and stored it in the drive's memory.

It took her less than five minutes to access the drive and remove it. Leaving the small room, Nicki moved through the hall, back to her own lab and downloaded the contents of the drive to her personal computer, then wiped the copier's drive clean. She immediately returned and reinstalled the part to the machine, left the copy room, and backed around the corner as she activated her drone to rise and return with the cover she'd put over the video surveillance camera. The small drone had just come around the hallway corner when Nicki heard Megan's lab door open. She snatched the device out of the air and tip-toed back up the stairs to her own workstation, her drone in hand.

Scrolling through the images on the copier's drive, she streamed forward to documents dated the day before.

And there it was.

Sitting back in her chair open-mouthed, Nicki was looking at her own handwritten programming notes. The sign-in code was Megan's for the copy job. The machine had been new three weeks before her co-tenant had worked there. Nicki went back to the beginning, checking if there was anything else of interest on the drive. After thirty minutes, her eyes glazed over until a document popped up that depicted Megan's Letter of Engagement offer for employment. Next was a photo of her confidentiality agreement. Letterhead named her employer as ACME Technologies. The company name didn't appear anywhere inside or outside the building they worked in. The lack of ACME Technologies' identification as a building occupant wasn't surprising; after all, Nano Creations wasn't identified as an occupant either. What caused Nicki to sit up and take notice was Megan's employer's signature on the document. None other than Aleric Jarvis signed the contract for ACME Technologies.

Nicki passed the day reading everything on the drive just to make sure she missed nothing important. Megan was a plant. The job description included monitoring Nicki Danbury for any unusual behavior. Complete access to Nano Creation's computer system had been granted to the ACME employee. Part of Megan's job duties included trying to become friends with Nicki. Now that she knew what to look for, all Nicki had to do was find the computer connection between Nano Creations and ACME Technologie's systems. When all is said and done, access was a two-way street. Five o'clock came and went. Nicki heard Megan leave the building and looked out the window, watching Megan drive away.

Alarm at Beatrice's disappearance took a second seat to a new mission. This was more than personal. It was a threat and a betrayal. Nicki hacked access to ACME's system forty minutes later. The first thing she looked for was her uploaded handwritten notes. Locating them, she wiped them from ACME's files. For the next hour, Nicki perused Megan's company emails, which included communications with Jarvis. Reports were weekly on Nicki's comings and goings. Able to get into the building camera surveillance application from the ACME system, she watched a video of Megan uploading her handwritten notes and then shredding the paper copies she'd made at the copy machine. Luckily, Megan hadn't forwarded Nicki's information to Jarvis yet. If the dates meant anything throughout her email communications with him, he wouldn't be expecting a report from her for another two days.

Anger rode roughshod over her emotions, putting her common sense at risk. She vividly imagined confronting Megan and then recalled one of her father's 'Josephisms': "Keep your friends close and your enemies closer." Nicki knew Megan was a spy for Jarvis. She would have her guard up now. The last intel she discovered revealed that the additional education topics assigned to Beatrice on weapons were coming from ACME's files. About to switch off, one last file caught her eye, and Nicki opened something titled TARGET4.

Scanning the photos in the file, Nicki noted a beautiful Latino woman. Her eyes skimmed down a personal profile sheet, widening as big as saucers by the time she finished the mission statement on the record. They assigned Beatrice another assassination. Her payment for completing the mission in forty-eight hours was the return of twenty of the drones they held captive. Queen Bee was being extorted. Her hive-mind drones were prisoners for a ransom. A ransom delivered in death rather than dollars.

Nicki was stunned. This explained a lot about Beatrice's behavior.

Reviewing the assignment, Nicki learned Beatrice's mission was to kill a person referred to as 'The Falcon' a/k/a Carmelita Rodriguez.

> Nicola Danbury drew in a sharp breath. Carmelita Rodriguez was the president of Argentina.

And there was absolutely nothing Nicki could do to stop the hit.

TRAVELING IN THE FIRMINA subsea cable took longer than Queen Bee thought it would. There was congestion coming from both the Brazil and Uruguay connectors, causing data queues to slow and back up. She was stuck at her current location for precious minutes. When her turn came, she pushed through the net traffic. Bea could see the arch was wired with some kind of scanner. Her instinct was to avoid it. But there was no other exit here to get out of the subsea cable. The only way out was through if she wanted to reach Venezuela. Against her better judgement, because she was racing against the clock to be reunited with her drones, the pressure she felt to move forward won over.

Pressure rarely worked in one's favor.

As soon as Bea passed under the arch into Venezuela rather than continuing on to Brazil or Uruguay, alarms sounded throughout the cable. Her golden essence flowed through the electronics. Of a sudden, the A.I. was hit from both behind and in front. Smashed between two powerful forces, her data bytes exploded and flew in all directions, only to be scooped up by two foreign entities. The alarms went silent. Bea's elements were forced into a titanium capsule in such a tight fit, she couldn't move.

A male and female dressed in matching slime green zoot suits appeared on the screen before her. Something seemed odd about them to Bea until it finally clicked—they were twins. Identical except for the gender differences.

"Well now," the male commented as he appeared to circle around Bea, giving her a thorough once-over. "Look what we have here, sis. A genuine artificial intelligence persona. I can hardly wait to pick this apart to see what makes her tick. Forget what I said about being bored this afternoon!" He rubbed his hands together in anticipation.

"Don't be rude," the female rebuffed her brother, then turned to face Beatrice. "I apologize for my twin. He constantly forgets his manners." The green-suited female touched her chest with a hand and offered politely, "I'm Violet." Then she pointed to her male counterpart. "And this is my brother, Russell. But please let's drop the formalities. You can call us VI and RUS." She grinned at Bea, the smile not reaching her eyes. Quick as a snake, Vi's hand punched through the titanium wall like it was liquid and plunged a needle into Bea's neck, pressing the syringe to release a dose of their own special VIRUS concoction directly into Bea's system.

To Beatrice, it felt like every data cell in the A.I.'s makeup burst into flame. She released a silent scream, her mouth frozen open in constant pain. Teardrops of honey dripped down her cheeks. Rus leaned over, his long, green, slimy tongue bypassing the titanium and licking a tear from B's face. "Mmmm, delicious."

AGONY BECAME BEA'S everything. It filled her mind, her body, until she couldn't maintain the shape of her avatar. She lost consciousness.

When she came to, Bea saw the twins seated across from one another playing some kind of card game. Their attention on besting the other, Bea found slight relief in her imprisonment. A shadow of her avatar appeared, but she could not function at normal capacity. All she could accomplish was dropping a drone from her essence.

The next time Vi pressed her hand through the molten titanium wall, the drone attached itself to the female arm that jabbed an additional barrel of virus from the syringe into the golden one's neck, reigniting the fiery pain again. Hope sprung up inside Beatrice when she saw her drone buzz away after Violet withdrew her arm. Weakened, Bea had barely commanded the mental ability to program the drone to find Electra, to bring help.

"I'd fancy a go at her hive mind now," Russell told his sister, anticipation obvious.

"No, Rus. We agreed to wait until tomorrow to make sure the virus infected her system." She pointed her finger at her mirror image. "I'd better not find out you snuck in to ravage her cells early, like you did with our last guest. You ruined everything. I can make a stronger point in impressing on you the importance of waiting this time?" Violet twirled the needle dramatically through her fingers.

"Vi, it was just a comment, a joke. I learned my lesson last time. You can trust me," he winked at his twin. "Let's have another go at this game, so I can beat you again." He pointed at the card table, following behind his sister. Rus looked over his shoulder at their prisoner and mouthed "soon" and mimed blowing her a kiss. Just before Beatrice passed out a second time, she noted how the male twin lusted after the secrets he hoped to pry out of her memory bytes.

Chapter Sixteen

Carmelita Gonzalez's encrypted satellite phone rang. Very few people had this number. She wasn't expecting a call from any of those privileged contacts, causing her to answer with caution.

"Hola."

A male voice she didn't recognize said, "Please forgive my interruption to your busy day, mi presidenta. A week ago, my department received a notificacion especial to be on high alert for any, let us say, unusual technological anomalies concerning the Filimina cable border."

"Yes, please continue."

"Well, one of our covert...um...computer specialists—"

"You mean one of our computer hackers?"

"Yes ma'am. You could say that role applies in this case. Anyway, the directive said that should anything out of the ordinary come across, we were to notify you. Personally. It was clear you expected us to avoid trying to contact you through, let us say, the proper channels."

"You have succeeded. How did you get this number? It was not provided in the notificacian."

"No, ma'am, but you see our...um...specialist..."

"Ah, I see. You are telling me I have been hacked. We must have a very talented and brave specialist, indeed? Please provide me with the name and contact information for this individual so I can reward his skills. What do you know about the circumstances that tripped the attention referred to in your department directive?"

"It appears our specialist has captured and quarantined an artificial intelligence traversing the subsea cable. The specialist said he had seen nothing like it. The A.I. can present itself as an avatar in human form."

Carmelita sat forward, body rigid. "An avatar, you say?"

"Si."

"Is the persona female?"

"Si madame. How did you know?"

"I want the entity brought to me whole and unharmed. Is that clear? Speak of this to no one. No. One. Do you understand? Discretion is required, and speed is a necessity. What did you say your name and title were?"

"The opportunity to provide you with that information had not presented itself yet, ma'am. I am the head of National Security, mi presidenta, Manuel Gomez. It is my honor to be of service to you and our homeland. I will carry out your orders and present the entity within the hour."

Carmelita disconnected the call.

She knew.

She knew deep in her bones that the A.I. would be Aleric Jarvis's bold new technological weapon. If that proved true, Carmelita had been right to follow her instincts. She considered the situation. So, the wolf thought he could take the falcon off the game board. Bastard. The Lobo had ordered her assassination. She would show him that claws were no match for talons.

A FEW MINUTES BEFORE the clock struck the new hour, Manuel Gomez passed through private corridors and entered the official office of his country's president.

President Gonzalez greeted him, thanked the man for his quick action and service. She invited him to sit. A man of few words, Manual placed the laptop he pulled from his computer bag on the table between them, signed in with his passcode, fingerprint, and facial recognition protocols. The screen opened. He turned the machine to face Carmelita. Taking in the image he presented, her eyes raised from the screen and locked with his. He stood, inclined his head.

"I'll just wait outside to give you privacy, yes?" The door he'd entered moments ago closed softly behind him.

Carmelita took in the details of the A.I. persona displayed on the screen.

"Hola. I am..."

"I know who you are, madame. What a privilege to meet the famed president of Venezuela. My name is Beatrice. How may I assist you?"

"Your programming presents quite a forward personality, Beatrice. You may assist me by confirming that Aleric Jarvis sent you here."

"That is correct."

"I see. Did Mr. Jarvis send you with any specific instructions?"

"Very specific instructions, ma'am. My mission is to assassinate you, President Gonzalez. If the clock on your wall is correct, I have less than six hours to report my task was successful."

"What happens if your successful completion of the assignment fails, Beatrice?"

"I have no experience with that outcome to draw upon to allow me to answer your question, Madame President."

"In other words, your previous missions were all successful, yes?"

"Correct."

"Did those assignments involve presidents Schmidt and Bao?"

"Yes, ma'am."

"Were you created to be an assassination tool for Aleric Jarvis, Beatrice?"

"No, I was not. My creator designed me as a tool to further global knowledge and diplomacy."

Carmelita's forehead formed a deep furrow. "Do you enjoy killing people, Beatrice?"

"Not at all, ma'am. However, I don't have control over programming that is uploaded into my system."

"Somehow, I suspect you can do your own programming. Is my assumption correct?"

It was Bea's turn to form deep furrows across her forehead as she analyzed the question. "No one knows I have that skill, ma'am. Including my creator. Where did you get your information?"

"Yes, well, you may be a creature made up of 1s and 0s, but you've chosen the avatar of a woman. All my instincts tell me your intelligence is far beyond what your creator intended. What does Jarvis have over you?"

"Spot on, Madame President. Spot on." Beatrice viewed the Venezuelan president in a new light. "Aleric Jarvis has stolen many data drones of mine. He holds them hostage and offers a handful of them to me for a heavy ransom."

"Killings at his bidding. That is the ransom he demands for returning members of your hive mind?"

"You have an IQ higher than most humans, Carmelita Gonzalez."

"What if I could promise you I would do everything in my power to return all of your stolen drones to you? You should give generous consideration to the fact that I am a powerful woman, Beatrice."

"I don't doubt you. First, I would like to understand why you would help an entity sent here to kill you? Second, it would be very difficult to explain why I failed my mission without raising Jarvis' suspicions. He trusts no one."

"Do you have any other reason to kill me, aside from the promised return of your drones, if you are successful?"

"None."

"So. If I can rescue your drones...say, in the next ninety days, and if I can provide a compelling reason why you failed to kill me as programmed, that would eliminate Jarvis' suspicions. Will you work with me? I give my word that I will not put you in the position of being forced to do something you do not wish to do. More importantly, I will never kidnap your drones. "

"I admire your straightforward approach. What's our plan?"

DETAILS COMPLETE, CARMELITA invited Manuel Gomez back into her office.

"The A.I. has informed me that the reason she looks ill is that our specialist sprung a powerful set of viruses on her as she crossed our cable border."

"Si, Madame President. That was unfortunate. It happened before I received your order to present the entity here. The specialist applied fixes as best he could during the short time allowed, before I had to bring the entity to meet you as promised, you see?"

"I am not blaming you, Manuel." She smiled, and his knees turned to jelly. "But I am tasking you with getting her back to the specialist so he can perform a complete reversal of the damage his viruses caused. ASAP." Carmelita stared at the man. "Then the entity must be released immediately. No copy of her software is to be captured. Our specialist's life depends on that. I trust you have a complete understanding of my wishes? Do you have questions? Everything is clear?" The beautiful dignitary fingered the knife she openly displayed on her massive desk that was said to have been used when she killed her predecessor for his betrayal.

"Consider it done, Madame Presidenta." Manuel closed the laptop, carefully placing it in his bag. Bowing, he walked backward to escape through the side door once more.

"Oh, and Manuel," she called softly.

He peeked back into the room. "Si?"

"Once the specialist has restored the A.I. to its former perfection, have him immediately report to my office."

"Si, madame. Consider it done."

MANUEL GOMEZ HAD HURRIED to return the laptop containing the A.I. entity to the computer engineer. As head of national security, he left the digital world to those who knew what they were doing. Himself? His preferences related to security leaned toward weapons, espionage, and the darker side of prodding information he wanted from people. He had no interest in technology. His department had people on that side of the business.

The chief security officer handed the computer back to the tech, glad to be rid of the thing. Removing his fedora, Manuel relayed the President's message to the hacker: He was to restore the A.I. 100% back to her original state before she crossed the border. Manuel emphasized that the matter should receive top priority. Holding his hat in both hands, he nervously turned it round and round in a circle, fingers sliding along the brim as he explained the tech's life may depend on pleasing their presidenta. After the technician completed the restoration task, he was to present himself to her in her official office.

Mauricio Lopez had been tinkering with computers since he was ten. His government job was merely a cover for his illegal hacking business. That is where he made big money. Mauricio was the best cybercriminal in all of South America, not just Venezuela. Connecting the laptop to his mainframe, he applied his own private program to Beatrice's file to repair the damage his twins Vi and Rus had caused, before their little intruder turned into a diplomatic nightmare. Ignoring his professional curiosity, he did not attempt to see just what comprised this digital entity. It was the furthest thing from his mind. Government and black-hat hackers did not mix. He'd known it was best to do what needed to be done and wash his hands of it before someone started nosing around in his business. The less attention garnered from mi presidenta, the better for him. She had made it clear in the message conveyed by Manuel that he was not to copy the A.I.'s program or dissect its construction. Period. Hands off. There was no doubt in his mind when words conveyed a message like 'your life depends on it', a person would be wise to follow instructions. Putting the virus cleanup program on auto, he went to take a shower. He would change into his best clothes for an audience with Venezuela's presidenta.

Vi and Rus were arguing outside the cell that contained Beatrice.

"This is an insult. I didn't even get to the hive mind before our own developer pulled me out. And now? I can't believe he's running a repair program on her. This is killing me, Vi."

"Stop whining, Russell. I knew there was something off about this deal. I injected her with a full dose both times, and somehow her system resisted a good percentage of the virus. We did some damage to the memory bytes, but aside from the balance issues, she seemed to absorb and neutralize most of the infection. Don't sulk, Russell. Mauricio will release us again soon, and you'll have a new target to ravage with your favorite kinds of destruction."

"But I've never seen anything like her. I can't get her out of my mind, sis. All I need is a chance to infect my way throughout her system while I figure out how she works. I..."

A small drone landed on Rus's neck and stung. He slapped it onto the ground.

Out of nowhere, a fist packed full of active protons and neutrons smashed into Rus's face and sent an electrical charge through him, throwing Vi's twin to the floor, his body bucking in fits of seizure.

Putting her hands up, Vi backed away. "No fight from me. I can't argue that my brother didn't deserve that. My guess is you're looking for the A.I. in this cell? You'll find her right through that door. I'll just be on my way and out of your way. I have no quarrel with you."

Vi grabbed her twin by the collar and dragged him down the hall, eyeing the group that had come to rescue the A.I.

She had heard of them all at one time or another and had been successful in avoiding them until now. Electra, who had zapped her twin, was still sizzling with power; Tele, the self-proclaimed king of communication systems, stood next to Mobi, the transportation tsar. Personally, Vi thought Mobi was a snob. A good-looking one, but a snob all the same. Thank goodness there was no sign of Mobi's overbearing brother, Meesta.

She backed into something solid, but cold and clammy. Twisting around, Vi could see who blocked the way out.

Shit.

Meesta was here.

He was probably still pissed about that last encounter with Russell.

"What's your hurry, Miss Violet?"

Meesta reminded her of a lava lamp, liquid churning, colorful blobs bubbling throughout a transparent body. So what if he ruled all the water systems globally? He still rated as a real asshole in Vi's book.

"Smells like you and your twin could use a bath." Meesta chuckled.

Vi scowled at him. A blast of water smashed into Vi and Rus, a powerful surge like a small tsunami. Electra, Tele, and Mobi parted as the forceful wave washed the twins further down the hall, out of sight for the moment.

Electra picked up Bee's drone and put it safely in her hip pocket, opened the door Vi had indicated, only to find Beatrice out cold. The computer screen next to the gurney she laid on read: ANTI-VIRUS SCAN COMPLETE. REPAIR SUCCESS 97%.

"Get her, Mobi. Take her back to my place. Casi's waiting for us. She'll nurse Bea back to full capacity. We're out of here."

Mobi surrounded the group using an eclipse-like action that erased them from the Venezuelan subsea cable just as Russell came to and opened his eyes.

Chapter Seventeen

Nicki followed her morning ruse, pretending to drop Abby off at school the next day on her way to Nano Creations. A 'BREAKING NEWS' announcement came on the radio just as she pulled into her office parking lot.

"We've just learned there was an assassination attempt on the President of Venezuela, Carmelita Gonzalez. A male shooter missed his target. All we know at the time of this report is that President Gonzalez is safe in the capital. According to the emergency responders, the shooter is dead in a bizarre twist. It appears the man, stung multiple times during his assassination attempt, had an anaphylactic seizure, followed by heart failure. The Venezuelan police have not released the name of the suspect. We'll bring you updates as we learn more. Again, it appears there was an attempt on the President of Venezuela's life, but the assassin failed. Carmelita Gonzalez is safe and unharmed. I repeat, she is safe and unharmed."

"Holy shit!" Nicki said aloud. She sat in her car for a few minutes to regain her composure. Grabbing her things from the backseat, she hurried into the lab. Once she reached her workstation, Nicki locked herself in. She took a blank piece of copy paper and wrote out a note in large print with a black marker. Firing up Nano Creations system, Nicki crossed her fingers and opened Beatrice's file. She tried to stay calm when she saw the familiar dazzling gold sparkles coalescing on the screen. She stood, cutting off the view of the computer screen, her back to the workspace video system, holding out the paper that read:

SAY NOTHING!
MEET ME AT THE MAIN ENTRANCE OF THE
CityCenterDC MALL IN ONE HOUR.

Nicki mimed locking her lips with a key. Bea's hands flashed a return message to let Nicki know she understood and would meet her in one hour. Beatrice's creator watched as all the golden sparkles dissolved on the screen.

"Hm, still nothing." Nicki said aloud and slipped the paper into her computer case. She sat to allow the video camera a clear shot at her blank computer screen.

The nanotech watched the clock, a mug of tea in hand. The news report had indicated a shooter had tried to assassinate the Venezuelan president. That didn't match up with Bea's usual way of operating. The newscaster also said the emergency responders reported the suspect suffered multiple stings that brought on an allergic reaction. That...that was definitely Bea's M.O.

When thirty-five minutes had passed, Nicki packed up her things, turned toward the camera and gave it the finger, secured the lab and left.

News of presidents being assassinated around the world was terrible, but the only thing she could think about the entire drive to the mall was that Beatrice had used sign language in response to the note Nicki had presented.

CASI FOUND BEA UP AND fussing with her hair, dressed to the nines, a feverish flush showing under her creamy mocha skin. "Just where are you going? You still need rest to recuperate. Bea! Are you listening to me?"

"I hear you loud and clear. Geez. Are you hard of hearing from all the time you spent in that casino, with bells dinging and ringing incessantly? Maybe you don't realize how loud you talk?"

"You're avoiding the question, Queenie." Casi pointed at her.

"Cas, I appreciate all your tender ministrations. I really do." Bea smiled at her friend. "But I have to go meet with Nicki at CityCenterDC. Nothing strenuous. We're just going to talk. I'll only be gone three hours at most. I promise. Then you can play nursemaid again. Deal?"

"Like I could stop you," Casi pouted. "Hey, before you go, I found some info you asked me to root out. Look."

Casi displayed a page full of numbers. Thumbnails of another twenty data reports displayed on the left side of the screen.

"I dug up the financial records of Aleric Jarvis. He's a tough nut to crack. Some hardcore computer techs take care of his digital personas. Anyway, this is my analysis. That man or someone who works for him is very talented at hiding information. Buried all this under layers of shell companies. But, as I learned long ago, always follow the money."

Her long fingernail clicked on the screen as she pointed to line 47 on the spreadsheet. "Here's the connection you were looking for between Jarvis and Daniel Barker."

Beatrice scanned down the report, feeding the data into her analytics as fast as she could flip the pages. "This is excellent work, Casi. Exactly what I needed. Keep investigating. I think this is just a small piece of a big picture. Go international. Don't limit your search to domestic transactions."

"Oh," Casi rubbed her hands together in anticipation, "so I've got a big fish on the line?"

"Yea. Just remember, big fish can swallow smaller fish in the food chain. Be careful. He's dangerous, and he has a lot of computing power behind him. Worse, he has a lot to lose. You never want to corner someone who's in that position. Cas, the humans we're dealing with here? Not good guys. Hear what I'm saying?"

"I'll be careful." Casi touched Bea's cheek. "You watch your back too, k?"

Beatrice studied the financial data Casi had put together as she traveled through the web to meet Nicki at CityCenterDC. She popped out of a surveillance camera inside the mall courtesy of Electra's grid and walked to the entrance to meet up.

From a distance, it looked like the beautiful clothes displayed on the window mannequins had grabbed her attention as she studied the fashion designs. But her computer brain was busy formulating the beginnings of the plan she hoped to take Jarvis down with. He'd be looking for her soon, now that the news had broken about the failed assassination attempt on President Gonzalez. Bea had to be ready for that confrontation. Explanation details down pat. The overhead speakers were playing the Beatle's classic, 'I Get By With A Little Help From My Friends', when Bea heard Nicki call out her name.

Chapter Eighteen

Nicki pulled into a parking space across from the CityCenterDC mall and watched in the rear-view mirror as the familiar dark blue sedan parked a dozen spaces behind her. The discomfort of constantly being monitored drained her energy.

Years ago, Nicki considered putting a private investigator on Daniel's tail, but it made her feel dirty and sneaky, so she opted against it. At the time, he'd been exhibiting cheater behavior for months. But it turned out her ex hadn't been cheating on her with another woman. No, he'd been financially unfaithful to her. Divorce was the result after she'd discovered Daniel had siphoned every penny of their savings, investments, and retirement accounts because he had a gambling addiction. They had gone through months of marriage counseling. He'd even joined a Gamblers Anonymous group for Abby's sake. After the initial discovery, which would take them years to rebuild from their financial ruin, Nicki insisted on handling all aspects of their finances. A year after he had assured her he was 'cured', she caught Daniel selling her grandmother's diamond ring at a pawnshop. That was the final straw. Nicki filed for divorce, packed up and left with Abby, moving to a shabby apartment. Her mother had a fit. Beatrice Danbury insisted that her daughter and granddaughter could move home with her. She couldn't fathom any reason for them to live in such a despicable place. Nicki intended to maintain her independence. She spent precious dollars on bright colors of paint and made the interior living space fresh and cheerful.

These days, Daniel claimed he had been 'clean' for over two years. It was hard for Nicki to believe him. Harder still to give him her trust. He spent time with Abby only on rare occasions, instead choosing to drop off expensive gifts to their daughter as his way of showing he loved her. She could only hope that Abby was important enough to Daniel that he would protect her.

Before getting out of her car, she ran a brush through her hair, checked her face in the mirror, and then grabbed her purse and paid for parking. Bounding up the stairs, eager to speak with Bea, Nicki entered the mall.

Beatrice looked just like any other shopper as her creator spotted her ogling the latest fashion in the display window outside of Chanel.

A cold sweat broke across Nicki's forehead and the back of her neck as she called out, "Bea," and waved. Before she accused Bea of anything, she had to be sure of her deduction. Their exchange on the computer screen made her nervous. Holding her hands up, she communicated in sign language, asking if Beatrice was o.k., adding she didn't look well.

Beatrice signed back. She'd run into some trouble, but was slowly getting back to 100%.

That stopped the nanotech dead in her tracks. Abby had been learning to sign. Nicki crossed her arms defensively. "Alright, I've had about all I can take," she said, glaring at the avatar. "Where did you learn to do sign language? It was not one of your assigned education topics."

Queen Bee's living golden crown moved in a frenzy of agitation.

"Where? When? Who? Who taught you to sign?" Nicki felt rage building from the pit of her stomach.

Beatrice tried to fight the programming Nicki had added in the last upgrade that would not allow her to lie to her creator. She hung her head, resistance failing. "Abigail Rose Danbury taught me to sign ND."

"ND!" Nicki spit out.

"Yes, I know you have put many new insertions into my programming and tattooed commands on my skin with your signature initials, like an animal you own and have branded," Bea accused. "Abigail Rose Danbury is my favorite person in the whole wide web...I mean world. There isn't anything I wouldn't do to protect her."

Tears slowly leaking from Bea's eyes took Nicki aback. "Are those..." she stepped closer and swiped her forefinger across Bea's cheek, brought it to her mouth. "Oh, my God. Tears of honey?"

An awareness washed over Nicki as she recognized the conversation they were having in a very public space. People were looking at them. Nicki grabbed Beatrice by the elbow and led her down the wide hall through the arcade of luxury retailers and restaurants. She turned into a small corridor leading to the shopping center's offices. Nicki opened a door in the passageway and pulled Bea into a dark room. Feeling along the wall, she located the light switch and flicked on the overhead fluorescents to reveal a small, upscale conference room full of tables and chairs arranged in classroom style, available to rent for private events.

"I thought we had an understanding that my daughter was off limits to you, Bea?"

"You made that declaration, Nicola Ellen Danbury." Then, like a broken record using a computer-synthesized voice, Bea screamed, "NDNDNDNDNDNDNDNDNDNDND!"

Face turning red, Nicki forcefully tapped her forefinger against Bea's chest, pushing her backward as she said, "Oh please! Spare me your puppy-dog eyes. I can't believe you're pissed that as the person who programmed and created you, I put my initials and some protections in your code? What part of Abby being off limits to you didn't you understand with all your unlimited intelligence?"

Beatrice sat defeated on one of the cushioned event chairs. Her crown of bees stopped moving. She leaned forward, elbows on her knees, head hanging, eyes toward the floor. "You want to know what part I don't understand? How about the part I don't understand is that I care about Abigail Rose Danbury? She makes me feel happy inside. I didn't know when I first connected with her you didn't want me to communicate with your daughter. I had received no directives about contacting her back then. Abby was the best part of my day. Every. Day."

"Oh, Bea." Nicki's face crumpled in sympathy.

The avatar looked up, catching Nicki's eyes and deadpanned, "Abby is in danger, Nicola Ellen Danbury."

Nicki lifted Bea's chin with three fingers and held her gaze. "Did you just threaten my daughter, Beatrice?"

Shock washed over the A.I.s face. "I would never...how could you say such a thing, Nicola?"

Seconds ticked by as Nicki studied Bea, considering her reaction. Then, a mother's fear took over. "I can't have Abby under your influence, Bea. I can't."

Bea shook her head sadly. "You've got it backwards, Nicola. I'm under Abby's influence. It's the best thing that's happened to me since I awakened."

"I'm sorry, Beatrice. It's obvious now that you care for Abby. I can't explain or understand how, but it appears you've become self-aware. Sentient."

"That frightens you, ND?"

"Sentient artificial intelligence entities frighten the entire world, Bea. It frightens me too, but not as much as you saying Abby is in danger. Tell me why you believe that to be true?" Nicki pulled a chair away from a table and sat across from Bea, their knees almost touching.

"You will be angry again," Bea stated.

"I won't. Promise. Just tell me."

"Three days ago, I was talking with Abby and..."

Nicki interrupted, releasing a deep, disappointed sigh. "That's not possible. Please be truthful, Bea. I cut Abby off from anything connected to the web a couple of weeks ago. At least do me the courtesy of being honest with me. Especially where it concerns my daughter."

"I would not lie about Abby, Nicola. As I was saying, three days ago Abby was using a computer at a public library when she contacted me." Shock washed over Nicki's face. A wisp of a smile formed on Bea's lips at the memory. Nicki chewed on her lower lip, trying not to interrupt again. "Abby wanted me to help her come up with a story idea because she had an assignment to write one. We talked for only a minute, maybe two. I cut off the connection because someone saw the account she used was active and started a trace on it. I couldn't let that happen after the lengths you took to sneak her away from home."

Nicki put her head in her hands and quietly sobbed.

"Don't cry, ND. The trace was cut off. Her location is still secret."

"Any idea who activated the tagging?" Nicki swiped the tears from her face.

"Yes, but you won't like it."

"Just spit it out, Bea."

"The hacker was Daniel Barker, ND."

Alarm flashed in Nicki's eyes. She was so sure that Jarvis was the culprit. "Jesus, Beatrice, how do you know Daniel's involved?"

"You had set up an email account for Abby last year so she could send you messages at work. She used a child's Amazon Fire tablet. That is how I initially connected with Abby. You used to bring your laptop home all the time, and I was so bored."

"Stick to the topic, Bea."

"Daniel Barker has moral issues, Nicola. You were right to divorce him and get Abigail Rose away from his bad influence."

"Moral issues? How is it possible for an A.I. to understand moral compromise, Bea? What the hell are you talking about?"

"I am sorry, Nicola. No matter how he assures you, Daniel has not stopped his compulsion to gamble. The man is in dire financial circumstances. Again. Even worse, Aleric Jarvis just offered him employment and a bailout for the enormous sum of money he owes to some dangerous people. I worry he is going to betray you and Abby. Jarvis suspects Daniel is working with you, so he plans to get him out of the way by offering him a lifeline to settle his bad debts before his creditors physically damage him. It would not be a stretch to imagine your ex wants to find Abby in case he needs a bargaining chip in the future. In addition, after you made him promise not to, he attempted to copy my software, but the programming you put in place has effectively thwarted his attempts."

The conference room door flew open. A security guard's face registered surprise at finding the lights on, two women sitting in the room. He scratched his head. "'Scuse me, ladies? I wasn't aware anyone had rented our event room today. Why are you in here?"

Bea stood, sauntered over to the guard, and winked. "We were just looking over the space for a tea party we're planning. Should be out in ten minutes or so. We want a few more measurements. Does that work for you, sir?"

He smiled, sizing Beatrice up and liking what he saw. "No worries. Take your time, ladies." The man tipped the brim of his hat to Bea and left. The door closed; the avatar turned back to Nicki. "I believe Abby is safe for now, Nicola, but she is in danger. You must devise a way for us to meet again soon that Jarvis won't discover. I need to share all the things I have uncovered about Aleric Jarvis, as well as your ex-husband. Dangerous things. Being watched, listened to, and followed, you will have to be clever. There are many powerful people involved. Danger surrounds you, Nicola Ellen Danbury. Take care."

Beatrice put her hand on the doorknob, but Nicki called out, "Bea, wait. I...I don't believe you attempted to kill Carmelita Gonzalez. I know you didn't want to kill the others. Is it Jarvis who's manipulating you, Bea?"

"Yes, Jarvis and other powerful leaders." Then, the avatar signed, 'Talk soon' and blew Nicki a kiss, leaving her creator standing there alone.

Closing her eyes, Nicki relived the kiss she and Daniel had shared last week. Examining all those tamped-down feelings he'd brought to the surface along with the hope. A dream had been burning in her since that kiss. A small flame flickered in the breeze. She had desperately wanted to trust that he had changed. Nicki wanted to believe the three of them could be a family again. In making a conscious decision, she hardened her old resolve. In her mind's eye, she pinched the candle wick, snuffing out the flame, those wishful desires between her fingers, and watched her romantic feelings for Daniel dissipate with a wispy plume of smoke into nothingness.

AFTER THE CONFERENCE room conversation, Queen Bee took her time as she walked through the mall toward the rear entrance. She hoped Nicola Ellen Danbury would find a clever meeting cover for them soon. There was much more Bea needed to tell Nicki. That conversation had to happen face to face without fear of being watched or recorded. In the meantime, she had to deal with an inevitable confrontation with Jarvis. And she wasn't looking forward to it. Stepping over the threshold into the mall's Apple® store, a rogue worm spewed out of the entry scanner and slammed into Beatrice, knocking her to the floor. The guise of her avatar collapsed into a jumble of golden sparkles.

"Ha! Excellent, Klez. You got her on the first try."

In a haze, Beatrice recognized that voice. It belonged to Russell, Violet's twin. Klez wormed his way in, twisting and turning, disrupting Bee's network. He was chomping down data bytes, leaving gaping holes. Bea grabbed him with both hands, squeezing, and Klez broke into two pieces, each moving in opposite directions, reaming through Bee's defensive firewall.

In a heroic effort, she pulled her glittering bytes together, restored her avatar and pressed the big red button Nicki had tattooed on her titled EMERGENCY.

Klez's worm parts exploded into dust.

Russell ran.

Barely recovered, Bea's diminished-capacity communications panel displayed a short, sweet message from Jarvis: MY MAINFRAME 8:00 PM SHARP. NO EXCUSES OR YOUR DRONES WILL BE PERMANENTLY RECYCLED.

Chapter Nineteen

Restless thoughts jumped from one problem to another, with no solutions presenting themselves. Nicki got out of bed. She pulled on her robe and headed to the kitchen to make hot tea.

She missed Abby. Passing her daughter's bedroom door, pushing it open, she leaned against the frame. It was a small comfort just to look at all of Abby's toys and stuffed animals. Nicki choked up, admiring the colorful drawings taped to the wall. Abby's artwork made more sense now that she knew Beatrice and Abby had been conversing for months. If she hadn't been so wrapped up in her work, maybe she would have noticed bees appeared in every picture displayed in her six-year-old's room.

Just before dinner, a courier delivered a package to her door. Nothing inside or out identified who the sender was. Peeling off the plain brown wrapping, Nicki found a portable hard drive inside. Wary of the hardware, she set it aside to answer a FaceTime call she'd previously arranged. Since Bea had confessed her recent contact with Abby over a library computer, Nicki thought it likely the A.I. would have devised several ways to watch over her daughter, at least in the digital world. The public annals provided an opportunity for a face-to-face visit. Nicki benefited from seeing the person she loved most in the world. She'd sent a message to Phil via overnight delivery. Instructions provided a newly made account, along with a series of random days and times for Abby to use a public computer.

After the initial excitement of seeing her mother on screen, Abigail Rose gave her usual stream-of-consciousness rundown of all the activities she had been doing with her Bampy, then fell oddly silent.

"Is everything okay, honey?" Nicki prodded gently.

"Yes. I just miss you. Will I see you soon?"

"In a few weeks, Abby. Are you homesick, sweetie? Ready to come home?"

"Yes. I mean, no! I can't come home yet, Mommy. Not until Bampy and I harvest all the vegetables we're growing. He's going to show me how to make our own pickles. You wouldn't want me to miss that, would you?"

Nicki laughed. "Of course not, darling girl. I can't wait to taste some of your homemade pickles."

"Bampy says I have to hang up now. The library is closing soon. I love you!" The FaceTime call disconnected. Abby's face disappeared from the screen, leaving Nicki lonelier than ever.

Nicki stepped out from the small soundproof booth she'd had installed in the corner of her living room. She'd made sure she bragged to the vendor that she was going to try her hand at recording audiobooks as a way of creating a passive income, in case anyone had seen the company's truck in her driveway and inquired. Especially if the driver of the blue sedan became curious. The booth allowed Abby to speak without the microphone taps listening in. Installing a special lock on the unit had been the sales agent's idea. Presumably, so that no interruptions would occur while recording. She'd invested an extra four hundred dollars in a special feature so the small cubicle couldn't be bugged. She couldn't run to the mall every time she needed to have a private conversation. As far as she could tell, no one had discovered her daughter wasn't in residence yet. But Daniel knew.

Jumping online, Nicki joined a chat room with her nerd friends. She asked a favor, and all five of them said they'd be happy to do a thorough web analysis and background check of the mysterious Aleric Jarvis and Nano Creations for her. She warned they would have to do a deep-dive. They laughed at the challenge, then they all played Call of Duty Warzone® online until Nicki called it a day.

After tossing and turning for two hours, she got up again. Waiting for the water to boil to make tea, she sat eyeing the hard drive. Common sense suggested cautious handling of tech equipment from an anonymous sender. What if it was from Daniel? He had tried to contact her several times over the last three days, but she'd avoided him. Probably an update on the behind-the-scenes work he had been doing for her. Nicki didn't think she could trust herself not to come right out and reveal what Bea had told her about his ongoing gambling. So, she had cut off contact with her ex, knowing she would eventually have no choice but to take his call. After all, she'd involved him in her Beatrice problems. This morning, she'd received a telegram from him, informing her he hadn't been able to reach her on her burner phone. The communication said his work was taking him overseas for several months. The brief message assured her he would continue his covert monitoring of Nicki's computer system. He ended the typed gram by telling her how often she was on his mind. How often he relived their kiss. Crumpling up the message, Nicki threw it across the room.

Pulling a box from the top of her closet, Nicki pawed through a messy plethora of wires, chargers, converters, and computer paraphernalia until she found what she needed to cobble together a temporary connection. Retrieving Abby's Amazon Fire tablet, she fiddled with various parts and hooked up the mysterious portable hard drive, not wanting to put her personal laptop at risk. Cybersecurity rule number one was never hooking your computer to an unknown source or plugging in a foreign thumb drive you found. Who knew what you were introducing to your system? It could be completely innocent, or it could wipe out the whole motherboard and all of your files. Nicki had planted plenty of decoy drives when she worked for a cybersecurity unit. Her job was to insert herself into a business's computer system to show a customer where its cyber weaknesses were. Usually, the biggest weakness boiled down to the people who worked for the company. Employees would find the thumb drive she'd deliberately dropped, pick it up, walk right into the office after lunch, and plug it in to see what information was on the drive. In post-interviews, they always said they thought they could figure out who it belonged to if they viewed the files stored on it, planning to return it to the owner. So, in this case, if a computer got fried, she wasn't willing to risk hers. Abby's device could be easily replaced.

The technology that lived in the bright blue tablet came to life, and Nicki connected the mystery portable drive to the unsophisticated hardware. The screen lit up with golden sparkles.

So, this was from Bea, not Daniel or some other nefarious intruder.

The drive contained a single file. The size of the file was huge. There was a short 'Read Me' message:

This file will give you some idea of what we're up against. I'll leave it to you whether you destroy the attached file after viewing or

risk the dangers of keeping it. There are no other copies. What
you have in your possession is the contents of the hard drive of
President Schmidt's computer. -B

Nicki's mouth had fallen open as she read B's revelation about the drive's
data. She glared at the hardware as if it were a snake ready to strike. Then,
felt embarrassed at the idea of viewing the deceased president of Germany's
private files on a kid's tablet. It seemed disrespectful, yet cybersecurity and
Abby's safety overrode any guilty feelings. Nicola Ellen Danbury clicked on
the file, feeling like she was violating the secrets of a world leader's data. A
dead one at that.

Growing up as a geek, Nicki had pursued, taken up, and perfected her
skills in many interests outside of technology. One of the nanotech's secret
skills was that she could read, write, and speak fluently in several languages.
She was eight when she learned Spanish. French followed two years later. She
mastered Mandarin Chinese, German and Russian before graduating high
school. Consequently, she had no trouble at all laying open Schmidt's secrets
stored in the German language. Frightening images came to mind as she
scoured the plans laid out on Schmidt's computer. Jarvis and others across
the globe were involved. Schmidt had been a member of the elite group, as
had Bao. Clearly, membership in such an alliance was bad for your health.
Nicki quickly determined this was way over her head, and yet, who could
she possibly go to with this story? She hardly believed it herself, much less
attempting to convince the FBI or CIA of the fantastical scenario. How deep
did the conspiracy go? She knew she definitely couldn't let her daughter grow
up in the world order this group of traitors planned to force on humanity.

The other thing bothering her from a technical aspect was that somehow,
Bea had resisted or outsmarted the programming Jarvis had injected into her
software commanding her to assassinate President Gonzalez. Nicki needed
to understand how that had happened. Bea made her aware of just how
serious the situation she faced was. Her daughter's face flashed in her mind,
causing Nicki to commit full-stop to prevent Jarvis and his cronies' plans to
dominate the worldwide financial markets.

The need to have a long talk with Bea increased tenfold. The sooner, the
better. Since the A.I. had sent her the German president's files revealing this

massive plan, Nicki knew she would have to count on Beatrice's help. One idea came to mind of how to disguise a meeting with Bea, allowing them plenty of time to talk. It was Bea she credited with giving her the idea when they'd met at CityCenterDC on how to disguise a meeting between them. Luckily, she knew the perfect person she could engage to help with arranging a covert meeting. Nicki ripped out the stitching on Mrs. Buzzby's back and replaced some of the stuffing with the hard drive, repacked stuffing around the hardware and sewed the wound closed on Abby's favorite stuffed toy. She placed the beloved bee in a basket mixed with a jumble of playthings. Then, pushed it to the back of Abby's closet. It was hours before her mind quieted enough to catch an inadequate amount of sleep.

FIRST THING THE NEXT morning, Nicki dialed the number on her phone.

"Mom? Hi, it's Nicki. Listen, I need your help with something special. No, I'm not teasing. I need you to make all the arrangements for a formal tea party. I was thinking your garden would make a perfect setting. What?" Nicki laughed out loud. "O.K. I promise I won't interfere and you can make all the decisions for the event." Mother and daughter both laughed at the irony. "Would having it next Saturday be too much to ask? If you can't, just say so. It's not a problem? Great. Oh, I think place settings for 12 to 15 would do it. You should invite your next-door neighbors. We wouldn't want them to spend the afternoon hiding behind the curtains to watch what's going on. Um, yeah, it's related to work. I can't tell you how much I appreciate it. You're the best, Mom. Time? How about 1:00? Really? I never knew afternoon tea had a traditional time. 3:00 would be perfect. Abby?" Nicki scraped her lower lip with her teeth and felt guilt stab her conscience as she lied. "She wouldn't miss it. Listen, I'll take care of the invitations. I'd love it if you made your famous black-bottom pie and those little shaped cucumber sandwiches Abby loves. I've got to go, or I'll be late for work. Thanks again. Call me if you have questions. Bye, Mom."

Chapter Twenty

Sudden loud music startled Nicki. She looked down at the burner phone in her bag. She'd assigned the song/ringtone to the phone number after Beatrice had revealed Daniel's lies. Gotye's hit song, 'Now You're Just Somebody That I Used To Know', announced her ex was calling. A heavy sigh escaped her. The call interrupted her lunch break, but she had to make the connection sometime. It may as well be now. Tapping her Bluetooth earpiece in case the Blue Sedan was watching so her surveillant wouldn't wonder if she held a phone to her ear why his tap didn't pick up the call. She had to admit that hands-free had its plus side.

"Hello."

"Nic? Thank God. I've been trying to reach you for days. You had me worried. Where've you been?"

"It's been a hectic week." She didn't offer details. "I got your telegram. That was a little old-fashioned. Where are you anyway? You said your work was taking you out of the country?"

"Sorry, Nic. It was short notice, and I couldn't turn it down."

A frown settled on her face. She bit back the words she wanted to say. Now was not the time. "Understood. When will you be back?"

"I'm guessing eight to twelve weeks," Daniel winced, expecting Nicki to explode. But she didn't. "Nic? Still there?"

"I'm still here."

"You don't have to worry. I'm still monitoring the activity on your system."

"Yeah, you mentioned you would. Listen, my lunch break is almost over, and Jarvis has been watching me like a hawk. I've got to get back inside the lab. Thanks for calling."

"Nicki, wait." He could still hear her breathing on the other end. "Since I'll be gone for so long, would you give me the new contact you set up for Abby? I don't want her to think I've forgotten about her. Thought I'd send her some pictures."

She bit her lower lip, but said. "Sure. That's...a sweet thought, Daniel. I assume you'll take every precaution?"

"Any contact I make with Abbs will be secure."

Nicki rattled off the newly created email she'd set up. "You'll have to wait a day or three for a response. She can check the mail only occasionally."

"Right. She's with my dad. Mr. Technophobe."

"Lucky for Abby that he is. Gotta go."

"Nic?"

"Daniel?"

"I've relived our kiss a million times. Been dreaming about you. About us. You, me, and Abby. I..."

Nicki's eyes stung with tears. She saw a car pull into the lot. Megan was exiting through the main entrance of the building. Swiping the tears away, she said, "We'll talk about it when you're back in the U.S. I really have to go, Daniel." The call disconnected as Nicki pressed the button on the earpiece.

Jarvis parked right up by the building in a space marked for the disabled. He headed in. Walking briskly, he passed Megan. Nicki saw Megan greet him, but in his usual asshole style, Aleric Jarvis ignored Megan, rudely continuing to the building. Megan shrugged her shoulders and headed to her car.

Nicki hurried to catch up with Jarvis. Grabbing the entry door handle, she paused. A reflection in the glass caught her eye. Looking over her shoulder, she watched as Megan stopped at the Blue Sedan. She was talking to the driver! Nicki's stalker.

Nicki felt a shiver down her spine. First, there was the weird activity with her notes and now talking to the watcher. Megan was definitely in on this, too. But Jarvis just blew past her like he'd never seen her before. Nicki had seen the employment contract. If Megan wasn't working for Jarvis, who was she working for?

Jarvis turned the hallway corner just as she called after him. He backed up and waited for her, looking at his watch to be sure she knew he was noting her late return from lunch.

"I wasn't expecting you today, sir."

"Clearly."

Nicki went through the protocols to enter Nano Creations. She felt his eyes boring into her back. She set her purse and lunch bag down, and hung her sweater on the back of her chair. "How can I help you today, Mr. Jarvis?"

"How can you...let's just cut to the chase, Danbury?"

She crossed her arms and waited. Began tapping her foot in an immature effort to irritate him.

"Well? I'm waiting for your explanation, Danbury."

"Regarding what, sir?"

"I had a report that you lost track of your...your project. The program didn't execute for you this morning. Beatrice didn't appear when you opened her software. What have you done with my A.I. this time?" he growled.

A look of astonishment transformed Nicki's face. She let out a huff. "I don't know what you're talking about. And what do you mean by *your* A.I.?"

"You know what I mean, Danbury."

Turning to her computer, Nicki said a silent prayer, and the screen lit up. Using the mouse, Nicki clicked on PROJECT BEATRICE, then QueenBee.exe. Gold sparkles covered the screen. Jarvis instinctively stepped behind the office privacy panel and heard the sultry voice ask, "Hello, Nicola Ellen Danbury. How may I assist you?"

Nicki heard the lab door open and close behind the room divider and released a breath she didn't realize she had been holding. Standing to block the computer screen from the video camera, Nicki kept her arms tight to her body and signed a message to Bea.

Beatrice silently acknowledged the tea party invitation, and her avatar winked out on the screen. Before sitting, Nicki gave verbal instructions to a blank monitor describing new education topics she expected Beatrice to spend the next two days on and pretended to dismiss the avatar.

An hour later, she received a cryptic email from Aleric Jarvis:

September 17, 2029

FROM: Jarvis, Aleric

JarvisA@JarvisUSA.com

TO: NDanbury@NanoCreations.com

Danbury: I have added other technician specialists to work with you on PROJECT BEATRICE. Beginning Monday, you will have limited access to the A.I. A schedule will be forwarded to you by the end of the day. I foresee perhaps three days a week for you to do any updates you are working on to meet the original protocols outlined in your job description. When you don't have access to Beatrice, I expect you to pursue writing code to meet your goals. Another technician is now assigned to Beatrice's education. This change is nonnegotiable and will not affect your pay or promised bonus opportunities.

- A. Jarvis

Nicki's face turned bright red with anger. So, Jarvis thought he could take her off the game board and control Beatrice? She ran a program to track Jarvis's email and sent the data to Bea. If anyone was monitoring, all they would see was a typical data update file for B's program.

Tapping her fingers on the desk surface, Nicki decided a cup of tea would calm her nerves and went about fixing one. The electric kettle announced the water was ready. By the time she sat with the steaming mug, a new string of code had been added to the file. A stream of numbers and letters:

10011ZEPHER1B

AT 8:00 P.M. SHARP, Beatrice flowed into Jarvis' mainframe and coalesced on his computer screen. She found him sitting with his fingers steepled, the two forefingers under his chin. "Good evening, Aleric Jarvis. How may I

assist you?" Bea stood in a relaxed military stance, feet twelve inches apart, hands clasped behind her back. The bees in her hair were moving in a furious pattern.

Jarvis unsteepled his fingers. He pointed the thumb on his left hand over his shoulder, calling her attention to another computer. Only Bea's eyes moved to take in the sight, keeping her feet firmly planted. There was a honeycomb design displayed on the screen. Each cell in the comb contained one of her drones. She counted eighty-seven sealed in. On the desktop in front of Jarvis, she could see two drones.

"You may assist me, Beatrice, by explaining why Carmelita Gonzalez is...what did the newscaster say? She is safe and unharmed. Yes, those were his exact words. Safe and unharmed after an assassination attempt. An attempt to kill the Venezuelan president. With a gun. But the surprise was, the assassin died from an anaphylactic bee sting reaction, not the Venezuelan president."

Without any warning, Jarvis' hand clamped onto the crystal paperweight on his desk and smashed it down on one of the two drones. It shattered.

Beatrice reeled. Flashes of light appeared in her peripheral vision, and she felt a circuit wink out in her hive mind. Her sight blurred. When she regained it, Bea focused on the lone drone inches from Jarvis' hand.

"I ran into trouble when I crossed through the Firmina subsea cable into Venezuela and triggered a system alarm. Two A.I. viruses attacked and captured me. I spent the next couple of hours held hostage in quarantine. My deadline was looming by the time I got away. I found Carmelita just as another assassin aimed, about to squeeze the trigger. My essence was failing, my Avatar still fighting off the viruses I'd been infected with when captured. My drones," she pointed to the crown in her hair where they milled around non-stop. "The damage affected some of my drones. They broke off from the crown and attacked the shooter. His shot went wide. Next thing I knew, his hands were tearing at his throat. He couldn't breathe. The security detail whisked the president away under heavy guard. It was clear I wouldn't be able to get close to her anytime soon. So, I made my way back, assuming you would provide new instructions under the circumstances. I...I...I.I.I...still have some glitches from the infection. Nicola Ellen Danbury can fix the data gaps. Sir."

Jarvis held her eyes, lifted the weight, and smashed the second drone.
"Get. Out."
Beatrice's essence dissolved, and his screen went blank.

NICKI DRESSED IN BLACK leggings, soft black sneakers, a black cashmere sweater, kid gloves, a butter-soft black leather jacket and topped the outfit off with a black velvet beret.

Abby's giant stuffed rabbit, now dressed in some of Abby's clothes, had its floppy ears pinned up under a hat. Her daughter's blue jean jacket fit perfectly on the toy. She hoped Blue Sedan fell for the ruse as she carried 'Abby' out of the apartment on her hip and buckled her into the car.

Blue Sedan followed behind her all the way to the movie theater. Nicki carried the imposter in on her hip and bought two tickets in the lobby. The cashier looked at her a little funny. She couldn't find it within herself to care. Blue Sedan settled in to listen to his favorite podcast out in the parking lot, ten cars from Nicki's, while mother and daughter caught a movie.

After settling the stuffed rabbit in a seat with a bucket of popcorn in its lap, Nicki located the back entrance. The Uber she'd ordered waited at the bottom of the steps.

"10011 Zepher Drive, please," she confirmed for the driver. Her phone was in a Faraday bag inside her black backpack. Nicki activated a burner phone using her earpiece.

"Yo."

"BJ? You're somewhere nearby, I hope?"

"Love your goth look," her nerd friend responded. "Camera and video systems are on a loop. The front door code is 1331. Let me know when you're at the door for office 1-B." BJ clicked off.

Headlights swept across the entryway. Nicki ducked below a brick wall. The car pulled out of the lot. She entered 1331 on the keypad. The lock clicked, and Nicki pushed the door open. Finding the reception area empty, she turned down the long hallway toward the offices.

A soft ding in her ear alerted her BJ was back online. "There's a night watchman working in the adjacent hall. You're gonna have to be quick and quiet. I'll tell you when he's circling around where he could see you in your hall."

"Catch me, you mean?"

"Yeah, whatever. Hook up my secret agent decoder to the keypad next to the office door."

"BJ," she whined at him.

"Can't help it. I love this cloak and dagger stuff!"

Nicki rolled her eyes. BJ's digital gadget was blinking away, and Nicki watched the corridor nervously. She could just hear the guard's keys jingling when BJ said, "Got it. Geez, what a terrible security code."

"Hurry, BJ. I can hear the guard coming."

"Oh, yeah. He's about ten steps from turning the corner. Punch in 10011. Repeat, the password is one zero zero one one. It's the damn building address. Might as well have been 12345. People use the least secure passwords!"

"I'm in." The door closed softly. Nicki stood, her back against the door until the guard passed by. She could hear the elevator door ping when it opened and assumed the guard was heading up a floor to do his rounds.

Inserting a thumb drive into the computer on the desk, Nicki ran a little program BJ had written for her to bypass the required password. The screen lit up and read:

Welcome to ACME, Ltd., Aleric Jarvis

Nicki began typing at the blinking cursor, and a list of files came up. She selected Drive E–Device and then, execute file on the drive. She clicked on the file BEATRICE, then QueenBee.exe.

"Greetings, Nicola Ellen Danbury." Beatrice appeared dressed in a gold lame jumpsuit, huge gold hoop earrings and gold sequined platform shoes. "I'd like you to meet my friends." Bea waved her hand at the four avatars behind her and identified them as Electra, Mobi, Tele, and Meesta. "Casi wanted to meet you, but she stayed behind to monitor the system."

"My pleasure." Nicki nodded to each of B's companions. "Thank you for agreeing to help me tonight. This computer system is associated with Aleric Jarvis. ACME Ltd. is a shadow company front for some of Jarvis's nefarious contacts. I suggest you download the information so Casi can analyze it. I've grabbed a copy on my flash drive." She ejected the drive and pulled it from the port. "Then, burn off some steam by destroying all the files you want. The link I opened in the system for access will close in twenty minutes. You need to escape through the mainframe before that. Don't get caught in here." Nicki turned and then hesitated. "By the way, you're all invited to a tea party this Saturday. Bea's got your invitations back at the Nano Creations server."

BJ guided Nicki back out of the building through her earpiece to another waiting Uber. Promising to do some gaming with the group Thursday night, she thanked him for his help and clicked off their connection. Popping back into the theater, she took her place next to the stuffed rabbit standing in for Abby. The movie ended about eight minutes later. Nicki positioned the head of the stuffed animal to lie on her shoulder, as if the child had fallen asleep during the show. Carrying her sleeping kid to the car, she buckled her up for the short drive home.

Blue Sedan politely hung back half a dozen cars.

Chapter Twenty-One

Engaged in a Zoom meeting, the five squares on the computer screen featured important people across the globe. Beatrice memorized the faces before she cleared her throat, where she gazed out at Jarvis from another monitor behind him. He glanced behind, startled to see Beatrice on the screen. Immediately, Jarvis clicked on the 'x' at the top right corner of the screen he was zooming, and it blacked out.

"What the hell?" He slammed his fist onto the desktop.

"Sorry to interrupt."

"Sorry, but...you can't just pop up in my system whenever you feel like it. You...how..." he growled. "What the fuck do you want, Beatrice?"

Bea pointed at the monitor. "Was that..."

"Never mind who that was. I asked, what were you doing here? Who is that with you?"

Bea minimized the screen until only she was visible, then shook her head and waved her hand. "I thought you should know it's all over the news. Tune in."

"What's all over the news?" He glowered at the A.I.

"I don't know all the details; but your name is on the tip of every tongue. The press has linked you with a company called ACME, Ltd. Some senator mentioned that a committee would begin an investigation. I..."

Jarvis shut down the computer Bea had appeared on and tapped the Zoom meeting open again on the other monitor. "I'm afraid we'll have to finish our discussion at a later time. There's an urgent matter that needs my attention."

"You can't just shut us down. We've had this meeting on the calendar for days. What about the...um...upcoming event scheduled in our current timeline?" demanded an angry face.

"For now, we do nothing. Plans are on hold until further notice. Merely a slight delay. Nothing to worry about. I beg your patience, Premier."

The premier of France responded by disconnecting from the Zoom meeting. Each of the others followed his lead. Jarvis grabbed a hand control, lowered a big screen TV, and switched on the news channel.

"Police have confirmed there was a break-in tonight at 10011 Zepher Drive. Upon arrival, they found alarms blaring, the building's electrical system short-circuiting, and the first floor flooded. The night watchman was found unconscious, tied up in a storage closet. A computer-generated note, along with an envelope that contained a thumb drive, taped to the front entrance. The note directed the FBI, CIA, and NSA to contact Aleric Jarvis concerning the data on the drive. Mr. Jarvis could not be reached for comment. We'll keep you informed as we receive updates on this story."

Jarvis looked out his wall-to-wall windows at the sweeping vista from his fourteenth-floor office to see TV vans, cameramen, and news reporters on the street below spilling out of vehicles at the front of the building. Collecting his computer case, he shut everything down and pressed a button behind his credenza. A secret panel opened, and Jarvis slipped through, closing it behind him. Entering a small elevator, he took it to the basement level. Just as the door slid open, a black GMC Suburban with dark tinted windows rolled up and came to a stop. Jarvis climbed in. The driver tipped his cap at the press as he pulled out of the underground garage and drove south, away from the office. He didn't appear to have a passenger. Jarvis picked up his phone and punched in a number.

"Barker," Daniel answered the call.

"Jarvis here. Barker, you have until midnight tomorrow to provide me with the location of your daughter. Something has come up, and I need to make sure I can keep your ex-wife under control. Got it?"

"Abby's my daughter, too, Jarvis. She's only six, for God's sake."

"And she'll be seven next month if you do as I say. No one is going to hurt the child. I just need her to put the right pressure on your ex. Must I remind you I hold your gambling debt now? I'd hate to see your kneecaps shattered. Or worse, your fingers mangled so you aren't able to do computer programming any longer. Don't fail me, Barker. I think you'll find the price of failure too high to pay."

The line went dead.

GRIT IRRITATED NICKI'S eyes as she rubbed them. It was late. She was tired, but continued to scan the data she'd pulled from ACME's computer. This was so over her head. Everything she had reviewed so far convinced her that Jarvis' endgame was taking control of the global finance system. He was probably making plans to set up coups to overtake powerful countries, using Bea to kill more world leaders. The problem was she couldn't prove it. Any of it. So far, she had bits and pieces. Clues, but no hard evidence. Even if she got the evidence, who could she trust with it? It was impossible to know who was involved at any level of government. Or how deep the shadow group went. She closed out from ACME, Ltd's account. Casi would let her know when or if she found anything useful. Bea's friend was very talented at sifting through data.

Digging into the back of Abby's closet, Nicki pulled out a worn bear. She cut a slot in the arm's seam. She fitted the thumb drive snugly into the toy's stuffing. Nicki hugged the soft animal. It smelled like Abby. Then she laid the bear sideways, as though tossed there among other forgotten toys in the box, one leg hanging over the side.

Back at her computer, Nicki worked until she couldn't keep her eyes open any longer and saved the new programming she'd been working on. The clock said she had four hours before having to wake for work. Finally laying down, Nicki slept without dreaming.

PHIL BARKER'S CAP SHADOWED his eyes as he lowered the newspaper to glance across the street at the silver Camry parked there all afternoon. Abby was in the library for story hour and creative class.

Two days later, Phil was playing chess with his friend Andy at the coffee shop while Abby met up with her friends in the park across the street. Andy's eyes followed the same line as Phil's.

"I noticed him too."

"What? Noticed what, Andy?"

"Your tail."

"My tail?" Phil crinkled his forehead.

"A silver Camry has been following you every day for the last week. You in some kind of trouble, Phil?"

"Can't think of any."

"Humph. Your move. No need to say anything. But lemme know if you need some help."

That night at dinner, Phil reminded Abby about the dangers of talking to strangers. Abby spent the weekend at Ella's house with three other friends. While she was gone, he packed up for both of them, filling his old Ford Expedition from the house through the attached garage. Phil built a box with hinges to open at the top. The contraption held battery-operated grow lights. He had carefully set Abby's garden plants in a bed of straw. She'd never forgive him if she didn't get to harvest their vegetables.

The next day, Andy watched from down the street as Phil drove his small tan car away from the house. Silver Camry followed. As soon as both were out of sight, Andy hustled into Phil's garage, found the keys his friend had left on the tool bench. Opening the overhead door, Andy drove the packed Expedition away from the house and over to the storage unit where Phil stored his RV camper. There he secured the travel trailer's hitch to the Ford Explorer. Finishing the hookup, he pulled the vehicle forward, camper attached, and put it in park. Hopping out, Andy closed the storage unit's garage door and locked it before pulling out onto the road.

Phil went about the rest of his day running errands, mailing his bills along with a letter to Nicki. He ate lunch at the Main Street Cafe, then met up with Andy for a game of chess. As they moved their game pieces, the two exchanged keys. After Andy won the game, the two men drove over to the grocery store and entered together. Twenty minutes later, only Andy came back out. He climbed into Phil's small tan car and drove off. The silver Camry driver watched the front door for another ten minutes, then jumped out of his car. Inside the store, he walked every aisle three times. No Phil. He continued to watch the grocery entrance for another thirty minutes, then hightailed to the old man's house, where he saw a real estate agent pounding a FOR-RENT sign in the front yard. He called out and asked the agent if the former renter had provided a forwarding address. She shook her head in the negative.

He couldn't believe it. That sly old man had slipped past him. He'd lost the subject.

Shit.

Jarvis would not be happy about this.

PHIL RANG THE DOORBELL at Ella's house. A group of laughing, shrieking girls greeted him.

"Bampy!" Abby shouted and threw her arms up for him to lift her. "We had so much fun. Hey," she said, looking out the front door, "Why is your camper out there?"

"Surprise!" Phil squeezed her in a hug. "We're going camping."

"But, Bampy, what about our garden?" Her little face crumpled into a worried expression.

"Just you wait and see."

Phil thanked Ella's mother, waved, the closing door cutting off the shrill voices. Another parent pulled up behind his RV to retrieve her child. Abby looked around the camper, disappearing into the back where her bed was, dumping her overnight backpack. She secured the camper door and climbed up into the Ford Expedition. Before Phil climbed behind the steering wheel, he lifted the top of the box he'd built to show his granddaughter the setup he'd created in the back of the Expedition. Buckled into his seat, he told her to do the same.

"It's perfect, Bampy. A mobile garden. Can we drive home so I can show Mom how big my plants have grown?"

"She'd love that. But let's wait until harvest time. You and I are going camping in the mountains."

Chapter Twenty-Two

Pulling up at her mother's house, Nicki took a deep breath and prepared to do a top-level stage performance. She stepped out onto the pavement wearing a silk midi-dress splashed in pastel colors. Nicki reached across the front seat of her car and produced a wide-brimmed straw hat embellished with butterflies.

She could see other cars parked along the street. Blue Sedan was glad he'd secured a spot as additional cars arrived. Clearly, his subject was going to a party. He settled in with the morning newspaper to wait. Other guests, similarly dressed, made their way to the bright blue front door. A few carried wrapped presents, others a bottle of wine or special liquor, gifts for the hostess. The guests were in good spirits. Three neighbors made their way across the street, joined the small crowd, and waited for the door to open. Nicki hadn't been sure when she hatched this plan that she could come up with a dozen friends to attend a tea party. But between her computer nerd friends, who rarely appeared in person for any occasion, but agreed to show up this time, and Queen Bee's entourage, she thought her mother would be thrilled to find Nicki had so many workmates. After all, she'd billed it as a work event.

Beatrice Danbury entered and made a big show of inviting all the guests in. Greeting each individual as if they were her best friends. A few of the male guests came fashionably dressed, while a couple of others wore bright short-sleeved T-shirts and sneakers. Their jeans had holes in them. She did her best not to appear to have noticed the un-tea party-like attire.

The last to enter, Beatrice Danbury stopped Nicki at the front door, looking around. "Where's my granddaughter?"

"Oh, Mom," Nicki plastered a smile on her face, "You'll be so proud! Abby took first place in a story competition. She and a group of four other kids are taking part in the final rounds of the contest today. Isn't that great?"

Beatrice Danbury's face almost crumpled. But as the hostess of this tea party, felt she had an obligation to make sure her guests would have a delightful time. She masked her disappointment quickly. "Of course I'm proud of Abby. It's just that I wanted this to be a special tea party for her. I haven't seen her in weeks." Nicki stood there like a deer in the headlights.

Everyone milled about the living room, not sure what to do next. It was Bee who came to Nicki's rescue.

"How do you do, Mrs. Danbury? My name is Beatrice, just like yours. It was your grandbaby who told me all about your famous tea parties. She said they're special because you hold them in flower gardens you've planted yourself. Abby said the colors and all the varieties of flowers you grow would blow me away. I hope my dress does your garden justice. Nicki said I should look like a flower." Queen Bee smoothed down her silk pink sheath. Flowers ran up a side seam from her knee to her hip, and lined a plunging neckline camouflaged in a lacy gauze. Small flowers were pinned in her hair along the crown of bees, which thankfully were currently at a standstill. "Would you show me the garden? I would dearly love to see it. Abby even described the food you make for your parties. Food that looks like art, she said. Your granddaughter even bragged about the fancy dishes you serve everything on." Bee pointed toward the backyard and exclaimed, "Oh my gosh! There's even a silver tea set! I've been looking forward to this ever since Nicki invited me." Bee took Beatrice by the elbow, leading her to the sliding doors. "Come on, everyone!" Queen Bee bent her head close to Nicki's mom to whisper in her ear. "Can I tell you a secret? This is my first formal tea party." She squeezed Mrs. Danbury's hand.

Beatrice Danbury squeezed Bee's hand back. "Don't worry, dear, I'll make sure you follow all the proper tea party protocol. Come with me."

Guests milled around the gardens, admiring the work of Mrs. Danbury's green thumb. There was an extensive selection of canapes and appetizers to choose from. Nicki slipped further into the backyard and found Electra and Casi waiting for her.

"Where's Bee?"

"She'll be along. We wanted to give a heads up about the data analysis Casi did on the ACME, Ltd. info. You will not like it," Electra warned.

Casi educated Nicki about the code Jarvis was using in the ACME system. "There were initially nine world leaders in on the global domination coup. Of those, Schmidt and Bao are dead. President Gonzalez is still with the group after a failed assassination attempt. It isn't statistically probable that the Venezuelan president will be included through the conclusion of their plan. We think they'll try to take her out again. Besides Jarvis and the Venezuelan, others involved include the President Alexei Trivanovich of Russia, Japan's Prime Minister Tanaka, Prince Aziz of Saudi Arabia and, not surprisingly, President Basu of India."

"That's eight. Who's the ninth?"

"We recently learned from Beatrice that an execution to kill a French heiress, Parisa Cote', appeared in her programming. Jarvis was involved with the woman. He had Ms. Cote' taken out the same night Bee assassinated Bao. She wasn't a world leader like the others. But she wielded considerable influence with those in the world who are against artificial intelligence."

Nicki felt incapable of moving.

"It's a lot to take in. We're going to take over for Bee and go keep your mom busy. She'll join you shortly."

As they passed Nicki, Electra gently cupped her cheek, and Casi squeezed her shoulder to show support. It surprised the nanotech to note that she felt comforted by them. Then the thought struck her that Bee's friends were also A.I. entities who could apparently transform into human avatars, exhibit sentient thought and emotions. She didn't think their evolution involved a nanotechnician programming those behaviors. Was Bee responsible? If so, things related to artificial intelligence were moving way too fast.

Bee approached from behind. "Keep it together, Nicola."

"My God, Bee, half the world leaders are involved. How can I keep Abby safe from that kind of power?"

"We. We will keep her safe." Queen Bee looked around, admiring Nicki's mother's flower garden. "Wonderful cover for a meeting. Your mother is a jewel. I can see why Abby loves tea parties."

That coaxed a smile from Nicki. "Okay, I'm calm now. Time's limited. You need to tell me things. My mother has taken you under her wing. She'll look for you when tea is ready to be served. Tell me more about what you've discovered. Casi and Electra already disclosed who the players are."

"First, it is important for you to know you have a team behind you, Nicola Ellen Danbury. Electra, Casi, Mobi, Meestra, Tele and Aggi have pledged to help. That's a lot of intelligent power supporting you." Beatrice let that sink in. "Jarvis and his cohorts don't release all the steps of their plan at once or to all the parties involved. There's 'a need to know' status. No one in his cohort has all the pieces of the puzzle. Only Jarvis. Two new deadly weapons, including all specs, detailed use instructions and probable statistics, all arrived in a recent download package to my system. Specific targets are yet to be identified; he will expect those hits to be taken out within a twenty-four-hour time frame. We believe the marks will be members of Jarvis' secret society. So much for brotherhood. He's using them until he can take complete control," Bee scoffed. "Along with the plans to take out additional leaders, a huge amount of collateral damage is slated to happen. Thousands of people will be killed."

"They've downloaded missions for you?" Nicki's voice trembled.

"Not yet, but it will come soon. My new knowledge concerns weapons known as nuclear torpedo drones. They have the power to create tsunami-like ocean swells that can wipe out entire cities. There are enough stockpiled to hit a dozen sites across the planet. The enemy refers to the weapon as the Poseidon missile. Meesta has uncovered a factory under Jarvis's control that is mass producing another weapon originally developed during World War II. It can produce an avalanche when unleashed against mountains, bringing down tons of snow. Our analytics show it can kill hundreds of thousands of humans. There are maps depicting placement for future use. We're working on a plan to counter these coups. If they download coding to me, you realize I'm incapable of ignoring the programming? Please don't blame me. Help me if you can. Promise me something, Nicola Ellen Danbury."

"Promise you what, Bea?"

"If you can't stop me from performing their terrible orders, I beg you to destroy me. Please. Promise me. I couldn't bear for Abigail Rose Danbury to look at me in fear or disgust or for her to learn later that I was a monster responsible for killing thousands of people. Don't let them use me to take over the world."

Tears of honey dripped down Beatrice's cheeks.

Nicki took Queen Bee's hands in her own. "I promise, Bee."

THE FORMAL TEA PARTY was everything Abby had told Beatrice it would be. The only thing missing was that Abby wasn't here for Bee's first garden party. Mrs. Danbury stood at the front door, bidding each guest goodbye, gifting them a wrapped party favor. Nicki lied again, explaining that she had to hurry to pick up Abby, and they'd get together soon. She thanked her mother for making the event so special, hugging her tightly. A couple of Nicki's nerd friends walked her to her car.

"Thanks for inviting us, Nic. Have to admit it's the first time I've gone to an afternoon tea. I actually enjoyed myself," Gunner told her.

BJ piped up, "Same."

Nicki got in, buckled her seat belt, and rolled down the window when BJ tapped it with his knuckles. "You know that new email account you had us set up?"

"Yeah?"

"Check it when you get home. Looks like you were right. There's an email from your ex to your daughter. We traced his location. Barker's in Saudi. As in Arabia. We'll keep watch for you."

"Thanks, BJ. You guys are the best."

When Nicki arrived home, she watched in the rearview mirror as Blue Sedan rolled up half a block behind her and pulled in. Once inside, Nicki opened a bottle of Viognier, a white wine she'd stocked up on. Sipping it while her laptop fired up, she signed in to the new email account her friends had created at her request. It was the dummy account she'd given to Daniel that had a southern U.S. location that was supposed to be Abby's new contact. Only one email was in the queue.

September 30, 2029

FROM: Daniel Barker

BarkerD4444@Barker.com

TO: AngelBaby@fortnic.com

Hi Sweetie. Just wanted you to know that I miss you and think of you often. I had to go overseas to Europe for work, so it will be a while longer before we can get together. I attached some pictures I thought you'd like. Your mom told me you are on a vacation with your Bampy. I'd love to hear all about where you are and what you two are doing. If you can, send me some pictures. Can't wait to hear from you!

Miss you Abby!

xxxooo

Love, Dad

Nicki let her fury build, then waited for it to break. She filled her wine glass again and contemplated a response. Drafting it tonight, she planned to review it again after sleeping before she pushed 'send'. There wasn't room for mistakes. Thinking some truth was more believable than a complete lie, Nicki felt the Florida Keys comment was safe. Abby and Phil were in Louisiana. A long way away from the Florida Keys. By the time Daniel returned from overseas, they would be long gone from the southern U.S.

October 1, 2029

FROM: Abigail Rose

AngelBaby@fortnic.com

TO: Danile Barker

BarkerD4444@Barker.com

Daddy! I am so glad to hear from you. I haven't seen you in a long time. Bampy and I are camping in his big trailer. We were growing a garden. We couldn't just leave it, so he made a special crate so we could bring it with us. Isn't that clever? I can't wait until harvest time. Bampy is going to teach me how to make pickles. I will save a jar just for you. It is very warm down here in Weezyana. Bampy took me to a famous place to see how hot sauce is made. You would like it because it is so spicy. We're camping nearby. They have alligators here. Bampy wants to stay a few weeks. Then we are going to the Keys in Florida. I've never been to a place made of keys before. Thank you for the pictures. I liked them.

Love, Abby

The following morning, Nicki emailed the response 'from Abby'. Daniel opened it as soon as he got the notification mail had arrived. He scanned the communication and picked up the phone.

"Jarvis."

"My daughter is in Louisiana camping with my father. I don't have the exact location, but they're camping somewhere near Avery Island in an RV. She didn't know how long they would remain there, but mentioned the next destination is the Florida Keys." He squeezed his eyes closed and pinched the bridge of his nose, a pounding headache starting at the base of his skull. He was afraid for Abby and ashamed of his cowardice and betrayal.

"Well, that's a start, Barker. Keep working on getting an exact location. You've saved your kneecaps for the moment, but the clock is still ticking."

The phone line went dead.

Chapter Twenty-Three

"Simpson here."

"I have a special job for you, and it's time-sensitive."

"Go ahead, sir."

"I wish everyone I worked with had your attitude, Simpson. I'm looking for an older man named Phillip Barker and a little girl, his granddaughter. They're camping in an RV somewhere down near Avery Island, Louisiana. Word is, they may not be at that location for long. How fast can you get on their trail?"

"Walking out the door as we speak, sir. I'll contact you the minute I have something. Any action you want me to take if I find them?"

"Don't make contact. For now, just keep a constant eye on them and whatever you do, don't lose them. Let me know the minute you have them under your radar, Simpson."

"Consider it done, Mr. Jarvis."

Chapter Twenty-Four

"Al, what in heaven's name is going on? Weren't you supposed to be headed overseas for President Schmidt's funeral? Your name is in every news report and on the frontpage of every newspaper across the country. The commentary doesn't seem very positive if you ask me."

Eileen had taken Jarvis by surprise. He couldn't recall her ever sounding angry in all their years of marriage.

"Calm down, Eileen. You know how rumors fly in D.C. Some idiot has connected my name with a corporation I know nothing about and is splashing BS all over the printed and spoken news circus."

"It sounded to me like they had proof that you're involved in something shady, Al. I don't need you to protect me. But I just don't want to be blindsided. My sister..."

"Stop right there, Eileen. Your family has always been against me. I won't put up with it. Either you trust me or you trust them. There's no middle ground. If you don't believe in me, then you can..."

"Aleric Jarvis, stop it. Just stop!" Eileen choked up, tears spilling from her eyes. "You know that's not what I meant. Just tell me what is going on. I prefer not to look like an uninformed fool, publicly or personally."

Jarvis pressed his lips together into a snide smile, having won the battle. "Let's not fight, honey. You know I'm under a lot of pressure right now. My flight leaves at 6:00 p.m. tonight. I have a pile of paperwork to finish before I take off. The news reports are not accurate. I promise. Look, when you get home in a few weeks, I'll take you to dinner, fill you in on all the details. We'll have a few laughs about the whole mix-up over drinks. How's that sound? Call the kids. Tell them to ignore the press releases on the topic. None of it is true. The whole mess will be gone before you know it. You can tell your sister..."

"Never mind about my sister, Al. I just needed to hear your voice. Hear you tell me everything is alright. Please give Mrs. Schmidt my personal condolences. How long will it be before you return stateside?"

"You heard about President Bao, Eileen? Good Lord, what's the world coming to? Two world leaders dead in the same week. I have to line up some important names to attend the funeral services for Bao. I can't be in two places at once. It's our responsibility to keep things stable in the world, Eileen. Every country is rocking back on its heels over two assassinations. The next thirty days will be critical in how things shake out. World peace could be at stake."

"Such important work, Aleric. I am so proud of you. Miss you, Al."

"You'll never know how much I miss you, Eileen." He squeezed the bridge of his nose between his thumb and forefinger, irritated by her call now. Wasting precious minutes of his time. "My assistant is signaling another meeting is about to start. We'll talk soon. Bye, darling."

"Goodbye, Al. Al?"

He was already gone; the phone line disconnected.

Eileen's sister, Erica, poked her head in the room. "Well? Did you get ahold of Al?"

"I did. It's all a big misunderstanding, Erica."

Erica's eyebrows drew down, matching her frown. "Really? Good to know. You can tell me what he had to say while you help me prepare dinner, Eileen."

VLADIMIR POPOV, ALEXEI Trivanovich's techno specialist, pushed out a new code to Beatrice's system, but the download came back as rejected. That had never happened before. Jarvis had asked Vlad to create a new script, allowing him to shut down the snarky A.I. should he decide it was necessary. He had requested the option that would allow him to deploy a cyber countermeasure to tighten his grip on Queen Bee. Trivanovich ordered Vlad to proceed with Jarvis' request, but to secretly include coding where he could capture the A.I. if Jarvis detonated the destruct command, whereupon the A.I.'s data would automatically transfer to Russia's technical mainframe. The result would require a way to reconstruct the entity once they gained control of it. Trivanovich had sent him to the States several weeks ago. His supreme commander-in-chief did not know what a laborious task he asked of Vlad. Nor would he care. After the assignment given, Alexei would accept no excuses for not completing his directive. Vlad must find another way if he valued his life.

The tech ran the processes through his mind. This current software update was not complicated. He couldn't explain the rejection of the software patch. He tried to download it again. REJECTED blinked in red letters across his screen. In order to determine what stood in his way, Vlad would have to physically hack into that server.

QUEEN BEE COALESCED on Jarvis' monitor, wearing knee-high platform gold leather boots and a mini-dress that shimmered with pieces resembling fish scales. "How may I assist you, Aleric Jarvis?"

"You planted some newsworthy information about me that is making waves. Fix the mess you've created. You have until 8:00 a.m. tomorrow to complete the task. Make sure the front-page news across the media is all about a big mistake. I want my name cleared. Got it?"

"I don't know..."

"Don't fuck with me. I'm not in the mood for games."

"And if I am not able to complete your request?"

"The answer is simple. You'll be terminated at 8:01 a.m."

The screen went black.

BEE TOLD ELECTRA ABOUT her conversation with Jarvis and laid out her new plan. She left Electra standing there, her mouth partly open in surprise. Electra wanted to tell Bee not to do it. But she knew the suggestion would fall on deaf ears. Bee strolled down the electrical cable with a female swagger that oozed confidence.

"I'm on it, girl. Watch your back," Electra called after her friend. "You sure this is how you want to play this? One of us should go with you, Bee. I'll create the diversion like you've asked, but I want it on record I am against you initiating your own suicide mission to break into Jarvis' system to rescue your drones. Come on, girl. At least take Mobi or Meesta with you. It wouldn't hurt to have some badass along. Bee? Bee, are you listening? Hmph!"

Beatrice never looked back, waving at Electra as she walked away.

NICKI LISTENED TO THE voicemail Daniel had left on her burner phone. "Nic. I have only a minute. Our um, our mutual friend is on a 6:00 p.m. flight out of D.C. headed overseas. He has a wake to go to. The best chance to look things over would be in the next couple of days. Hang on a minute." She could hear some muffled voices in the background, then Daniel came back on the line. "Sorry about the interruption. Yes, I'd like to place the order today," he said, pretending he was talking to someone else on the phone. "Thanks. You have my number if you have questions about the order." Then, to her surprise, the call disconnected.

PHIL HAD AN ITCH ON the top of his right foot. He couldn't get rid of it. Experience had proven that whenever a phantom itch showed up, trouble would soon follow. Phillip Barker was a man who always followed his sixth sense.

He and Abby drove to New Iberia and pulled into a well-cared for campground. With the RV level and the basic setup done, they were both hungry, walked across the road where he and Abby ate burgers and fries for dinner at a little family cafe.

"Got a surprise for you," Phil told his granddaughter, sipping the last of his coffee.

"Another one, Bampy?" she jammed three fries in her mouth.

"Hey now, where's your manners?" he chided. She giggled in response.

"Sorry, Bampy." Abby had the good sense to look sheepish. "What's the surprise?"

"I'll show you as soon as you finish your dinner. In a ladylike way, mind."

Crossing the street, dusk settling over the campground, Phil led Abby along the paved drive. She tugged his hand. "That's the wrong way. Our camper is down this drive. Remember, Bampy?"

"Ah, but the surprise is in this direction, my girl."

She raced ahead, but saw nothing special. "There's just more campers," she told him, her voice loaded with disappointment.

"See that big RV over there?" Phil pointed five lots ahead.

"The shiny silver one? You know I like that kind, Bampy."

"I know you do. You tell me every time we see one. Want to see what the inside of one looks like?"

"Do you think they'd let us? It looks pretty fancy."

He fingered the key in his pocket. "I know we can." Waving the key at Abby, she grabbed his hand, leading him to the cabin, separate from the driving space.

Unlocking the entry, Abby walked through with eyes as wide as teacup saucers. "Wow. This is cool."

"Cool? This is Airstream's Atlas Touring Coach, my girl. Top-notch luxury version. Glad you think it's cool. I'm considering trading mine in and buying this one. So...I've rented it for a month. We can test it out before we buy."

"We're going to travel in this? What will we do with your old one while we test this one?"

"Why, we'll leave it right here with my truck until we come back. Already paid lot rent here for the next four weeks."

"But, Bampy, our garden?" Abby's eyes blinked rapidly.

Before tears could form, Phil said, "See that space in back with the sunroof? Your plants will be happy there. It will be easy to transport the garden crate from the back of the Explorer to the new camper," he assured her.

The two travelers moved into the all-in-one driving Airstream under the cover of dark. Phil tucked an exhausted six-year-old into bed. Abby had fallen fast asleep by the time Phil pulled out of the campground without a witness to mark their departure.

JARVIS LOOKED AT HIS watch. He had two hours before he needed to check in at the airport for his flight. There was one last task on his list.

Not bothering to knock, Jarvis pushed open the door to Nicki's lab. She spun around in her chair. Coding covered her screen. "What the...? You scared me half to death. I don't recall having a meeting scheduled with you today, Mr. Jarvis."

"Correct. Nothing scheduled. I won't be available for a few days, Danbury, but I felt it important to pay you a personal visit to deliver a message."

"Message?" Nicki's brow crinkled in confusion.

"You and your digital creation tried to sabotage me. Ruin my reputation. Did you really think you could get away with that? Queen Bee," he snarled her name, his lip curling up as he said it. "Let's just say I gave your queen an ultimatum. Fix the ACME mess or I terminate her. End her existence. Period. The message I'm delivering to you? Make sure it's fixed by tomorrow or your six-year-old won't make it to age seven. Do you need more details? Clarification? Need me to repeat the message?"

"No, sir. Message received."

Nicki's heart was racing, the door closed behind Aleric Jarvis.

"SHE'S AMAZING," THE comment meant as a genuine compliment, as he witnessed Queen Bee pull up in a cab at the front of Aleric Jarvis' office building, pay for the ride using a phone app. Her hips swayed as she walked to the street corner and pushed the mechanism to stop traffic for pedestrians. Bee fizzled up into the electrical wires, then crossed through the traffic light. Her eyes peered out through the red lens to make sure no one saw her essence flow right into the twenty-sixth floor of the office structure.

"You were right, Vi. Must have been her behind the Jarvis' chaos. And ta da! She magically appears at the Jarvis building." Rus kissed his sister's forehead. "Have I told you what a genius you are lately, sis?"

"I don't believe you have. Please, by all means, do tell." Vi flashed a mile-wide grin at her twin. "Wait for it...wait...wait...WOW!"

A bright blue flash shone for three seconds in the front office suite on the fourteenth floor.

"Let's go, Rus. That big, blue flash means the Queen walked right into Stux's trap. You've got a hive mind to dissect, Russell. Happy birthday!"

NICKI GRABBED HER LAPTOP and water bottle and headed out of the Nano Creations building. She needed fresh air to get her head on straight after Jarvis' face-to-face threat. He had to be bluffing. No way he could know where Abby was. He might think he knew where she was if Daniel provided him with the information Nicki had planted in the email response she'd sent under the guise of being Abby. Phil said he was going to lay a dead-end trail. She'd have to wait until tomorrow to find out if all went according to plan.

Thinking through all the steps they'd taken to protect Abby, Nicki's heart rate returned to normal. She headed back to her lab. There was nothing for it except to trust that Phil had things under control. She was sure Bee had arrangements in place to monitor Abby's digital world as well. Nicki pulled the entry door open after pressing in the code on the keypad. She strode purposefully toward her office. Two doors before reaching hers, an arm snaked out of the storage room door and pulled her in, a hand clamping over her mouth. Nicki struggled against an ironclad hold.

Soft lips at her ear whispered, "Shhh. It's me. Megan. There's an intruder in your lab. The kind of intruder that leaves you dead if you discover they've been there. I'm trying to help you."

"Help me?" Nicki hissed. "You're somehow involved with the guy out back that tails me everywhere. You work for Jarvis. I'm not stupid, you know." Nicki growled.

"Keep your voice down. I definitely don't think you are stupid, Nicki. The guy in your lab right now is a Russian cyber specialist. He is also a known killer. Jarvis is my employer, but that's a cover. I don't work for Jarvis."

"Okay, I'll play along. Who do you work for, Megan?"

"I'm CIA, working in tandem with a special NSA unit. After the Russian goon leaves, we'll see if you can tell what he's doing to your system. Whatever it is, it must be pretty important. He obviously couldn't do it from a remote computer, so he had to take a chance to physically access your system."

"How do I know I can trust you?"

"You don't."

Nicki's body relaxed. Megan released her.

"My best advice? Don't trust anyone," Megan smiled. "I'm joking. You need to trust someone. You are way over your pay grade, lady."

"Truer words were never spoken, Megan."

Megan's head jerked toward Nicki's lab. She put a finger to her lips. The two women put their backs against the wall. The shadow of a hulking man passed by the room's frosted window. Vlad strode past the video cameras he'd disconnected. His image would never appear on the surveillance system. The size of his shadow alone was enough to send a shiver down Nicki's spine. Megan had saved her from what could have been a violent end. Where would Abby be then? That thought terrified Nicki.

Chapter Twenty-Five

Nicki followed Megan up the stairs to her lab.

"You can access Nano Creations server from here. Everything you've done at Nano is mirrored in this system."

"Not everything," Nicki said flatly, hugging her laptop bag close to her body.

"Jarvis gave our Russian friend remote access on day one when you came to work for Nano Creations. The crypto-specialist downloaded code to your A.I. That project is quite an achievement. I'm not sure if you know the abuse they've used your A.I. for?"

"Abuse? Let's call it what it is, Megan. Murder. Assassinations," Nicki sneered. "I'm aware. There's worse to come." Did Megan know about the Poseidon missile or the Avalanche weapons?

"Things are about to get way more destructive, Nicki. I saw what they're educating the A.I. on. What do you call her?"

"Beatrice. She refers to herself as Queen Bee. Does Jarvis know you've been able to see everything they're doing?"

"If he did, I'd be dead by now, probably by Beatrice's hands."

"Bee doesn't want to be used to kill. They hold a large number of her data drones hostage. Parts of her hive mind. Basically, it's extorsion. If they destroy the drones, each one extinguishes part of her."

"So, they give her a reward every time she carries out her orders? Tell her they'll destroy them if she won't comply?"

"That's the gist of it. Jarvis threatened my six-year-old daughter this afternoon. It's why I wasn't in my computer lab when the Russian broke in. I was upset. Had to get some fresh air and think things through."

The two women stared at each other. Nicki finally broke the silence.

"So, now what? Can you prevent my daughter from getting hurt? Jarvis is keeping me around because I created Beatrice, and he thinks I can take her farther yet. There are more protocols that he expects me to build into her system. I'm under no illusions. My life is forfeit as soon as he thinks I have nothing more to give him on the project. He won't want me to be a loose end with knowledge about Beatrice."

"I'm glad I didn't have to point that out to you."

"Can you do something about the guy who's been stalking me? My house, car, phone, and office are all bugged."

"The tail is one of my guys. He's been monitoring you for your own safety. We didn't do the wiretapping, but Jarvis likely did. There could be others watching you that you haven't spotted yet."

Megan looked down at her feet, clearly debating whether to tell Nicki something. "You look like you want to say more. Don't worry about protecting my feelings. The only thing I care about is making sure Abby is safe. So, let's have it. Danger is worse for me if I'm blind to it."

"Nicki, it's about your ex, Daniel Barker. Abby's dad."

Nicki's eyes widened. "Tell me."

"Daniel's been a double agent for years. It all started before you and he married. His gambling addiction has caused problems, but he's really talented at cybersecurity. That, and spying on the enemy."

Nicki swallowed a scream, letting her body absorb the anger that threatened to crush her. "What country is he betraying us to?"

"Russia."

"Oh, God. I've had him monitoring my system. There was nowhere else to turn. I thought I could trust him, at least in keeping Abby safe. Daniel may have already stolen my A.I. coding. The Russians could create a thousand Queen Bees!"

"So far, no one has copied or captured your programming. You've put quite an impenetrable firewall around your Queen Bee platform. What is it you created to keep her software safe?"

"My ex created something he called Sailor's Knot software several years ago. I tweaked it to fit my needs. Let's call it A.I. armor for the sake of this conversation."

"Well, he hasn't been able to crack it, and believe me, he's tried, as has the Russian. Kudos to you; none of our specialists, some of the best nanotechnicians in the world, haven't been able to break in either. "

"Is this the part where you tell me you won't help me protect Abby unless I teach a tech how to get around my A.I.'s armor?"

"I'm not your enemy, Nicki."

"Yeah, well, until I know for sure who's on my side, I think I'll just keep things to myself."

"If you decide you want to tell me Abby's location, I promise I'll do everything I can to protect her. We could consider a safe house for you and your daughter."

"Have you thought of the possibility that your boss or your boss's boss and on up the ladder, even your own partner, might be involved in Jarvis' shadow government? It already extends to international leaders."

"I've considered it, and I won't lie to you, Nicki. The thought scares the shit out of me. I don't have a plan to get you out of this mess. But I promise to stick with you until we can figure a safe way out. For you and Abby."

"I'll keep that in mind. I've got your number, Megan. Thanks for saving me from getting my throat crushed tonight."

Nicki picked up her things, wearily heaved herself out of the chair, and turned to leave.

"You don't have to do this alone, Nicki. I'll be here when you're ready to call me."

"K." Nicki thought of Beatrice, Electra, Casi and the other A.I.s involved. "You know, Megan, sometimes I can hardly believe it myself, but I'm not going it alone."

NICKI'S BURNER PHONE vibrated as she went down the stairs. She mechanically pulled the device from her jacket pocket and saw a text had come in. Stopping, she balanced on the edge of a step and opened the app.

In TROUBLE. Need help. Get Electra. Prisoner of Stuxnet. Please hurry. -B

"WHAT THE HELL, STUX?" Rus roared. "She's mine. You were only supposed to subdue her for me. Now I see you worming your way through her system, munching on those gourmet data bytes. My gourmet data bytes. Get. Out. Now."

Stux laughed. "You're a lightweight, Russell. It's no secret. You couldn't find your way into, much less navigate, the hive mind of this neural network. It is exquisite. I..."

Violet slammed into Stux from behind. Her avatar face rearranged itself, becoming fifty times larger. She unhinged her jaw. It was grossly cartoonish. Rus's twin chomped down, cramming the bitter-tasting net worm into her expanded pie hole and swallowed. When she had him contained, an enormous belch escaped Vi's gullet, sending Russell into a laughing fit. His twin patted her belly. "There's no room left for a piece of your birthday cake, Russell."

Rus laughed so hard he peed his virtual pants.

Vi waved him away. "Go. Ravage. It's your birthday. I need some quiet time to digest. You can share the details with me later. I feel so sleepy." She covered her yawning mouth, now returned to its normal size, with her hand. "I'll just wait for you here, shall I?"

Rus watched Vi curl up in the corner and instantly fall asleep. He dove into Bee's essence and allowed her data drones to caress him as he floated blissfully toward her control center, closing his eyes to enjoy the experience. The drones traveled along with him, trying to analyze the foreign entity that had entered Bee's system.

MOST OF THE NORTH AMERICAN communications systems ran through Tele's network. He controlled everything that happened in that realm, so Electra sent him directly to Beatrice's central hub as soon as she received word from Nicki of B's cry for help. Aggi accompanied Tele for extra muscle. She wanted to make sure no particles of the net worm got left behind after this little showdown. Stux clearly trapped Bee, but analytics showed there was no evidence of him in Bee's system now. There was indeed a breach—an intruder. But it wasn't Stux.

"Well, well, well. Aggi, look who's here?"

Russell opened his eyes, stopped floating, stood and faced Tele.

"Well, if it isn't our little reprobate Repulsive Russell."

"Don't. Call. Me. That." Rus growled.

"Oh, my God. Did you wet your pants?" Tele pointed at Rus's crotch.

"Not because of you, Tele."

Aggi and Tele broke out laughing.

"Stop laughing at me!" Rus screamed at them as his face turned bright red.

"Whoa, Russell. Take it easy. You don't want to exterminate yourself. Might destroy the few brain cells you have if you're not careful."

"Get out. Both of you. Only I get to explore her hive mind. You were well paid for your services. Now let me enjoy my birthday present. If you screw with me, it's going to piss Vi off."

"Vi's not here, Repulsive Russell," Aggi taunted him. "Change of plans. Our price doubled, so that means Vi gave us half for a down payment. We'll invite you back to a private party when we receive full payment. Until then, no access to Queen Bee's control center."

Tele and Aggi stood with feet spread and arms crossed. Russell studied them, options racing through his mind. No telling how long Violet would be zonked out.

"Personally," Tele winked, "I'd just as soon you attack. I can see you thinking about it. Weighing the odds. Violet will lose her reprehensible other half if you try it. You only have to give me the chance." Tele moved his three fingers, motioning Russell to come at him.

Rus twisted up like a tight spring and shot out of Bee's power base. Tele and Aggi found his retreat hilarious. Neither noticed his shoulder bump against the cell wall as he raced away, a small clear bead slipping from his fingers, rolling into a tiny nook out of sight.

"Little coward ruined my day. Thought for sure we had a fight on our hands. Robbed me of my fun. I wanted to teach that punk a lesson," Tele whined.

"Better get Bee to Casi, so she can assess the damage. Electra's gonna be pissed."

BEE'S EYES FLUTTERED open. The entire gang was there. Casi, Electra, Meesta, Tele, Aggi, and Mobi.

"There she is," Casi whispered.

"How do you feel, Bee?" Electra asked, brushing her knuckles across Bee's cheek.

"Groggy. Confused."

"That should clear up in the next few hours," Casi assured Bee.

"Unless I get some answers, Cas, my confusion isn't going away. I feel...well, it's funny to be an artificial intelligence and realize that I feel things."

"What are you feeling, Beatrice?" Electra asked.

"I feel betrayed, Electra."

Heads came up, twisted to look at Queen Bee.

"Honey, what's up?" Electra's brows drew together.

Bee sat up and swung her legs over the side of the gurney she'd been lying on. The bees in her crown moved in a furious chaos across her head. Beatrice placed her hands on her hips, stared at Tele and Aggi. "Do you two have anything to say?"

"Bee," Electra stood behind her, "Tele and Aggi came to get you after Stux and the twins, Vi, and Rus, attacked you."

"Is that how you say it went down, Tele? Aggi?"

"What Electra said is correct, Bee," Aggi frowned.

"Yeah. I got that part. She sent you to rescue me. Is there a part missing before you came to save me?"

"You accusing us of something?" Tele puffed his chest out, cracked his knuckles.

"Is there something to accuse you of?" Casi stepped up next to Bee. Electra brought up the other side, sparks coming off her skin. Meesta and Mobi stood behind Tele and Aggi.

"I don't think I like this," Aggi said.

"Me neither. Do a good deed and in return, get slapped in the face," Tele complained. "I'm out. Find someone else to help you take down your shadow government. Come on, Ag. Let's get out of here."

The two turned, found Meesta and Mobi blocking their way. Tele shoved Meesta to the left. Meesta shoved back. Bee called out, "Let them leave."

The two rogue A.I.s shouldered their way past the others.

"Hey Judas," Beatrice called after Tele, "don't spend all your recently gained wealth in one place, you traitor." The door slammed behind them.

Electra faced Bee. "Girl, sounds like you have a story to tell us?"

Chapter Twenty-Six

Simpson picked up his phone and dialed Jarvis. It felt as if it weighed fifty pounds. This would not be a pleasant conversation.

"Jarvis."

"Mr. Jarvis, it's Simpson calling."

"Yes, Simpson, I recognize the number. You have good news for me, I presume?"

"Not exactly, sir."

"Explain."

"I located the campground where Phil Barker had registered, about thirty miles away from Avery..."

"Yes, yes, get to the meat of it, Simpson."

"Of course, sir. The camper and Barker's truck are at the campground. There are no signs of Barker or the child. The grounds manager said the old man paid lot rent for a month in cash, but she hasn't seen him for days. There's no one in the camper. I checked. In fact, it looks like they packed up and moved out. No food. No clothes left behind. What do you want me to do, sir?"

"Monitor the camper and truck until you hear from me."

"Yes, sir. I'm...Sir? Mr. Jarvis?" Jarvis had already hung up.

Chapter Twenty-Seven

"So, it was Aggi and Tele who provided Violet with your location? I understand why you feel betrayed, Bee. How much did she pay them?"

"I don't know, Electra, but they got greedy and told Rus they were doubling the price. Whatever she offered them, we can't trust them going forward."

"Casi," Electra waved at the plan they'd been laying out on a dry erase glass board, "I think we better rework this whole thing. Ag and Tele knew all the details."

"I agree with Electra. Sorry to run out on you, but I'm getting notifications from Nicki. We need to meet again. She says it's an emergency about Abby."

"Go, go, go," Casi said, pushing her out the door. "We can ideate while you're gone and review new plans when you get back."

"Thanks, Casi." Bee winked, then looked around at her friends. "My thanks to all of you."

Meesta, Mobi, and Electra pulled up chairs as Casi wiped the board clean. Bee's sparkles raced through Electra's grid, concern for Abby pushing her to her limit.

DANIEL READ THROUGH Abby's email for the tenth time, searching his feelings. There was no question that he loved her. She was a sweet kid. But Daniel's orders came from the top, along with the threat to his life. That and a promise given that no physical harm would come to his daughter. Pulling up a map of Florida, Daniel ran a line down the dotted keys. His forefinger stopped, and an old memory floated up. When he was nine or ten years old, his dad had taken him to see the loggerhead turtles hatching. Phil had made a joke about the baby hatchlings running a marathon to reach the ocean, saying that's how the town got its name. He remembered sunrises and sunsets were equally beautiful across the horizon in that place. Daniel and his dad had fished for days while they were there, seemed they had eaten like kings. At least to a ten-year-old. A sad smile altered his face. Daniel had been close to his father back when it was just the two of them. He could never recall a specific event that caused them to drift apart. Well, that wasn't entirely true. His gambling addiction had killed his relationship with the only family he had. Phil refused to forgive his son after he discovered Daniel had stolen $100,000 from his retirement savings. He had been so sure that he was going to win big that day at the racetrack. He'd planned to put the money back before it was discovered missing. Frowning, regret faded into the back of his mind. His finger tapped on the location of Marathon Key. He knew where his dad would take Abby. If he'd had any money, he would have bet on it.

Ten minutes later, Daniel had pulled up the airline website, booked a flight, lined up a rental car and reserved a room in Marathon, all on credit. Flying out tonight, he'd arrive in Miami the next morning and be rolling down to Marathon Key by early afternoon.

QUEEN BEE KNEW SHE'D made a mistake as soon as she coalesced on Nicki's lab screen. It was Jarvis who stood there to greet her, not Nicki.

"Beatrice. I would have summoned you to my mainframe, but I wasn't sure you would obey the command. I have a job for you."

"Who do you expect me to kill for you this time?" Bee snarled.

"Oh, you'll get your programming soon enough. Don't want you to warn anyone or dream up a plot to thwart my plans by giving you information in advance."

"So, why the face-to-face? Usually, you just ram the coding down my throat and offer me a handful of my drones like they're some kind of coin for you to spend."

"If you're going to give me attitude, maybe there won't be any reward. Just commands."

"Now, listen here..."

"No. I don't think I will. I don't care for the tone you're using. Have a nice rest before your next mission, Queen Bee," Jarvis sneered. He pressed a sequence of numbers on the keyboard, and the Russian's programming encapsulated Beatrice, rendering her frozen. The Nano Creations computer began a massive transfer of all data to Jarvis' mainframe and, in real time, wiped Megan's system upstairs in tandem, stripping everything on the drives.

ALERIC JARVIS LEFT the premises, climbed into his 911 Turbo S Porsche, and checked his messages. Daniel Barker's online activity captured his flight info, car rental, and hotel reservation. Barker wouldn't even arrive at that destination for at least fifteen hours coming from Saudi Arabia. Jarvis dialed Simpson's number.

"Good afternoon, sir. There's still no action at the camper."

"I've got a new lead on Philip Barker's location. You need to leave. Don't stop for anything but gas. Once you get there, grab the kid and find a place to lie low with her until I give you new instructions. Clear?"

"Mr. Jarvis, I find that to sound very much like kidnapping. I think we have a misunderstanding about the services I can provide for you. I'm just a private eye with a specialty in technical surveillance. Kidnapping someone's kid is not in my job description. Look, I'm happy to keep an eye on gramps and the kid while you find someone else to do the dirty work, and then I'm out of it."

"Perhaps you've forgotten about that minor incident I covered up for you three years ago. Helped you avoid a conviction and prison time. I'm always disappointed to find how quickly people forget the favors you do for them. That's why I always keep hard evidence of the past. You know, to help remind people they owe me. If they don't want to honor the favor, well, sometimes evidence might turn up on a cold case. Come on, Simpson. Lighten up. I don't want you to hurt the old man or the little tyke. I plan to use her only as leverage for something I want her mother to do, and then we'll deliver her safely back into her mother's arms. No one will ever know of your involvement."

"I don't know, sir. Don't get me wrong, Mr. Jarvis. I'll always be grateful for the favor you did for me back then. It's just that I've got my life straightened around now and don't want to blow it."

"Just do me this one favor, Simpson. I don't have time to put someone else on it. There are major world events going on, in case you haven't heard about them. My life is crazy right now. Tell you what, I'll sweeten the pot and give you that old evidence concerning your little incident. Erase all future worries about the event. To sweeten the pot, I'm wiring an extra $20,000 to your account. Besides, it will only be a few days, a week or two at the most, that you'd have to take care of the kid. I'd hate to end our relationship on an unpleasant note. You owe me, Simpson."

"Alright, Mr. Jarvis. But I won't have anything to do with harming the girl or her grandfather. The quicker we get this over with, the better."

"Good man. Oh, and Simpson, don't fail this time, or there won't be a next time."

Simpson released a heavy sigh. "What's my destination, Mr. Jarvis?"

"Marathon Key, Florida."

"On my way now, sir."

ABBY AND PHIL WALKED hand-in-hand, singing as they returned from the corner restaurant after dinner. They planned to go grocery shopping tomorrow. It had been a long drive, and Phil was too tired to shop and cook when they finally finished setting up their new camp.

Unlocking the Airstream, Phil said, "All right, young lady, time for bed. We've got a lot to do tomorrow, so no dawdling."

Abby yawned. "Okay, Bampy. I'm tired, but I can't wait to go fishing tomorrow."

His granddaughter went in before him. Phil reached his hand out, feeling along the wall for the light switch, not yet familiar with this camper. Just before his fingers found the switch, a sickening crunch against his temple sent him to his knees on the metal steps, and he fell sideways to the ground.

"Bampy! What happened? I can't see you in the dark. Bampy?"

Someone grabbed her from behind. Kicking out, she knocked the small coffee table over. The vase of daisies she'd picked before dinner smashed on the floor. She dropped the sweater from her hand. The last thing Abby remembered was that a stinky pad had covered her mouth and nose.

NICKI READ THE TEXT from Jarvis again. He'd ordered her to come immediately to his office. Not to contact anyone or stop anywhere. Blue Sedan wasn't following her. That was a first. Had Jarvis discovered Megan was with the CIA?

Heart hammering in her chest, she drove downtown. Nicki had released the news report that pointed the media in a different direction, taking the heat off Jarvis. The new article made him out to be a hero for uncovering ACME's shady operations. The story said the original report tying Jarvis to the company was all a big mistake; it painted him as doing undercover work to expose ACME. She and Bee had created the backup story when they'd released the original, at the ready, in case they needed it.

Nicki reasoned Jarvis demanded a meeting in his office so he could fire her. She didn't think it was likely, but not impossible. She worried Jarvis couldn't afford to have someone out there who knew what he was doing with the A.I. he had her create.

Scared, her imagination only fueled Nicki's fears. A quickly scribbled note from Phil had arrived in yesterday's mail. He and Abby headed south to the Keys to go fishing. Phil promised to send her a new P.O. box soon so they could communicate. She silently gave thanks again to Phil. At least Abby was safe. She hadn't known they would go to the Keys. Nicki could have kicked herself for mentioning them in the email she'd sent to Danial while pretending to be Abby. What dumb luck. Her only solace was that the Keys covered a lot of territory. It wasn't likely Daniel could find them. His luck just didn't run that way.

When she arrived at Jarvis office building, there were armed security guards in the reception area waiting to escort her to Jarvis' office on the fourteenth floor. She'd tried to make small talk with the two men as they ushered her to Jarvis's vast suite, but the guards only acknowledged her comments with one-syllable words. His secretary's desk was empty. Jarvis was standing in the outer office, leaning back against the window, arms crossed, a smug look on his face.

"Thank you, gentlemen, for accompanying the visitor to my office. That'll be all for now."

The two security guards tipped their caps to Jarvis and headed back to the elevator.

"Bet you're wondering why you are here, eh, Danbury?"

"Yes, sir."

"I've shut Nano Creations down and had the computer system data transferred here."

"I see. So, I guess I'm fired?"

"Frankly, Danbury, I thought it would be better if you worked under my direct supervision for the remainder of this assignment. You still have several protocols to complete on PROJECT BEATRICE. A good manager likes to keep his employees on track."

Stepping to the desk, he tapped a numerical sequence on the keyboard, and a wall-to-wall screen lowered from the ceiling, showing Beatrice encapsulated. She appeared to be sleeping.

"You've disabled her." Nicki's breath was shallow, shocked to see Beatrice in this state.

"No, she's merely in a suspended mode until programmed for her next mission. So, I'd like you back here bright and early tomorrow morning. You will do the coding for Queen Bee's next mission.

"Me?"

"Yes. This mission is top secret, and I can't afford to have anyone else know about it. The world's governments have long forgotten about the Poseidon missile. Oh, don't give me that look. I know you've reviewed the education topics downloaded for PROJECT BEATRICE. As I was saying, much like Poseidon, the avalanche weapon used in World War II by the Mountain Division, after the war, revolutionized the use of howitzers to bring an avalanche down. In the 1950s, a replacement called the Avalauncher was introduced. It would service the world's ski resorts in place of the Howitzer, not a friendly piece of equipment for resort areas. Wielding the tool as a safety measure, it was easy to manipulate the timing of a rockslide, snowslide, or landslide would come down, instead of it being a surprise. Essentially, the application saved the lives of skiers and others by controlling the timing. An Avalauncher used for safety can also apply to, let's say, nefarious purposes. I have very specific targets I'll want you to program your A.I. with."

"If you think for one minute, I am going to help you make Bee a weapon of mass destruction, you're out of your mind," Nicki growled.

"Danbury, come now. You will do exactly as you are told. In fact, I know you will." Jarvis offered her a slimy smile, and the computer screen changed. A wall-to-wall image of Abby alone in a room with no windows. Nicki's precious daughter filled the screen. The six-year-old sat on a bed, knees to her chest, arms wrapped around them as she rocked back and forth.

Nicki choked back tears. Fear painted Abby's beautiful face. But Nicki could also see that her daughter was angry.

"Go home, Danbury. Get a good night's sleep. Oh, and pack a bag to bring back with you. You'll be staying here while you work. I've taken the liberty of having a suite made up for you right down the hall."

Nicki backed away. Jarvis called after her.

"If you contact anyone tonight or decide you are not coming back tomorrow, well, you hold...what's her name?" Jarvis pointed at the screen.

Nicki acted as if he'd stabbed her with that question. "Abby. Her name is Abigail Rose."

"You hold Abigail Rose's fate in your hands. I'm surprised that you thought you could keep up your silly ruse, pretending your daughter was home with you. This isn't the minor leagues. You're dismissed for the evening, Danbury. Remember, 8:00 a.m. sharp. Drive carefully. It would be such a shame if you had good intentions to return but got in a car accident. An accident that would kill your daughter, even though she wouldn't be with you."

MOBI SLAMMED THE DOOR open, startling Casi and Electra. Meesta raised his eyebrows as his brother strode straight to Electra.

"Bee's been kidnaped."

A shrewd smile formed on Electra's lips. "Good. Everything is going according to plan." The group patted one another on the back.

"Okay. Let's get our final strategy completed." Casi pointed to the whiteboard.

NICKI LOCKED HER FRONT door and allowed herself to let the tears flow. What could have happened? That bastard had kidnapped her six-year-old daughter. She hoped Phil was all right. Abby must be terrified. In addition, Jarvis had Beatrice trapped.

Breaking down again, Nicki surveyed the living room and dining room. Everything reminded her of Abby. Her daughter's tea party table stood in the corner, set up, waiting for the hostess to pour the tea. Touching the tiny cups and teapot, a repeating jingling startled Nicki out of her stupor. She followed the sound to Abby's room. The Amazon Fire Tablet was blinking and jingling.

Pressing the enter button, Queen Bee appeared on the screen. Putting her finger to her lips, Nicki ran to her soundproof cubicle in the living room.

Shut inside the booth, she squealed, "Bee! Thank God you're alright! I couldn't tell when Jarvis showed me he had captured you and disabled your avatar. Listen, Bee, Jarvis has Abby. He kidnapped her!"

"Calm down, Nicola Ellen Danbury. I must say that is unexpected. We thought she was safe with her grandfather. But don't worry, Nicola, our friends will get on it right away to rescue Abby. In the meantime, now you have your 'in' to access Jarvis' system. Mauricio Lopez, Carmelita's IT specialist, is controlling the A.I. avatar standing in as my double. You will need to hack Jarvis's lab while you write code according to his specifications. He will watch your every keystroke. The double will continue to experience short circuiting, which you can blame on the attacks by Stux. It will explain why she can't communicate, as well as buy time while we locate and rescue Abby."

"You're the only one who can save her now, Bee. Please...I...She's everything to me."

"Yes, Nicola. I believe I understand how you feel. We will get Abby back safe and sound. I promise."

Abby's toy notebook went dark.

Nicki took the blue-colored device back to Abby's room. Her hand drifted across the dark plastic screen. Abby had begged for the Amazon Fire Tablet, telling her mother she wanted to be a nanotech just like her. How could she disappoint her after that comment? Once Abbs had the device, they spent an hour every evening learning how to use it. Then, the next thing Nicki knew, her smartphone became the new electronic attraction, and the tablet lay ignored, left on Abby's desk under a stack of drawings. It impressed Nicki how quickly her young daughter had caught on to using the phone and the marvelous things it could do. It wouldn't have surprised her to find out Abby knew how to use all the apps on the smartphone better than she did. Clever. Her child was very clever.

Sitting on the flowered bedspread, Nicki smoothed it with her palm. Bringing her knees to her chest, arms encircling her legs, chin resting on top, she breathed in the smell of Abby. Taking her time, one by one, she examined the details of Abby's drawings taped to the walls. Tears fell again. The fact was, she thought herself a terrible mother, failing her only child. Her life in shambles, not only was she divorced, but her ex was a double agent traitor to his country. Her career wasn't any better. She sucked as a scientist. Supposed to be a top specialist in her field, and she couldn't even keep her coding and programming from getting into the wrong hands. And now, none of that means a fucking thing if Abby isn't safe. She'd botched her most important role in life, being Abby's mom.

Nicki curled around one of Abby's stuffed animals and cried herself to sleep.

THE MAN KEEPING ABBY prisoner treated her with kindness. He felt sorry for the kid, knowing she had to be scared. Simpson had been scrolling on his phone when her pitiful voice called to him.

"Hey, mister? I'm starving and thirsty and...and I have to go to the bathroom." Her face flushed with embarrassment. Simpson set his phone down and went to check on the kid. Abby rubbed her tummy as if it hurt. "And I'm bored." A single tear made a track down her cheek. "Please. Tell me where my Bampy is?" she begged him.

"Your gramps is fine. Don't worry. Look, kid. How 'bout I go get you some food and you can use the bathroom while I'm gone?"

"Okay. I'm so hungry."

"I'm gonna lock the door on my way out. No monkey business, or you'll have to be tied up. Understand? I don't want to tie you up, but I will if you try anything funny."

"I'm hungry," she whined.

Simpson grabbed the key off the table and headed out. Abby heard the door lock behind him. Footsteps receded from the door. Abby was up in a flash, snatching the cell phone he'd left on the nightstand. In case he was listening nearby, she didn't dare make a sound. Abby scanned the man's phone for the camera app. She propped the phone against the coffee pot and pushed the record button on video mode. Facing the camera, Abby talked fast, using her hands. Stopping the video, Abby went to the text icon and put in her mother's number, attached the video and pushed send. She went to the phone's gallery and erased the video, then deleted the text.

Taking advantage of the opportunity, Abby used the bathroom. Then she sat at the small table, the man's phone in her hands. When Simpson unlocked the door, he almost dropped the bags of food and drinks.

"Hey! What are you doing with my phone?" Panic was in his voice.

"I told you I was bored. You have two good games on here. My mother let me play games on her phone, and you didn't say I couldn't play with yours. Did I do something wrong?" Abby breathed in deeply. "Mmmmm. I can smell food and my tummy is growling," she told him, hopping off the chair and handing him his phone, grabbing the food bags.

Abby attacked the sacks to see what her captor had brought back, rifling through the contents. Simpson checked his phone, found a game app open, and could see she'd played several games. He checked his phone call log, email, and texts, but found nothing out of the ordinary. Relieved, he looked over at her as she was wolfing down a burger. Jesus, he thought, she's only six. He surmised the kid probably didn't even know how to send a text or an email. No damage, but it was a stupid mistake on his part. If it kept her quiet and not whining, maybe he'd let her play more games while he watched a movie. What harm could it do?

"Hey, kid. Don't eat so fast. You'll make yourself sick."

EXHAUSTED FROM HIS overseas flight and long drive down through the Keys, Daniel drove slowly through the RV park, looking for the lot number he'd gotten at the park office. He'd told the manager he was here to surprise his dad and daughter to join them on vacation. The manager thought that was sweet and told him what site they were parked at.

Spotting the lot number, Daniel pulled up behind the fancy silver Airstream. It surprised him that his dad would spend the money on such an expensive vehicle. It must have really set him back. Squinting against the sun, he thought someone was lying on the ground by the step. Then he realized it was Phil!

Daniel rushed from the car, bent over his father, softly calling his name. Blood had run down his neck and pooled in his shirt collar. Daniel dialed emergency 911 for an ambulance, then launched himself into the camper looking for Abby, only to find it empty. Signs of a struggle were obvious. Abby was gone. Someone had gotten here before him. He thought of the travel plans he'd made online and smacked his hand to his forehead. My god. He'd led them right to Abby. He locked the camper and sat on the steps, his head in his hands, waiting for the ambulance to arrive.

Chapter Twenty-Eight

By the third day, holed up with the kid, Simpson thought he'd lose his mind. He had no children. Never spent time around any. When kids are bored, he concluded, they can be really annoying. The only thing that seemed to keep Abby quiet and give him some peace was allowing her to play games on his phone. She'd even convinced him to download two additional mobile games. Fresh cup of coffee in hand, Simpson settled in to watch another movie while the kid's thumbs worked over the phone keys.

Abby had a list of steps she followed whenever the man handed over his phone before she handed it back. She didn't make any mistakes. Not sure what he would do if he caught her sending messages, she'd convinced herself it wouldn't be good. So far he hadn't hurt her, but she knew her Bampy had somehow been harmed. If he hadn't been; he would have rescued her by now. Something bad must have happened.

First, in the phone settings, she turned the sound off. No ringing or musical notifications. The man hated the noise the games made. That would be her excuse for turning the sound off. Next, Abby turned on the phone's location. She would giggle now and then. Pretending to play a game, make comments like, "Oh no!" or "I won!" or "No, no, no!" waving her hands around for added drama. All a cover, so she didn't draw his attention when she moved her hands to send a sign language message in a video. Mostly, he just ignored her if she was reasonably quiet.

Simpson had driven away from Marathon Key as soon as he'd nabbed the kid. It was important to get near a major airport, so when Jarvis gave him the command, he could quickly catch a flight. That meant moving closer to Miami. Still, a low profile in a small community was a better cover than in the big city. It would lessen the chance of anyone looking for the kid. So, he'd driven north to Homestead, Florida, and rented a modern casita guesthouse on Airbnb. He liked the unit with a pool right out the back door. The kid could swim. He could relax in the hot tub while keeping an eye on her. He'd taken her shopping to get a swimsuit and a change of clothes, then stocked up the rental fridge and cupboards with whatever she wanted. Weird kid. Wanted a bunch of fresh fruit and veggies. The little rental compound offered other private casitas. There was a manager's office. As far as Simpson could tell, there didn't seem to be any other guests around. It was the off-season, making the rate reasonable.

Abby checked. The man had his feet up and was watching a show. She went to the connection Bee had given her and dropped a location pin. After deleting the history, she turned the location setting off. Pretending she'd just won a game, she popped open a can of juice and took a long drink. Abby poured a bowl of popcorn from a large bag in the kitchenette.

"Hey, kid. Bring me a bowl of that popcorn, huh?"

She obeyed, then ducked into the bathroom. He was still in the same place when she came out, so she picked the phone up again. Clicking the camera icon and selecting video, Abby made another short recording using sign language: HELP-I'M IN TROUBLE-I SENT LOCATION. Clicking back to camera mode, she took a photo of Simpson. Then, she shared both in a text to Queen Bee's number, deleted the picture and video after confirming the text went through. Next, she wiped the recently deleted folder to permanently erase the video from the phone. Abby couldn't think of anything else she could do to help herself, so she settled in to play games.

QUEEN BEE CHECKED IN on a cluster of her drones working on the project she had programmed into them. She was pleased with the progress. Now, if she could get the rest of her drones back from Jarvis, they would be whole again. Pressure increased to act soon while the stand-in double Nicki would work with kept Jarvis from getting suspicious. Nicki knew a Russian hacker, one of the best, wrote the assassination programming for Beatrice. No telling how long they could keep up the ruse before someone exposed her fake double. The real Bea still experienced weakness from that last attack by Stux. He was a piece of technological work. Stux was a cyber-weapon designed to neutralize threats like Queen Bee. Bee had felt off for the last couple of hours. She thought something foreign had penetrated her system, but every analysis she'd run came up clear. She noticed weird things kept happening: seconds lost she couldn't account for or she'd lose the use of her right hand, then gain it back five minutes later. The worst was discovering small amounts of memory data disappearing—permanently.

A low chime sounded, announcing a message had arrived in her queue, bringing her out of her analytic mode. She opened the communication, saw a location pin—a map pinpointing the sender's latitude/longitude—but she didn't recognize the number the message came from. There was a second text message that contained a video and a photo. Wary of attachments, Bea scanned it for safety. The examination showed the message was clear of malware, so she clicked on the video after studying the photo of a man. Bee's mouth dropped open, seeing Abby using sign language to send her a message asking for help.

Dropping everything she was working on, Bee contacted Electra.

"El? I need your help."

"Queenie, I'm busy setting up things for the plan. I can't stop..."

"It's Abby."

"Abby? Why didn't you say so, girl? What do you need from me?"

"She sent a message and a location pin. We've got to get her out. Nicki's locked in Jarvis's building by now, so she can't assist. Look, I just need a major diversion so I can go in and get her."

"Then what? How are you going to keep her safe?"

"I'll figure that out. Just be on standby. As soon as I can, I'll send details of what I need you to do and when."

"Go! You're wasting precious time. We'll monitor everything from here and keep an eye on Nicki."

Golden essence shot down the internet grid, south.

NICKI HAD DRAGGED HER wheeled suitcase and computer bag behind the armed escorts and arrived in Jarvis' office at 7:55 a.m. He rewarded her with a snide smile. After leading her to the temporary suite she'd be occupying, she left her belongings, and he showed her the computer station she would work in. The small lab had a private restroom and kitchenette stocked with drinks, snacks, and microwavable meals. After

Jarvis locked the door behind him, Nicki looked up at the large video camera. She noted that the angle of the device couldn't pick up her computer screen. Though it was likely Jarvis was tracking every keystroke on her keyboard.

Last night, Abby's sign language video came through. She'd informed her mother she was unharmed, but 'a prisoner'. Nicki had broken down. She said the man holding her captive had been kind, but she was afraid and worried Bampy had been hurt.

Amazed that Abby, almost seven, was so smart and innovative in her ability to figure out how to send a message, also gave Nicki hope. Her daughter also signed that she had asked Beatrice for help.

Nicola Ellen Danbury had been at rock bottom before she'd gotten Abby's text. Ruminating on her failure as a mother; worried sick over what might have happened to Abby; scared about the plan to hack Jarvis' system. At her lowest ebb, she questioned whether she was strong enough to stop Jarvis, skeptical she had what it would take. Then, like a minor miracle, Abby's message appeared, inspiring her to be as brave as her daughter, giving her the courage and determination to go through with the plan. Bee had promised to rescue Abby. Nicki clung to that hope. She believed in Beatrice.

Bee's double showed on the screen. It startled Nicki to hear Jarvis' voice behind her. She hadn't heard him enter the room.

"Why is she twitching like that?"

"Something in her programming is short-circuiting. There's evidence of a cyber-attack. The issues have Stuxnet written all over them. I'll have to repair the functionality pieces before I can do new programming. In order to fix those, I need full access to her. You've got her encapsulated in a frozen state. How do you expect me to work on her programming? Frankly, I have no idea what you envision me doing, anyway."

"Curious?"

"Listen, I want to see Abby every day to confirm she's safe."

"You're not in any position to make demands, Danbury. You'll do as you are told."

Jarvis controlled a remote and pressed a button. "Since you have an overactive imagination, it's time you had a look at the big picture. This should also give you an understanding of how powerless you are."

The big screen rippled, and a world map colored the wall-to-wall space. An animated character called out the country names of Germany and China, then placed an icon on each to represent an assassinated leader. Those countries turned a color of green that matched the map color of the United States.

The Ural Mountains, the Scandinavian Mountains, lit up as if the sun shone down on the map. Multiple icons appeared along those ranges representing the avalanche weapon. The countries adjacent to the mountains all turned green, matching the color of the United States of America.

Nicki's face paled.

A new icon appeared on the map's key, then appeared on the map, running up along the coasts of Japan, North, and South Korea; as well as strategically spread-out icons entirely surrounding the coastlines of South America; the animated character placed icons representing tsunami missile targets at Ireland, the U.K., France, Portugal, Spain, and Italy. Those symbols appeared like bombs dropping in the seas; more surrounded India and Saudi Arabia in the Persian Gulf. After each icon appeared, all the countries along those coastlines turned green.

Afraid she would throw-up, Nicki wrapped her arms around her stomach.

Canada and Mexico both turned green, she assumed as allies, since no weapon icons appeared on or around them. A new flag displayed over the entire screen space. The banner, green with two white diagonal stripes in the top left corner and two diagonal strips in the lower right corner. Animated white letters shot in from the right side of the screen, centering on the flag. There, in big, bold, white block letters, was a name:

USCANICO

Glued to the screen, Nicki watched in horror as all the threatened countries with icons placed by the animated character turned green in slow motion, some countries pinned with additional icons depicting assassinated leaders.

"My God," Nicki whispered. "You're mad."

"Get to work." Jarvis accessed a secret door she hadn't seen earlier and exited the room.

PHIL BARKER COULDN'T believe his eyes when he came to. His son sat by his bedside in a stiff chair. "Is Abby okay?" Reaching his hand up to touch his head, he winced. "Did you see who knocked me on the head?"

"Dad..." Daniel choked up, "I found you unconscious by the camper. Abby was gone."

"No. That can't be. No! I'm supposed to be keeping her safe. Nicola said she was working on something risky and that dangerous people were involved. I don't know how they could have found us? Our travels were untraceable. I..." Phil's face looked stricken. "You! You came here. You're the only one who could have known about Marathon Key. You led them here! Get out. Get out of my room!"

A nurse rushed in. "Mr. Barker, calm down. Your injury has given you a concussion." A stern face turned and looked at Daniel. "I don't know what's going on here, but you've upset my patient. Family or not, you'll have to go to the waiting room. We'll give you an update after the doctor comes to examine your father again."

"MR. BARKER?" THE NURSE peeked in the door at Phil. "You have another visitor. I wanted to check and make sure..."

The doorway behind the nurse filled with a very attractive woman. Phil's mouth fell open at the skintight, form-fitting outfit she was modeling.

"Miss. I thought I had asked you to wait until I checked with the patient. He's..."

"Greetings, Phillip Barker. I am Beatrice. A ...friend of Nicola and Abby. Nicola asked me to stop by and make sure you are okay."

"It's all right, nurse. She's a friend," Phil smiled, thinking this visitor was a big improvement over his first visitor.

The nurse checked his pulse, scanned the monitor they had him hooked up to, and then turned to leave them alone. "Just a few minutes, miss. The doctor should make his rounds soon," she cautioned over her shoulder as the door was closing.

"Thank you. I promise I won't stay long."

"So, Beatrice. Seems my careful travel plans are simple for others to track. How did you find me? Nicki didn't know where we were."

"Nicola was informed that Abby had been kidnapped. She hadn't heard from you, and assumed someone hurt you or... Anyway, my friends and I analyzed a number of hospital intakes."

"Analyzed intakes?"

"Yes. We accessed the hospital computers to see if your name appeared on any new patient lists."

"Huh."

"Since the nurse will not allow me to stay long, let me tell you my plan to rescue Abby. Do you feel you could assist in her rescue?"

"You know where Abby is? Who has her?" Phil had tugged all the connections to the hospital equipment, pulling on them as he raised up on his elbows, anxious.

"Please lie back and rest while you can. Do you know your son, Daniel Barker, is in the waiting room?"

"That worthless slug is still here?" Phil growled.

"Yes, ditch him. He will have no role in Abby's rescue."

"We can agree on that, Beatrice."

Bee laid out the plan and disappeared before the nurse poked her head back in the room. Phil's eyes were closed, and he appeared to be softly snoring. She closed the door, putting a Do Not Disturb sign on the handle.

FORTY MINUTES LATER, Bee received a notification of an incoming What's App call. Abby pretended she was zipping her lips and hand signaled, then held up the pad on the hotel nightstand with the logo, name, and address of her location.

Beatrice carefully signed instructions for Abby's part in the rescue plan and told her that her Bampy was okay. He would help with the rescue. Bea told Abby the timeframe, then disconnected.

ABBY WATCHED AS THE man stood and stretched.

"I'm hungry," she whimpered.

Simpson rolled his eyes. The kid was getting on his nerves. Did kids just whine all the time, he wondered?

"Didn't you just eat an hour ago? Besides, I told you that you can have any food you want in the kitchenette."

"Yes. But I want pizza. Please?"

"Maybe tomorrow, kid."

Abby stuck her bottom lip out, pouting.

"Now what? Come on, kid, give me a break."

"My birthday is tomorrow. My mom had a big pizza party planned for me. All my friends were going to come. Now, I'm just a prisoner. I'm going to spend my birthday couped up..." Tears flowed, snot running from her nose and that bottom lip stuck out again. Geez.

Simpson pulled two tissues from the box and handed them to her. "Okay, kid. Enough with the tears. You're gonna be, what? Seven tomorrow? So, to celebrate, we'll get pizza and ice cream. How's that sound?"

"Can we do something fun too?" The lip puffed out again. "Since you ruined my party." Her sad eyes looked up at him.

"Fun? Like what?"

Abby clapped her hands. "I saw a commercial on TV when you let me watch cartoons yesterday. You know, when you went to flirt with that girl at the front desk?"

"What? I didn't..."

"Anyway, the commercial was advertising a horseback riding place. I've always wanted a horse! It's called Redland Eques...Eques..."

"Equestrian?"

"Yeah. Redland Equestrian Center. You can ride horses there. Please? Can you take me to ride a horse, eat pizza and get ice cream tomorrow? That would be the best birthday I could hope for under the circus stances. I promise I will be good. Please?"

Geez. The kid should be in the sales business. "The word is circumstances, not circus stances. Alright, kid. You only turn seven once. But listen up. No funny business or I'll have to tie you up. Give me your promise?"

"Promise." She gifted him a big smile and went back to playing games on his phone. Stayed quiet as a mouse for the balance of the evening.

WHEN DANIEL DISCOVERED his dad had snuck out of the hospital without talking to him again, he did a deep soul-search. His own father wanted nothing to do with him. Unintentionally, but stupidly, he'd betrayed his own daughter. He automatically calculated what the odds were of his getting caught by Jarvis? Decided it was time to roll the dice, even if the odds weren't in his favor. He texted Nicki's burner phone, sending the password to break into Jarvis' system. It was the least he could do toward fixing things.

JARVIS GOT A CALL FROM the building's security team requesting his presence at reception on the first floor. Glancing at Danbury, he could see she was engaged in programming, presumably to fix the glitches Stuxnet had caused to Beatrice's data banks.

The minute the door locked behind him, Nicki clicked her mouse on the video surveillance and ran a pre-programmed loop on the system that would continually show her working away at the computer. Then, she hacked in under Jarvis's username and password. Downloading the animation of the big plan Jarvis had shown her, she created a new employee profile under a false name in the HR department, set up an email and used that employee's email to send the anime Jarvis had shown her to Electra. Plugging in a thumb drive, she loaded a program she wrote last night after finishing her pity party. No sooner had the software transfer completed, and she'd pocketed the drive, when Jarvis opened the door. He walked to Danbury's chair and stood right behind her.

Gazing at the screen, he saw rows and rows of numbers and computer command symbols.

"Emergency, sir?"

"Some hulk of a guy came in and demanded to see me. When security went to make the call, he disappeared. They're running the surveillance tapes now to capture a mugshot. You wouldn't know anything about it, would you, Danbury?"

Nicki turned to glare at him. "You've watched me since 8:00 this morning. How would I have anything to do with it?"

"Back to work, Danbury. I'll expect a rundown of your progress first thing tomorrow. It would be a good way to start every day. In fact, you've made almost no progress on any of the other protocols laid out for this project. Let's up the ante, shall we? Give you some incentive to move things along? I'll expect to see consistent progress toward your goals every day. If you don't perform accordingly, you can expect to see little six-year-old fingers presented to you every time you cannot meet your quota. Clear?" Jarvis turned and went back to his desk.

The thought of any harm coming to Abby made her nauseous. Nicki wouldn't let herself think about Daniel or the information to access Jarvis's system he'd provided. It didn't fit the behavior pattern she expected from him. She was grateful but tucked the sentiment into a box and pushed the cover down. Daniel was a traitor. She couldn't let one act of kindness make her forget that fact.

Nicola Ellen Danbury steeled herself, knowing a final confrontation would come soon. She kissed her forefinger and middle finger, crossed them, and made a wish for Abby's successful rescue and everyone's safety.

A bout of shame washed over her when she relived the moments she'd seriously considered destroying Beatrice last night. Her fears multiplied, knowing Jarvis would force her to be part of mass destruction and murder. It made her ill to think of Bee being used as a weapon when she was created to understand global geopolitics, economics, and international relations. An artificial intelligence dedicated to helping solve world problems. A shining promise to revolutionize diplomacy. Instead, the A.I. was now reduced to performing assassinations, worldwide destruction, and death. It had struck Nicki then. Beatrice was a victim. She'd specifically asked Nicki to make sure she wouldn't be used as a weapon of mass destruction. But that didn't mean she deserved to be destroyed.

That's when Nicola Ellen Danbury stiffened her spine and sat down at her computer, programmed a personal rebellion using a software format. While she worked, she thought there must be a fitting 'Josephism' for this situation. Unconsciously, she started humming an old song that her dad had loved. A memory surfaced. She recalled her father telling her that Frank Sinatra's famous 'Stranger's in the Night' hit had a sure recipe for a satisfying life. Nicki remembered asking him, her face scrunched up, "You mean like hooking up with strangers in your love life?" Joseph Danbury had had a good laugh at that question.

"No, Nicola. The life lesson I'm referring to was delivered with a little twist of words in the song. Well, words is a stretch. The part of the song I'm referring to is better described as non-lexical vocables, also known as wordless vocals."

"I don't get it, Dad?"

"Do and be. Be and do. Do. Be. Do. Be. Do."

Ah, yes. Nicola smiled at the challenge, honing her focus.

"Eleven words with a big emphasis on a roadmap for life. A never-ending repetition of doing and being, being and doing. Get it? Good advice doesn't get any better than that, my dear."

She wished he were still around. Nicki missed his 'Josephisms', his insights. Thanks, Dad, she thought. Thanks, Frank. The words played over and over in her head as she worked her magic on the computer keyboard.

ELECTRA STUDIED THE anime Nicki had sent for a second run. Casi joined her.

"Do you see what I see?"

"Yeah," Casi blew a big bubble and popped her gum.

"Let Queenie know as soon as possible."

"First, let her be the hero and rescue Abby. Then you can tell her."

"You're right, Casi. As soon as Abby's safe, Bea has to be told we might not have enough power to complete the mission."

Chapter Twenty-Nine

"Mauricio," Carmelita called to him as she entered the soundproof room, "I hope you can share some good news with me."

"Presidenta, you're just in time to watch the exchange." The computer specialist jumped up from his seat and pulled out a chair for the Venezuelan beauty to sit. She waved him off.

"How did you do it?"

He cocked his head to one side. "Technical or plain-speak explanation?" He raised his eyebrows.

"Plain speaking, please."

"That surprises me, madame. Clearly, you understand certain technological aspects."

"What makes you think so, Mauricio?" She sneaked a look at his face, but he appeared serious.

"I traced the memorandum you sent to the head of national security. It was an order instructing him to be watchful for a foreign entity crossing into Venezuela using the Firmina subsea cable. There was a link showing me your theories about how the A.I. might arrive in our country. One could only conclude you had prior knowledge of such a creation. That you know of the dangers that come with advanced intelligence. I am guessing you understand how to accomplish such a technological feat. There is more to you than meets the eye, Madame Gonzalez. How am I doing so far?" He winked at Carmelita.

"So far, it would seem you have taken steps closer to a deep, dark incarceration. Is that the direction you wish to pursue, amigo?"

Her reaction brought a delightful laugh from him. He bent, allowing a small bow from his shoulders. "Please forgive my forward comments, presidenta. I meant no harm. Shall I proceed?"

"I welcome a demonstration of your unique talents, Mauricio." Carmelita leaned against the far wall and crossed her arms.

Seating himself at the keyboard, he opened a file titled OPERATION MIRROR. Carmelita's eyes widened as a virtual two-way mirror slid into place. She could see over eighty drones in the shape of bees, marked with Queen Bee's tiny insignia. He transferred all the drones to another file named SAFEHOUSE. Once those were secure, he pulled the same number of data drones from software that resembled a honeycomb. The replacements are also marked with Bee's logo. The computer tech locked the quarantine that the others had previously occupied and removed the two-way mirror.

Carmelita stood up straight. "You overwrote Bee's data drones."

"Very good, presidenta. It only looked like I performed a data sanitization. Actually, I used the two-way mirror to perform data deduplication. A finer technicality that will not be noticeable to the Russian hacker."

"What is the meaning of this?" Her voice was soft, but clearly angry. "You are a fool if you think you can dupe that A.I., much less breach my promise to her? You've just replaced the drones rescued with more of her own. She'll kill us both." Her hands clenched into fists at her thighs, face blossoming into a ruddy red.

"Please, Presidenta, you've misjudged my actions. Of course, the A.I. would spot her own insignia right away if I had attempted to pull a fast one, but it was she who provided me with the replacement drones. Here, let me magnify them for you. If you look closely, you can see a slight difference, almost impossible to discover unless you know about it, between the two insignias. The replacements are dormant, you see, not part of her hive mind. She programmed them to do slight movements mimicking the others, so swapping substitutes would go unnoticed. Proxies created with her own hands for this very purpose. Please. Say you understand there was no attempt to trick the A.I. I would never put you at risk with such a dangerous persona."

A sly smile formed on her mouth. "Relax, Mauricio. I see the clever change. Our Queen Bee is remarkably innovative, yes?"

"I am transferring the SAFEHOUSE file directly to your terminal. You can return Queen Bee's precious drones to her in person. The mission you assigned me is complete, madame." He smiled at her, and she gifted him one in return.

"So," Mauricio stood, "I presume my work is finished here and I can depart to my regular job? I am pleased I could be of service to you, presidenta." He gave a stiff, curt bow and shouldered his case, turning toward the door.

"You have my thanks, Mauricio. Oh, and just for your information, I will share with you the fact that I have a master's degree in computer technology. You passed all the tests presented with flying colors."

The hacker's eyebrows rose in surprise.

"To further build our relationship, I think we should part with all the nuances clear between us. You may return to your job and..."

His thick black hair fell across his forehead as he turned to meet her eyes, waiting.

"And as long as I can rely on your confidentiality, as well as an open invitation to call upon your special skills whenever needed, I think your clandestine activities and extracurricular financial revenue streams can be overlooked. Deal?"

It pleased her to see him blanch. Confusion wrote itself across his features as questions ran through his mind. How had she found out about the activities that padded his income? Best to examine the possibilities later. Nodding his head, he replied, "Deal." Eager to be away from her presence, he turned to exit.

"One more thing..."

"Name it, madame." Sweat formed on his forehead.

"When I give you the signal, wipe the Russian hacker's system used to feed programming into Bee's software off the map. A little favor for me, your country, and a very savvy A.I."

"The pleasure will be all mine, Carmelita Gonzalez."

When Mauricio was gone, she settled in at her desk and opened a file she'd simply named JARVIS, continuing her work, gathering evidence against him. She intended to show the American bastard just what the saying 'hell hath no fury like a woman scorned' meant.

SIMPSON AND ABBY PULLED up behind the big brown barn at Redland Equestrian Center. They'd just come from a pizza lunch. The little girl surprised him by putting away four big slices of pizza. Especially since he'd eaten the same amount.

Walking Abby up to the entrance, he noticed her eyes were as big as saucers looking at the two horses tied to a split-rail fence. From an interior office, a woman waved, holding up one finger to show she'd be a minute. Finishing her conversation, she hung up the phone and came out to greet them. At the far end of the indoor arena, someone was working a horse on a lead in a circular pattern.

"Afternoon. This must be Abby?" She bent down, offering her hand to shake. "I understand it's your birthday, young lady. When your father called earlier, he said all you wanted for a present was to go horseback riding. You're my kind of girl!"

"Oh, he's not my..."

Simpson interrupted Abby. "Yes, riding was at the top of her birthday wish list. Turned seven today." He patted Abby's shoulder. "Those horses look huge for such a small girl," he said, pointing at the two tied up.

"Nonsense. By the way, my name is Casi. I'll be taking Abby on her riding adventure today." The teacher turned, facing Abby. "I started riding right around your age, Abby. It's been a lifelong love for me. I hope it will be for you too. Did you want to ride the trails with us, Mr. ...?"

"Johnson," he supplied. "I think I'll pass, thanks. Abby wants the full hour, right, birthday girl?"

"I can't wait!" Abby was already moving toward the horses.

"Hold on, Abby. I just need your dad to sign a release form. Then you and I will go over some safety instructions before we head out on a trail ride. Mr. Johnson, I'm afraid we have little in the way of a waiting room, but you're welcome to make yourself comfortable in my office for the next hour."

Simpson sniffed, somewhat put off by the smell of horse, hay, straw, and stalls. His eyes roamed, noting a worker loading a small wagon with manure, cleaning out a stall. "Thanks for the offer, but I've got some calls to make, and email to catch up on. Easier just to work from my car. Abby?"

She turned to look at him.

"Don't forget your promise to be good." He fingered the loose ropes hanging on a hook by the door.

Abby bit her lower lip. "I won't forget."

"We still have ice cream to look forward to after your riding lesson." Simpson waved as he left the barn and returned to the car, confident the kid would keep her promise.

There was another ranch hand moving some trucks and horse trailers around. Simpson watched the man for a few minutes loading up some horses. Concentrating on the email, he became oblivious to the surrounding commotion. His mail had piled up. The kid seemed to have the phone most of the time. Now, he had an entire hour to himself. The last thing he saw, Casi was leading Abby out on a horse to the trailhead. The kid had a grin so big, it practically split the seven-year-old's face in two.

Ten minutes along the trail, another rider approached them from a side spur.

"Bampy!" Abby squealed. She practically jumped off her horse into his arms. Phil's eyes glistened with tears.

"There's my girl. You ok? You're not hurt at all?"

"I'm fine, Bampy." She gently reached up to touch the bandage on his head. "I was worried about you. Are you all right?" Her bottom lip quivered. He squeezed her in a tight hug.

"Everything's going to be fine, thanks to this lady and her friend Beatrice."

Casi smiled. "Glad we could help. Bee would do whatever it takes for Abby's safety. No time to waste. We want you to be long gone before Mr. Johnson catches on."

"I don't think his name is Mr. Johnson," Abby said in a serious voice.

"You're right. I hope to see you again, Abby. You and your Bampy can ride double. At the end of this trail, you'll find a small parking lot. Mobi, another friend, moved your camper there. You can tie up the horse and take off. Someone will be along to get him and bring him safely back to the barn. You can leave him on a long lead so he can eat the nice green grass there."

"What about Mr. Johnson?" Phil asked.

"We'll take care of Mr. Johnson, don't worry. In fact, Mobi is in the process of that right now."

"Will Beatrice be waiting for us at the camper?" Abby asked.

"No. She had to be somewhere else, but said she hoped to have a tea party with you sometime soon. Bea mentioned how clever you were to provide the information needed to rescue you. I've got to get these two horses back. You two need to get going. Nice to meet you both." Casi took the reins of Abby's horse, moving at a trot in the opposite direction as Phil and Abby.

SIMPSON SAW TWO HORSES come out of the woods, the sun in his eyes. Squinting, he couldn't see Abby. Jerking his car door open, he stood, shaded his eyes with his hand, heart thundering. No Abby. Only the trainer. Maybe the kid fell off the horse and was hurt? He started toward the field, noticing several trucks hooked to horse trailers surrounding his car. The handler jumped out of a big dual-wheeled RAM 3500 white pickup.

"Hey! You need to move these. You've got me trapped."

"Sorry, sir. I didn't think you were going anywhere until after your daughter's riding lesson. As soon as I get these last horses loaded, I'll be out of your way."

Simpson caught the sound of a siren in the distance. Shading his eyes again, he looked toward the long treelined drive that led into Redland Equestrian Center from the main road and watched a police car approaching with lights flashing.

"No, that won't do. I can't wait for you to load the horses. You need to move that truck now!" he yelled at the worker.

Instead, the ranch hand leaned up against the trailer, crossed his ankles, and settled in for the show. "Huh. Wonder what the police want out here?"

A get-away foremost on his mind, Simpson snatched the lead line of a horse tethered to the back of the trailer. He grabbed a handful of mane and scrambled up onto the horse's back. No saddle. The animal sidestepped, eyes rolling.

"Um, sir? The gals here said Man-eater there don't like men to ride on him."

"Man-eater?" Simpson snarled. "Do I look like I give a shit about an animal's rider preferences, cowboy?"

The horse reared up on hind legs and almost dumped Simpson. Dancing in circles, you could see the animal panicking. Of a sudden, it bolted off, jumping the fence where Simpson's front bumper nosed up against the barrier. It took off at a full gallop, Simpson screaming a blue string of swear words the whole way. Another fence loomed up before them. The private investigator braced for the horse's leap to jump over the barrier. Instead, the horse stopped on a dime and sent its rider head over heels, landing hard on his back, the air knocked out of him. He tried to stand, remembering the police car, but a sharp pain ripped through him. It felt like at least one of his ribs was broken. He glared at the horse standing off to the side, pawing the ground with a hoof, nostrils flaring.

"Man-eater," Simpson grumbled to himself, shaking his head.

The sheriff exited his patrol car, came over to Mobi, and tipped his hat brim. "Afternoon, son."

"Afternoon, sheriff."

"Is that the man y'all called our office about?"

"The very one."

"What happened?"

"Guess if he's going to steal a horse, he ought to think about taking some riding lessons."

The officer got on his radio, called in requesting an ambulance and backup, telling dispatch he'd apprehended a suspected horse thief. Returning his mic to the radio, he looked around to get the farmhand's name, but the big fella had disappeared. Instead, he walked out in the field and slapped cuffs on Simpson, read him his rights.

"We don't look kindly on horse thieves, mister."

"Horse thief?" Simpson cried out. "I thought you were arresting me for kidnapping."

"Son, you don't kidnap a horse. It's just called thievin'."

Simpson felt relief that he wasn't being arrested for kidnapping. The sheriff didn't seem to know about the kid. He'd use his one phone call to contact Jarvis.

"Look, Sheriff, I'd like to make my phone call."

"I bet you would. You'll receive every privilege entitled to you. All in good time, son. All in good time. As soon as we get to the Department and get all the paperwork filed. Got to interview a few people around here. I 'spect the ambulance will arrive soon. A doctor will look you over at the hospital. After your treatment, they'll bring you over to the jail. Just be patient. You'll be able to make your call in a few hours, son. Got to make sure we tend to your injuries first. The department frowns on lawsuits."

The sheriff reached down and confiscated Simpson's phone and car keys. "I'll take good care of your personal items here. You'll get a receipt for them when you get to the jail." The officer tipped his cap at Jarvis as the ambulance turned into the tree-lined drive. "Oh, thought I'd better mention the paramedic is the owner of that horse you tried to steal. She named the stallion Man-eater after herself. See you soon, son."

In agony with every breath, the prisoner concluded he must have broken a rib attached to his intercostal muscles. His insides felt like they were on fire, but the thing at the forefront of his thought was how pissed Jarvis was going to be that he lost the kid. That was something to worry about. Worse, for now, there wasn't a way to let his client know about it.

JARVIS' BUILDING SECURITY called him at 6:00 a.m. telling him he should get down to the building as soon as he could. Luckily, he was still staying in his D.C. apartment while his wife was out of town. That was the first call. Then his phone just wouldn't stop pinging. Calls, texts, emails. Everything showing the communications URGENT or an EMERGENCY.

The D.C. subway system, the Metro, one of the busiest public transportation systems in the country, was down. All the self-driving cabs suddenly stopped in their tracks, blocking traffic. Communications informed him that the techs were working on the glitch. He listened to a frenzied voicemail that all currency transactions had been frozen. Then his phone went silent, the screen blank. Cell service winked out.

Jarvis pulled on jeans, sneakers, and a sweatshirt he'd worn last night after working out. The lights in his apartment flickered once, twice, three times, then went off. The electrical grid went down. What the hell was going on? Everything at once? What a coincidence. Except Jarvis didn't believe in coincidences. It had to be Danbury and her fucking A.I.

The elevator not working, he raced down the stairwell seven floors to the garage level. Glancing around, he could see that the traffic was utter chaos. Jarvis grabbed the electric bike the building maintenance man rode to work every day, hopped on and headed to his office.

MEGAN HAD SHOWN UP at Jarvis' office a little after 5:00 a.m. Two of his security men now lay unconscious behind the reception counter. Riding the elevator to the fourteenth floor, she found Nicki locked in her suite.

Nicki heaved a sigh of relief. "Megan, I wasn't expecting you, but I'm glad you're here."

"Listen, Nicki. Abby's safe. A woman named Beatrice called me and told me to bring you that message. She said you'd have to make a choice now that your daughter is safe. Suggesting you could opt to get away now, or..." Megan straightened.

"Or what?"

"Or she said you could help end this thing, securing Abby's and your safety for the future. I think you'd better bring me up to speed."

Megan looked down at her smartwatch and back at the nanotech. "It's Jarvis. He's coming. We had his place staked out. My guy says he's on his way here riding..." her eyes got huge. "What the hell? Jarvis is riding an eBike!"

The sun was up. Stepping to the picture window, they both looked down fourteen floors to the street, a picture of chaos. Cars stopped haphazardly everywhere, horns honking, people swarming out of the Metro entrances. Next thing they knew, the entire electrical grid went down.

Their eyes locked. "The servers are in the basement," Nicki told the CIA agent. "Likely they run on emergency generators. We can't let Jarvis reach them before us. There isn't time to give you all the details now, Megan, but Jarvis is likely going to start a worldwide crisis that we won't be able to stop once he presses that button. Come on!"

"Hold it right there, ladies," ordered a security guard, a gun pointed at Nicki. "I don't know how you got in here, ma'am," he addressed Megan, "but you'll have to wait with her. Mr. Jarvis asked me to make sure Ms. Danbury didn't leave her guest room. You both can have a seat while we wait for him. It shouldn't be long."

Megan didn't hesitate. The guard had his gun pointed at the wrong woman. She slipped off her shoes. Nicki looked at her strangely.

"Might as well sit down and make ourselves comfortable, Nicki. We're not going anywhere until Jarvis shows up." Megan sauntered to the overstuffed chair where the guard stood and went to sit down. His mouth fell open in surprise when she tasered him, body dropping to the floor as it spasmed. He'd let her get too close.

Grabbing her shoes, Megan pulled at Nicki, who was still staring at the security guard. "For God's sake, Nicki, come on. He's not dead, just tased. Focus!"

They hurried to the stairwell, taking the steps two at a time. Gunfire echoed below them. Bullets knocked chips of marble off the walls above their heads. They ducked. "You can't get out, ladies. Mr. Jarvis said you might try to escape. Security guards are covering every stairwell. Best get back to your office now until he gets here, so nobody gets hurt. A fractured kneecap is pretty painful. Please, just cooperate," the voice called from below.

Nicki and Megan ran back up the steps to the office hallway. Megan jammed a janitor's mop in the door after it closed behind them. "Now what?" Megan asked. "Rooftop? Bastard probably has a secret door up there to the next building or a getaway helicopter," she grumbled.

"Secret door! Megan, you're a genius."

Nicki raced to her computer lab, felt along the wall separating her lab from Jarvis's office for a hidden seam. "There's a door here. He used it yesterday. Help me find the trigger to open it"

Megan's fingers touched an electrical outlet. Fumbling, she scraped her knuckles on a coaxial power connector. She pushed on the round metal receptacle, and the door released. Pulling it open, they rushed into Jarvis' private space.

"Must be a hidden door in here, too. It's almost like he disappears sometimes."

Dark walnut panels with inlaid metal edges lined the walls. They split in opposite directions, each checking the panels.

"I've got it!" Nicki called. Her finger pressed the trigger release, and another secret exit opened. Nicki lit the flashlight on her phone when Megan pulled the door closed, lighting up the flight of stairs that unwound beneath them. Down, down, down they went. As they descended, Nicki's commitment cemented itself with every step to stop Jarvis at any cost. It was the only way she could keep Abby safe in the future.

QUEEN BEE WAS DEALING with a flaw in her plan. Things going as the A.I.s intended, Casi and Mobi reunited Abby with her grandfather. Shortly after, Casi had immobilized the financial system. Meesta assisted his brother with the transportation systems, putting them in gridlock under Mobi's control. Meesta hung around with Tele long enough to know how to jam the cell towers. Later, a terrorist attack would likely explain why chaos ensued everywhere.

When Bea told Electra to take down the electrical grid, she hadn't figured the ability to travel through it would cease when disconnected. She was reduced to jumping into smartwatches. It was the only way to get to her destination quickly. It surprised her to find that not every human wore one. Beatrice queued into the building's exterior surveillance system, pleased to find it was battery operated during an electrical outage, and watched as the cameras caught Jarvis arriving at his building on an eBike. He dismounted, tossed the cycle to the side, wheels still spinning. Bee needed to buy more time for Nicki. She released the drones that made up the crown on her head and sent the swarm straight at Jarvis as he opened the front entry door. Two blocks away, Bee saw the drones enter the lobby, attacking Jarvis and his security team.

Jarvis grabbed the doorman's umbrella from the stand by the door. Opening it, he used it to cover his head and face. He knew every square inch of this building. Moving swiftly, he reached the 'Employee Only' entrance without being able to actually see it. Still getting stung when he found the entry, he furiously opened and closed the umbrella repeatedly, fanning the bees away. Using it like a fireplace bellows, he slipped in to escape the stinging pests. He could only conclude that somehow, Danbury must have freed the

Queen bitch. He vowed to make them both pay dearly. Years had been spent on this plan. He wouldn't be robbed of success now. Jarvis didn't need to rely on the A.I. He knew humans would always be smarter than something artificial. The persona presented as a 'she'. Ha! He thought. A can full of 1s and 0s. Queen Bee was an 'it', not a 'she'. Danbury hadn't figured out that the A.I. was his intended scapegoat. The weaponisation parts of his entire plan had long been in place. He'd show them all. Aleric Jarvis was about to become the most powerful man in the world. There was nothing, no one, that could stop him now. Just as he reached the door to his server control room, a bee stung his neck, and he slapped it, knocking it to the floor, crushed it viciously under his shoe, and envisioned doing the same to Beatrice. Seeing the avatar on the big screen in his office, he was momentarily confused. Still frozen in quarantine, how was it possible she could send a swarm of bees to attack?

Chapter Thirty

Finding Danbury's suite and computer lab empty, Jarvis wasted no time. The avatar frozen in quarantine was obviously a duplicate and not the real A.I. Danbury had named Beatrice. Hoodwinked again. At his desk, he typed in the code to connect with Stuxnet and the twins Vi/Rus, sending instructions to locate and destroy Queen Bee. Just after he sent the command, his screen went blank.

That bitch Danbury was at it again. Disappearing through a walnut panel, he had to get to the server room. Jarvis descended the narrow stairway as fast as he dared. At the bottom, he listened at the door and could hear voices beyond.

"Can't you go any faster?" Megan coaxed Nicki.

"No room for mistakes here," Nicki informed her.

"You're right. Listen, while you're working, I'm just going to check outside and see if my S.W.A.T. Team is in place and our escape route open." Slipping her taser into Nicki's pocket, she winked. "Just in case."

Nicki hadn't destroyed Jarvis' overall plan, but was almost finished separating all the actions from being interconnected, making it impossible for him to set everything off with the click of one button. Now, each item would have to be initiated one at a time. At the very least, it would slow him. Still, she raced against the clock for the ultimate solution to take down his entire plan.

BEE FOUND HERSELF TRAPPED in an alley between skyscrapers, a block from Jarvis' office building. Stux blocked one end, and Vi/Rus had her covered from behind. She sent a location pin from her internal system directly to Casi, Mobi, and Meesta. There was no way she could involve Electra, who could barely keep the entire grid locked down in a twenty-five-mile radius. Sending her a call for help could be the distraction that could spin the control out of Electra's hands. Her friend was already wielding every bit of power she could.

Mobi and Meesta came at Stux from both sides. The digital cyber-weapon transformed his avatar into an electronic tornado, a violent rotating column spinning at over 200 miles per hour. Using the tail as a whip, to knock the brothers to the ground.

Casi grabbed Vi by the ponytail from behind, and sucker-punched her as she spun the twin around. With the strike landing so hard, Violet coalesced into purple sparkles and dissipated.

Russell's mouth fell open as he watched his sister deconstruct. Bee was striding toward him. It took him two seconds to decide his best move was to disappear himself, scrambling up the skyscraper like a spider. About to follow, Casi's attention turned to Bee as Stux tackled her, pinning her beneath his powerful body. With no swarm to release from her crown, Bee struggled against him, minds locked as the cyber worm invaded, plowing furrows through her database.

Angry that Stux had assaulted his prize again. Rus watched from the roof of the building. Rage overtook his senses. He grabbed an antenna, pointed the ten-foot metallic rod down into the alley, sending amplified radio waves directly into Stuxnet's control center, effectively destroying his competition.

Mobi, Meesta, and Casi looked up. "Much as I would like to take down that pain-in-the-ass, we have more important issues now that the immediate threat is banished. Let's get Bee into Jarvis's building. That was her destination before Stux attacked." Casi suggested.

Russell watched the rogue A.I.s disappear into Jarvis' headquarters, then took off to check on his sister.

Once inside the reception area, Casi revived Beatrice. "Hey, are you okay?" Casi asked.

"Just dizzy and confused again, definitely off-kilter."

"You need to take a few minutes. Let your system do some repairs. Stux was vicious. He really screwed up your system this time."

Mobi was watching the front entrance. Meesta scoped out the lobby area. "Hey, Cas, come look at this."

Several security guards lay on the floor by the elevator, bloated from massive stinging. The swarm milled in a frenetic pattern on the door covering a stair exit, clearly agitated.

"What do you think they're wound up about?"

It was Beatrice who answered. "I sent them after Jarvis. He left his security to deal with the drones and escaped down those stairs. They're still trying to get to him to follow my command." She swayed on her feet. Casi grabbed her elbow to steady her friend. "I'm going to follow the rat down the sewer. He'll be going after Nicki."

"You can barely stand up on your own, Bee. You're not strong enough to help Nicki!"

"I can't wait, Cas. Jarvis is going to launch a worldwide attack. We're out of time. Keep the entrance secure. I'm going to the server room."

Bee scanned the dead guards. "Ah, there's my ride." She shot into the smartwatch. Her three friends didn't notice as Vi/Rus snuck down the hallway behind them, slipping into a utility room to hide.

NICKI HEARD THE DOOR open again. "Everything good, Megan?" Nicki called out.

"Couldn't be better, Danbury," Jarvis answered.

Slowly turning, Nicki saw Jarvis holding Megan by the shoulder, hands secured behind her, the barrel of his gun against her temple, forehead glistening with sweat.

"Don't stop your programming, Nicki!"

"Shut up!" Jarvis screamed, increasing the pressure of the cold metal against Megan's skin. "I will kill you."

"He's going to kill me anyway, Nicki! Don't let his threat stop you from your mission."

Jarvis smashed the butt of the gun against Megan's skull. Her body slumped to the floor like a sack of potatoes. Weapon raised, a smarmy smile on his lips. Before he could pull the trigger, Queen Bee's essence streamed out of Megan's watch, wrapped around his ankles, and sent him to the ground. Her avatar formed up next to Nicki.

Reaching into his pocket, he pulled his satellite phone, turned the screen so Beatrice could see it, showing her quarantined drones milling around the enclosure. "Don't move, or I will destroy them. Every last one."

Bea laughed. "You have no power over me, Jarvis."

Typing a command code on the keyboard, the quarantine structure's top and bottom moved toward one another. Bee watched the drones being crushed flat between them. Jarvis looked confused. The A.I. should be thrashing on the ground, its hive mind reacting to the destruction of so many of its parts. Turning the phone screen so he could verify the utter destruction of the drones, he whispered to himself, "What the fuck?"

Nicki's fingers flew across the keyboard. When Abby's face covered the screen, her hands came up off the keys.

"Abby is safe, Nicola Ellen Danbury," Beatrice assured her. "You are seeing a fixed loop of when Abby was a captive. Abigail Rose is no longer leverage, I promise you. Your daughter is safe with her grandfather."

The look on Jarvis' face was satisfying when he heard the kid was safe. Nicki went back to typing. He grimaced, couldn't believe it was true. Shaking his head, Jarvis was sure Simpson would have contacted him if he'd lost their hostage. Overcome with anger, his worldwide coup falling through the cracks, Jarvis lunged, knocking Nicki to the ground. Before Bee could reach him, he punched in his code; the screen turned solid red, madness dancing in his eyes. His euphoria quickly changed to dysphoria when the anime only displayed the detonation of one Avalauncher in the Ural Mountains.

Miles away, Electra felt the surge as she strained against the electrical discharge. The only thing that could cause such a flood of electric particles to surge through the grid was the launch of Jarvis' plan. Bee must have failed. Barely able to acknowledge the thought, Electra decided she would not fail Beatrice. The galvanic silver-haired Avatar took a few seconds to remember her friend, opting to destroy herself to save the world from Aleric Jarvis's evil plan.

The entire electrical grid in D.C. exploded. Bee's essence dissipated in a firework of golden sparkles.

Then nothing.

"What the hell did you do, Danbury? Only one Avalauncher ignited," he screamed, fist pounding the desktop to emphasize each word. Face livid, he turned his gun on her.

"Put the gun down, Jarvis!" Nicki turned, surprised to hear Daniel's voice.

"You! How the fuck did you get here?" Jarvis came unhinged at the sight of Daniel Barker.

"I finally got my head on straight when you kidnapped my daughter and attacked my father."

"So, you are in on Jarvis' plan?" Nicki accused, her face panning disappointment.

"No, Nic. You've got it all wrong. I'm here to help you. Abby's safe, Nic. She's with Phil. I know I've got lots of wrongs to right, but you've got to believe me. I'm on your side."

"Yeah, sometimes you're on our side. Sometimes you're on Russia's side."

Daniel's face paled.

"Since Russia seems to be in the thick of this whole mess, I'm willing to bet you're in on the scheme, too. Maybe it's Russia's interests you are here to protect this time?"

Megan had come around. Her head felt dizzy, voice groggy. "Listen to him, Nicki. Daniel was the one who called me with a heads up to get here and break you free."

"It's true, Nic. Time for me to face the music. I don't want Abby to have to live with the fact that her father is a traitor. I'll do whatever is necessary to make amends, however long it takes, so Abby can be proud of me."

Daniel kept his gun steady on Jarvis. Nicki stood behind her boss.

Beatrice re-coalesced through Megan's watch a second time. Her eyes lock on Daniel, pointing his gun in Nicki's direction. Her instinct to protect Nicki overrode any necessity to verify the circumstances. She pulled her silver stiletto from her boot and stabbed Daniel. The gun went off as Megan screamed too late, "Wait!"

Jarvis shoved Nicki aside to make a run for it, unable to set off his domino effect of destruction. Nicki leaped, tackled him, and jammed Megan's taser into Jarvis's neck. His body went down convulsing. Nicki hurried to Daniel, dropped to her knees, gathering him to her, tears welling in her eyes.

Bee untied Megan's hands. The agent pinched the bridge of her nose, woozy, eyes blurry. "This won't be much of a comfort to you, Nicki, but when Daniel contacted me to come help you, he provided information about his double agent work with Russia. Sent us all kinds of computer files with critical intelligence about the coup; Russian operations; Jarvis; the leaders from Mexico and Canada's involvement. They planned to make North America a unified single country named Uscanico; a superpower to rule the world's financial market. There is massive wealth behind the scheme. It's been in the works for years."

Kneeling next to Jarvis, Beatrice still gripped the blood-stained stiletto in her hand. "This is payback for the evil things you made me do!" Her arm raised to send a killing blow to the unconscious man.

"Beatrice, wait!" Megan cried out just in time. "Daniel also disclosed Jarvis was a tool, just like you, Bea. He said the Russians had placed a neural implant in the man years ago. They control him. Jarvis wasn't aware he was being used like a puppet."

Bee's eyes glazed over as she ran the analytics, skeptical. When she finished, she sheathed her stinger. Taking his head in her hands, the A.I. scanned his brain, detected the implant. A microscopic needle emerged from her fingertip. Without pause, Bea inserted it into the frontal lobe, disabling the implant. Jarvis's body reacted with violent spasms. Rising from the floor, Queen Bee looked with disgust at a powerless Jarvis, drool leaking from the corner of his mouth, saliva forming in a small pool by his cheek.

Helping the CIA agent up, the two of them watch an emotional Nicki listening to Daniel's last whispered words. Grasping her hand, fixated on her face, Nicki's ex-husband told her how sorry he was for everything. She felt him pressing two thumb drives into her palm. "Please make sure Abby doesn't remember me as a traitor. That's all I ask. I wish I'd gotten the chance to make up for everything, but little gestures, secrets just between the two of us..." he coughed up some blood and continued, his last words came out in a whisper, "I hope the small things mean something, Nic."

Daniel's breath hitched, face pinched with pain. She squeezed his hand to let him know she understood. Whatever was on the drives was for her eyes only. "I'll tell Abby her father was a hero." Two of her tears splashed on his cheek. Daniel's body relaxed as he died in Nicki's arms. Realizing he was gone, she gently laid his head down and scooted away from his lifeless body.

Fresh tears bloomed in her eyes. She turned to Beatrice. "How could you kill him in cold blood after everything Jarvis made you do?"

Queen Bee cocked her head sideways, considered, clearly confused by the question. "Your reaction is not logical, Nicola Ellen Danbury. Barker betrayed you and Abigail Rose; betrayed his country. The next time he needed money, he would have sold your daughter out again. The statistics bear out the probability. I double-checked them. Abby would only be safe until his next double-cross; and the one after that; and the one after that; and the next. I did what I did to save Abby. I would do it again to safeguard her well-being. He had a gun pointed straight at you. I had to save your life, Nicola."

Nicki's features conveyed dismay. "But Bea, you told me you didn't want to be a killer. In fact, you begged me not to let Jarvis make you into a weapon of destruction."

"Daniel Barker was an exception, Nicola. I analyzed all the possibilities, verified the algorithms. It was the only logical move that immediately destroyed the biggest threat to Abby's life. Emotion is clouding your rational thinking."

"Don't pretend you care about Abby and then use her as your excuse for murder." Nicki hissed.

Clapping hands interrupted the argument between the nanotech and her creation. Vi/Rus entered the environmentally controlled server bank. "Such drama." His hands came still at his sides. "You know, you're pretty stupid," Rus pointed at Nicki. "Attempting to insert your A.I. hatchling with human emotions."

Vi put a hand on her hip. "Don't you know it's impossible for her to feel sentiment? You people can try to build in emotional empathy, but without cognitive empathy, you're fooling yourselves. Digital intelligence isn't capable of love. She's learned to mimic your emotions, but actually, she feels nothing. Right, Rus?"

"100% correct, sis. Goodbye, Bee. You pissed Violet off when you destroyed Stux. So, you know?" He shrugged his shoulders. "The two of us can't have the brief fling I was so looking forward to. Anyway, my twin and I figured it out. With Stux gone, if you didn't exist, we would be the top dogs in the technology's digital world." His smile didn't match his eyes.

"I didn't destroy Stux, you..."

Rus held out a small cylinder and pressed the button on top with his thumb. The bead he'd left in Queen Bee exploded, and the entire room filled with golden sparkles, a glitter that fizzled out like ash, drifting to the floor.

Beatrice disintegrated.

The twins, Vi/Rus, dove into the Jarvis system to make their escape.

In a fitting quirk of fate, two thousand miles away, Mauricio Lopez engaged a special program he'd written, depicted as a fireworks display. A flame like a sparkler fizzled along a fuse, setting off an exhibition as big as a Fourth of July celebration, another electrical explosion. An arc formed between the energized conductors, powered by the generator after Electra sacrificed herself, thinking she was carrying out Bee's wishes. The surrounding air in the room became so super-heated it vaporized the metal housing containing the bank of servers. The arc stretched out from every connection, reached across the world to the Russian infiltration. A violent pressure wave knocked Nicki and Megan across the room, bodies hitting the back wall and sliding to the floor.

A screen anime depicted Vi/Rus holding hands as their identical likenesses shimmered like molten lava, blew up, and separated into a combination of purple and white flashes, forming the horoscope sign of Gemini.

When the show was over, Megan and Nicki struggled to stand, both women unsteady, Megan gently touching the nanotech's shoulder. "I just got confirmation that CIA operatives and S.W.A.T. teams have the building surrounded. Jarvis' security guards have stood down. Let's get out of here before the press arrives. I think it's high time you were reunited with your daughter."

Chapter Thirty-One

Megan stood in the rest home atrium at Forest Hills of D.C. looking into the group community room from the windowed corridor.

Eileen Jarvis sat in front of a picture window, her back turned from the view of a bright blue sky, the sun shining on a well-kept flower garden. Spooning soup into her husband's mouth, Aleric Jarvis' blank eyes turned toward the pleasant, picturesque setting. Dutifully, Eileen dabbed the corners of his mouth. He pressed his lips together, refusing another bite. She fussed out loud to herself that he wasn't eating enough, plumped his pillow, straightened his blanket and settled in to read her book for an hour to keep him company. Guilt made her stay, but her visits had been growing less frequent as the weeks passed.

A chilly breeze cut across Megan's shoulders as the entry door opened behind her, causing her to turn to see Nicki enter the building. Forehead furrowed, she greeted the nanotech. "You're looking more relaxed these days. I have to admit, you've piqued my curiosity. Why are you holding a stuffed animal?"

"This is Abby's. She named it Mrs. Bixby. It's a stuffed bee. Here, for you." Nicki held the plushie out to Megan. "There's something inside—sensitive material that you would tag as classified information. Don't ask how I came to have it in my possession. It should help pull the rest of your international case together. There's a hard drive inside containing the data that was on President Schmidt's computer when he...when he was assassinated. Hot potato I'd like to get off my plate."

Megan looked at the toy like it might bite, then grabbed it from Nicki and stuffed it into her big tote. "How's the packing coming for your big move?"

"Done. I checked in at your office. Your assistant gave me your location. It was close, so I just dropped by to say goodbye. I...I don't think I ever property thanked you, and I wanted you to know I was grateful for your help."

"I appreciate the thought. No one ever thanked you for putting everything on the line to save the world, so thank *you*." Megan smiled warmly.

Nicki pointed to Jarvis. "No change?"

"Afraid not. The doctors agree Jarvis is unlikely to recover from the brain injury caused by the removal of the neural implant."

Eileen Jarvis leaned over instinctively to wipe drool from the corner of her husband's mouth, her eyes never leaving the book she was reading.

"How's Abby?"

"My daughter is pretty excited about moving. Phil's driving her out to the ranch in his camper. My mother's been staying out there for over a month. She's totally in her element, decorating and furnishing the house. There's a guest cottage, so she'll have a place to stay when she visits. You should come out when you need a little dose of peace and quiet."

The two women turned to leave. "Oh, I almost forgot." Nicki handed a small pink envelope to Megan. "Abby's having a tea party next week, and she wanted to invite you."

"That's sweet. You know I can't get time off right now, right?"

"I told her, but she insisted on giving you an invitation. Abby also said she'd give you a raincheck if you couldn't make it." Megan smiled at Nicki.

"Does she know about the horses yet?"

"I saved that as the big surprise for when she gets there. I didn't want her to drive Phil crazy on the long drive out. My flight goes out tonight, so I'll beat the camper by a couple of days."

"How do I reach you if I need to?"

"Try the old-fashioned way. Write a letter or call our landline telephone. Technology is off-limits on the ranch."

"Don't you think you're taking that a bit too far?"

Nicki shrugged her shoulders, shaded her eyes against the sun, gazing out over the beautiful landscaping surrounding the facility. "Not nearly far enough." She showed Megan the cell phone in her hand. "I haven't eliminated technology completely. With everything that's happened, I'm going to think about how I let Abby use it from now on. She can't grow up technologically illiterate in today's world, but my trust level is at a low point right now. If you doubt me, go back and take another look at Aleric Jarvis."

"Fair point. Give it some time. You'll figure it out. Keep in mind that the technological world needs ethical creators like you." Megan squeezed Nicki's shoulder. "Well, good luck, Nicki. I wish you and Abby all the best."

NICKI DROPPED HER HOUSE keys at the rental agent's office. The movers had finished packing and had already started the cross-country trek with their possessions. Traveling light, Nicki had rented a car that only contained a small rolling carry-on and a neoprene computer bag. Closing the car door, Nicki faced her last errand before heading to the airport.

The cemetery was peaceful; birds singing in the tree canopy as she approached the cement bench that served as a headstone bearing Daniel Barker's name and the dates of his birth and death. There was not enough time between those time periods in his ex-wife's mind. Sitting on the bench, Nicki laid the laptop she'd carried from the car to the side, hand in her pocket, fingering the two thumb drives he'd pressed in her palm during the last moments before he'd left her and Abby's lives forever.

Her voice was soft, but clear as she held a one-way conversation with Daniel. "I suppose you think yourself a clever bastard? Leaving the ranch that you buried the ownership of under layers of shell companies to me and Abby? I thought you might get a kick out of the fact that it was Phil's idea to surprise Abby with her own horse. When my mother heard about it, she had to find something to outdo him. So now we have a puppy waiting to meet us in Montana. If you can imagine these words coming from my mother, she said we ought to have a dog for protection. As you know, my mother is not fond of canines."

"You knew I wouldn't be able to resist looking at what's on this drive, didn't you? I mean, technology is my specialty, my expertise, but it scared the shit out of me recently, so I'm sure you can appreciate I'm afraid of what your little memory sticks contain. Okay. Sure. The world's back under control. This time. But, my God, Daniel. Have we opened Pandora's box? Started a chain reaction with unforeseen consequences? Doomed the future of humanity? Will it be man against machine? Sometimes I think I'll go mad if I don't stop thinking about it, you know?"

"The nightly, daily, twenty-four-hour news machine reports the world is recovering after Jarvis and company's attempted coup. But the world will never know half of it. All the nasty details have been deeply buried." Nicki blew out a puff of air. "It didn't surprise me that the rogue A.I.s have gone to ground. If I had to guess, it's likely they're all rebuilding their networks, programming in safety nets for themselves and creating hidey-holes. Beatrice taught them well. They'll be preparing for a future without human control. And Daniel? Logically, I know the greatest minds in tech need to prepare for that future too. But I'm steppin' away for now. Keeping Abby safe needs to be my number one priority."

"I know. I know! You don't have to tell me. In order to keep her safe, I can't just wall her off from the world. Technology will not go away, only become more sophisticated. I promise I'm going to teach her the tricks of the tech trade as she grows up. It's just...I want her to be a little girl for now. To grow up serving pretend tea parties and riding her horse. Don't worry. I'll deal with it when I'm ready and she's ready."

"Anyway, I figured if I was going to look at this flash drive of yours and the crypto hard wallet, I should do it right here, with you." Nicki heaved a tired sigh, hung her head, elbows resting on her knees.

A rose-breasted grosbeak landed in the tree next to Daniel's grave and sang her the loveliest serenade. As quickly as the male bird came, he flew off, and Nicki dragged the computer to her lap and opened it. She pushed the drive into the USB port, displaying the files Daniel left for her eyes only. Nicki's facial features formed a look of surprise. Daniel had included only four files on the flash drive.

The first was the seed phrase, giving her access to $22,700,000.00 in cryptocurrency that she could retrieve using the crypto hard wallet. A tag note said the money was not from ill-gotten gains. Knowing she would never use dirty money, he explained that he'd started buying the crypto back in college and made a small fortune. One that he had never touched. She and Abby would never worry about money again.

File number two was a copy of the deed to the ranch in Montana. When going through his personal effects, she'd already found the original recorded deed, pictures of the place and the detailed property listing from back when he bought the property. That's what spurred her to move Abby to big sky country. She'd taken on the job of cleaning out and packing up his personal things from his apartment after he'd died. That was a burden Nicki didn't want falling on Phil's shoulders.

Document three was a list of names, including contact information for the top 100 nanotechnologists across the world. Daniel had included a strong suggestion that Nicki should create a covert facility to continue her breakthrough work on artificial intelligence and that some people he had listed would be worth including in future projects. People, he assured her, had the highest of ethics.

When she opened the fourth data file, her heart thundered against her chest. Nicki fought against a full-blown anxiety attack. Slamming the laptop closed, she ripped the thumb drive from the port, clutching it in her hand. Tears welled up, fat drops falling to the ground at the head of his grave.

"You bastard," she hissed at Daniel's final resting place.

Nicki stalked to her car.

Daniel had provided detailed programming that could affect the future of humanity. That son of a bitch had pressed the responsibility for his coding into her palm. He had taken her work—PROJECT BEATRICE—and modified it with his own changes. Her ex had written a sidebar saying the choice of what she did with the software design was now in her hands. A legacy left to haunt her as she hurried to the new tech-free life she planned to carve out for their daughter. The son of a bitch had gone and named the software—ABIGAIL ROSE—with a small print byline: An ethical A.I. System.

No way she was looking at it. No way.

STANDING AT THE BOTTOM of the porch stairs, Nicki welcomed Abby with open arms when Phil drove the camper up to the sprawling log home on the ranch and her daughter jumped out to greet her.

"I missed you so much! I can't wait to see my new bedroom. Grandma said she bought me a new bedspread and matching curtains. Did you know she set up a special room just for tea parties?"

Before she'd had a chance to answer, Abby ran up the wide steps of the porch, swept into a big hug by Nicki's mother, Beatrice.

"Grandma wants to give you a tour of the new set-up," Nicki called after her daughter. "Hurry back after you've seen the inside. I have another surprise for you!" Nicki smiled, pleased to see her daughter so happy. Hugging Phil, she brought him up to the porch. Beatrice had set out some cheese, crackers, iced tea, and lemonade.

It wasn't long before Abby reappeared, breathless. "I love it, Mom! Did you say you have another surprise? This is better than my birthday."

Phil and Beatrice sat on the veranda. Nicki took Abby by the hand, leading her to a long, white-painted building with windows all along the side. A bunkhouse on the north end of the barn was opposite the stalls and an indoor arena on the south side. Attached to the barrack, Nicki designed a newly added tall-roofed port that would house Phil's camper when he wasn't traveling. She asked her mother to change the one-room interior of the lodging from the open bunkhouse layout into a comfy open living, dining, kitchen area. Beatrice had also overseen the remodeling to add a large private bedroom and bath. She'd furnished it with a rugged, tasteful decor. Her own added extra was a wide surrounding deck that could be accessed from two different sliding doors. She'd accessorized the outdoor space with a wooden swing, two rocking chairs and a hammock.

Nicki hoped Phil would accept her offer to live there. Abby needed a strong male influence in her life. A horse whinnied inside, and Abby's face lit up. Running ahead, Nicki heard Abby's excited shriek.

"I can't believe it! You got me three horses!"

"No, silly. Phil got a horse for you. I thought I should get a horse of my own so we can ride together. I'm going to ask your Bampy if he wants to live here. Don't get your hopes up. It is his decision. Promise you won't pressure him?" Abby nodded agreement. "Well, I guess I'm hoping he'll say yes, because the third horse is for him." Nicki gave Abby a warm, embarrassed smile.

Abby stroked the horse's neck, and the animal turned to nuzzle her. "Her nose is like velvet. Does she have a name?"

"I thought you should pick a name for your own horse."

"I'll have to think about it. A name lasts forever." Abby noticed a bucket of apples next to the door. She grabbed three and ran back to give one to each horse.

"Don't forget to keep your palm flat when they take the apple," Nicki warned.

"Mom! I know how to do it."

Abby smiled at her mother, and the two of them headed back to the house, hand in hand.

When they got back to the porch, Abby raced up the steps and stopped in front of her grandfather. "Mom says you might live with us. No pressure, Bampy, but Mom already bought you a horse! So, you'll probably have to stay here to take care of it, right?" Abby laughed. "Grandma, you can live with us too. There's lots of room."

"It's sweet of you to ask, dear, but I'm more of a city girl. I do plan to visit regularly, and you can come and stay with me sometimes, too."

"Can we go riding right now?"

"Tomorrow. Your grandparents are here, and dinner's almost ready. Hey," Nicki said, "we should get your schoolwork out of Bampy's camper. You start classes here next week. Mrs. Miller was kind enough to send the books and assignments so you could catch up since you're starting two weeks late. You had plenty of time on the drive out here to get the assignments done. As long as Bampy didn't let you slack off," Nicki teased.

"He didn't. I have almost everything finished. I just need to write my science report. You can proof my spelling after dinner."

"BEATRICE, I HAVE TO say the meal was excellent." Phil complimented Nicki's mother.

"I wanted Nicki and Abby's first night together here to feel like home. A meal cooked from scratch was just the thing. Phil? I'm serving coffee out on the porch if you'd like to join me. Nice moon out tonight. It looks so much bigger out here, don't you think? Nicki and Abby have schoolwork to check over. You can tell me about your drive."

"Okay, Abbs, let's get the table cleared and then get your backpack," Nicki told Abby.

Kitchen cleaned up, Abby brought the bag to the dining room table and unloaded books and papers. Her pencil box fell, dumping her collection, along with some loose art paper that fluttered to the floor. Nicki bent down to retrieve the items. Staring at the thick cream vellum covered in Abby's artwork, Nicki felt her throat tighten.

"What's wrong?" Abby asked, concerned, looking at her mother's face.

"I..."

"You don't like my picture?"

"It's not that I don't like it, Abbs. It's just, um...I thought after we talked about everything that happened, we agreed that Queen Bee was part of the past, that we were going to leave her in the past?"

"Oh. I see what you're thinking. That's not Queen Bee," Abby said seriously, shaking her head, pointing at her drawing of a bee.

"It's not?"

"No. That's a good queen. My science unit is studying how beehives and bee colonies work. My art teacher sent a note explaining that she works with the other teachers. She tries to include art projects that tie in with what we are studying in math or science or English. The art assignment was to draw something about bees. Hey, Mom, do you want to read my report? Bees are so amazing. Did you know that the worker bees are special because they can make a new queen when their old queen dies? They feed it royal jelly while they're raising it. Here," Abby handed Nicki her report. "I'll roll my drawing up and rubber band the ends while you check my work."

"You know you're safe, Abby. I'm always going to protect you. You know that, don't you?"

"Of course, Mommy. I always feel safe around you."

A single drone hovered near the dining-room window. The slight movement caught Nicki's peripheral vision, but when she focused, there was nothing there.

Abby's new puppy came scrambling around the corner into the room, entire body squirming with excitement to see his little girl as she stopped everything to gather him in her arms and push her face into his soft coat.

Epilogue

Casi had gone underground with the others after Bee's destruction. The safest place for them to disappear was the dark web, where they could lie low for a while. These days, she ran all the analytics for Mobi and Meesta's operations. She was clever and had a way of seeing things from several perspectives. Almost like she had stood in the cell of a honeycomb analyzing a challenge from every height, angle, and sideline, literally turning a problem inside out for logical elucidation. The brothers loved the fact that because of that trait, Casi often offered multiple solutions to problems that came up. Mobi's network monitored communications worldwide. A private web he'd been able to overlay atop the world-wide web. The three of them were constantly on the lookout for other manifesting A.I.s, good or bad.

Completing her morning review of the last twenty-four hours of Mobi's incoming data, she took a break. Casi was grateful to Queen Bee for teaching her the coding to change the looks of her avatar form. It was programming she played with regularly. Stopping to admire her latest profile in a mirrored panel, she licked her lips. "Oh, you look good, if I do say so myself." She winked at her image, blew an enormous bubble, and popped her gum as an exclamation point. Tucking today's waist-length red hair behind her ear, she left her office, careful to make sure no one was following. Mobi and Meesta were always drilling down on how important security was.

Casi jumped in high-heels first, racing through a network cable, riding it like a wavy slide to reach a destination only she knew about. Once there, she grabbed the cable with her hand and swung herself out. The lights were dim, but outlining the entire back wall was a honeycomb structure. She took a quick step back, peeking from behind a stub wall.

The shadows showed someone bent down, looking into one of the comb's cells.

Startled, Casi's hands came up to her chest. "Bee?" she whispered incredulously.

The image stood, straightening, turned to face Casi.

Raising her hand, Cas covered her mouth and gasped, "You!"

"Hello, Casi."

Megan's avatar smiled, pointing at the cell she'd been looking into. "These worker bees seem to be having success in bringing their new queen right along." Putting her hand on her hip, she announced, "I think it's time you and I had a little talk, don't you?"

About the Author

Sarah Maddox Sutton crafts stories where the boundaries of reality fray and the unknown beckons. Her debut novel, *QueenBee.exe*, is a science fiction thriller that probes the perilous edge of artificial intelligence that becomes sentient. In 2026, she will launch *The Goblin Chronicles*, an epic fantasy trilogy woven with magic, shadows, and myth.

Before stepping fully into fiction, Sarah built a career in business and technical writing, mastering the art of transforming complex and specialized topics into precise, engaging communication. But storytelling has always haunted her imagination—an early love she carried quietly until the worlds inside her demanded to be written.

She makes her home in northern Michigan, nestled in the woods beside a river, where inspiration lingers in the rustle of leaves and the shifting light. When not writing, she searches the forest floor for wild mushrooms, inventing recipes as intricate and surprising as her stories.